TERMINAL
VISIONS

RICHARD PAUL RUSSO

With an Introduction by
Karen Joy Fowler

Golden Gryphon Press
2000

Contents

CONTENTS

for Candace

Introduction

"It's not often that someone comes along who is a true friend and a good writer."
—E. B. White, *Charlotte's Web*

For several years now I've felt as if I had a secret. While it's always fun to know something other people don't know, and this particular secret is a good one, a delightful one, still it distresses me to have it. So this collection particularly pleases me because the secret has been Richard Paul Russo's short fiction.

Richard's novels are not such a secret, having plenty of admirers, both inside the U.S. and out. *Subterranean Gallery* won the Philip K. Dick Award; *Carlucci's Edge* won the Philip K. Dick Special Award; and *Destroying Angel* was shortlisted for the Arthur C. Clarke Award. But his short stories, which are every bit as good, seem to me to receive less notice than they deserve.

Perhaps I ought to confess up front that Richard is a friend of mine. We met at the very first science fiction convention I ever attended; he may, in fact, be the first friend I made in the field. Over the years we have been to writing workshops together, as well as conventions, as well as each other's houses. I asked him to be on the Tiptree jury (an annual award made to a work of speculative fiction for its contribution to our understanding of gender—to date, he's been the only male chair) and I know he agreed, at least in part, because it was me asking.

I've also met a great many other writers and I've found the following to be generally true:

a) If you read the work first, you cannot reliably deduce anything about the writer from it. You're on a panel with the author of some hilarious tour de force and he spends the whole time complaining about the miserable state of publishing. He is not even imaginative about it. Or you find yourself at dinner seated next to an author whose work inspires your social conscience—I really should *DO* more, you think whenever you read her—and she turns out to be unable to talk about anything but herself.

But . . .

b) If you know a writer first and read him second you will invariably see bits of his personality reflected accurately in the work.

At our very first meeting Richard impressed me as serious, intense, smart, and grown-up, and so in his stories, he consistently proves to be. As I got to know him better, I found him the best possible sort of person with whom to discuss writing—ambitious with regard to his own future work, but modest and too self-effacing with regard to his past.

In a field that often rewards pyrotechnics, Richard's work is subtle and extremely spare. His stories may be set in outer space, the future, the jungle, or the realm of no-time; wherever, no one else creates landscapes with Richard's stunning economy of words. A few sure strokes—a piece of furniture, the view from a window, the ground beneath your foot—and a whole world emerges just out of sight, illusive, but utterly persuasive, and presented as if it were as ordinary as it must be to the characters themselves.

These characters have a similar elegant stripped-down essentialness. We learn almost nothing of their histories. They tend to speak little, to live in various kinds of isolation. They are caught in amber for us, struggling with problems that are touchingly human-sized. No one in a Richard Paul Russo story thinks he is saving the world, though with luck, with help, he might survive it.

"The Open Boat" is quintessential Russo. I think it the finest story in this collection (even though "Just Drive, She Said" is my actual favorite). In "The Open Boat" a tiny cast of characters—three men and two women—find themselves adrift in a tiny interstellar lifeboat in the nonuniverse. Their personal histories are quickly dispensed with; shared, we are told, in the early hours of their predicament, but meaningless in the nonuniverse. Equally short work is made of the events which led to their current situation. All that matters in the story is the nearly stationary, ever-slowing passage of Now.

As is often the case in a Russo story, the protagonist, Sara, is an artist. Sara is the one who tries to keep a record, find a shape for their circumstances. The others cope in their own particular ways: Jackal with expertise, Cass with pessimism, Bertrand with determination, Hallic with collapse. Their actions and conversations are sparse and repetitive, and yet, Richard's touch is so sure here, that we quickly come to know them completely. In a scene, sometimes in a sentence, we watch as each of them, one after another, is intimately unmade.

The story evokes a number of other works, including Sartre's "No Exit." But Richard's characters are so resolutely ordinary, the situation so randomly generated that "The Open Boat" creates its own unique chill. Hell is a literal place in the future where anyone might go as soon as technology has laid a road to it.

Although "The Open Boat" is grimmer than most of these stories, the usual mood in Richard's work is an undeniably dark one. The Russo vision tips a bit toward despair. But it is against this backdrop that kindness and connection become the stuff of drama. One of the things I admire most in Richard's work is the way he makes the moment of kindness more memorable, more worthy of a story, than the moment of cruelty. The Russo vision is tough, but seldom bleak.

This collection contains pieces driven by plot ("In the Season of the Rains," "More than Night"); by character ("View from Above," "Watching Lear Dream"); by setting ("Cities in Dust," "No Place Anymore"); by technology ("The Open Boat," "Liz and Diego"); by poetry ("Prayers of a Rain God," "Lunar Triptych: Embracing the Night"); and just plain driven ("Just Drive, She Said").

In sum, you will love these stories. And, if I'm right, if you do, then you have been let in on the best kind of secret, my favorite kind of secret, the kind you do not have to keep quiet about. You can tell anyone you like. You can tell everyone. I hope to hear you doing so.

Karen Joy Fowler
January 2000

Terminal Visions

Listen to My Heartbeat

CALE SAT OUT ON THE TERRACE CAFÉ, BESIDE THE rusted metal rail so he could watch the crowded street below. Though the table was shaded, the heat rose up from the street, drifted through the railing with dust, blew in at him with the hot, dry breeze. He wore dark glasses that turned the world yellow.

A waiter dressed all in white (presumably white; the man's outfit looked yellow to Cale) brought a chilled glass and an opened bottle of dark beer to Cale's table, poured half the beer into the glass, left. Cale drank deeply, refilled the glass.

Cale, too, was dressed in light clothing—a tan, short-sleeved shirt, tan cotton pants, and deck shoes that had once been a pure white but now were brick red from the dust of the dry clay streets. Sweat coated his forehead, and he wore no hat.

The babble of voices rose from the street along with the dust, but Cale did not try to understand any of it. Then a single word erupted from the babble, emerged in relief though it was not shouted. *"Endeavor."* Cale turned his head, listened, but the word was not repeated. He thought he could feel his heart begin pounding at the inside of his chest, catching at his breath. Then he turned back to look at his beer and tried to forget what he had heard.

Cale drank slowly, gazing out over the streets without seeing anything. He looked down at his right shoe, tapped it against the table leg. Red dust fell from the shoe, but the color didn't change. It was time to buy a new pair, he thought. Or to leave.

He did both.

First Cale booked a series of hopper flights that would take him to Frankfurt, then left the hotel and bought a new pair of white deck shoes at a shop a few blocks away. He continued to wear the old shoes, kept the new pair in its box.

The next morning he took a taxi to the airport, checked his one suitcase, then boarded the plane, carrying a small shoulder bag and the shoebox. Once the plane left the ground, Cale changed shoes, putting the old dusty red pair in the box, and the clean white pair on his feet.

Several hours later, when he arrived in Frankfurt, Cale dumped the old shoes into a trash can and bought a bottle of White Horse Scotch whiskey. He checked into the airport Sheraton, drank two-thirds of the bottle while watching German-dubbed American movies; halfway through *The Trial* (a film he had never understood, drunk or sober, in any language), Cale passed out.

When he woke, Cale could not remember where he was. Gray light came in through the windows, the curtains drawn wide. Morning? Afternoon? It didn't matter. The television was still on, almost inaudible; on the screen a cartoon woman poured a glass of low-alcohol beer for her cartoon child. Cale rolled off the bed, switched off the TV, then staggered into the bathroom.

After relieving himself, Cale undressed and climbed into the shower. He stood for a long time under the spray without moving, listening to the water against the tile and the glass door and running out the drain, trying not to think of anything at all. Then he slowly lowered himself and sat in the bottom of the stall, his knees bent, hot water streaming down his face and chest and between his legs, and quietly wept.

At the mirror, Cale ran fingers through the hair above his ears, dismayed at how much gray now nestled amid the dark brown. Too young to be graying, he thought. He breathed in deeply, tried to smile. He wasn't really that young anymore, and it was already too late for some things in his life.

*   *   *

Cale stood at the window and looked out over the airport, at what little he could see of the city in the gray afternoon light. Frankfurt. Christ, why had he come here? Everywhere he looked was gray—the tarmac, the block-shaped buildings of steel and cement, factory smoke in the distance, dirty snow, the overcast sky. In some ways the Germans never changed; just look at all that goddamn cement. He put on the dark glasses; even sick yellow was better than all that gray.

Cale knew, of course, why he had come.

He left his hotel room, descended to the station beneath the airport, and took a train into the heart of the city.

The building was old, run-down, but at least it wasn't one of the modern apartment buildings, bunker-like monstrosities of cement and steel and tiny windows. Easily a hundred years old, probably much older, it was built of discolored stone and dark wood, with large, multi-paned windows set in carved wooden frames; empty planter boxes hung beneath many of the windows. The other buildings on both sides of the narrow street were similar, though most were in worse condition.

Cale stood in front of the old building, looking up along its face. A freezing rain had begun, was turning what little snow remained on the street to slush. Cale tried the front door. It was unlocked, and he stepped into musty darkness; when he closed the door he shut off the sounds of the rain and the city.

Magret lived on the third floor, and Cale hesitated at the foot of the stairs, removed his sunglasses, looked up through pale light and swirling dust. He should have called ahead, but she probably would not have seen him, and he could not accept that. As it was, Magret might not tell him anything about Tracy. She might not even know.

Tracy. Sometimes Cale could not remember what she looked like, though it hadn't been that long since he'd seen her—six, seven months maybe. Perhaps Magret would have a picture of her.

Cale started up the stairs. Wood creaked with each of his footsteps; the bannister was loose, moved each time he gripped it. At the top of the second flight he rested a few moments before starting down the short, dark, carpeted hall.

On the right . . . yes, number 7. The wooden door was so dark it was almost black, and it had a small opening covered by a brass plate on the inside. Cale knocked. Silence at first, then quiet rustling sounds filtered through the door, then silence again. Cale knocked again, louder.

The brass plate opened almost immediately, and an eye appeared in the opening. Magret's eye. The eye widened a moment, withdrew, the plate clanked shut. Silence again.

Cale knocked one more time. "Magret, it's Cale. Let me in, please, I want to talk to you."

"*Ja, leck mich am Asch!*" Her voice was sharp and harsh. She switched to English. "So go the hell away, you bastard!"

"Magret, please let me in."

She pounded hard on the door in response, but said nothing.

Cale waited a minute or two, then knocked again. "Magret." His voice was calm, quiet. No response. "I'm not leaving," he said. "I'm going to wait here until you let me in. I need to talk to you."

Still no response. Cale removed his overcoat, draped it over his shoulder. He backed away from the door and leaned against the wall directly opposite it, waiting. A few minutes later the small brass plate opened; Magret's eye appeared for a moment then disappeared without a word from her, the plate clinking shut. The door did not open.

He waited for nearly two hours before she finally opened the door to him. She stood in the doorway, framed by dim interior light, looked at him with heavy-lidded eyes. Smoke drifted from a cigarette between her fingers. Magret wore a black button-down sweater and a knee-length skirt, and Cale found himself staring at her right leg which was, he now remembered, artificial from the knee down. Somehow he had forgotten. The leg was flesh-colored, but it did not look natural at all, and his chest tightened, hands going cold. Cale looked back up at Magret's face; expressionless, she stepped back to let him in. As Cale stepped forward, he smelled alcohol on her breath.

"I've been drinking while you've been waiting," she said. She inhaled on her cigarette, then closed the door behind him.

The apartment was warm, stuffy, smelled of stale smoke and sausage. The entranceway was dark, but Magret led the way, limping slightly, toward the brighter gray light of the kitchen. The smell of sausage, bratwurst probably, intensified as Cale stepped into the small kitchen. Magret waved at the wooden table pushed up against one wall, mumbled something about sitting down, then went to the cupboard above the sink.

"You want something to drink?" she asked.

"Do you have Scotch?"

Magret laughed, nodded. In the light from the two windows, Cale could see the gray in her auburn hair, more than in his own though he was sure she was a few years younger than he was. She took a glass from the cupboard, set it on the table.

"Sit down. Right back." She crushed her cigarette in the table ashtray, then limped out the side door.

Cale hung his coat over the chair, sat at the small table and leaned against the wall. The stove, refrigerator, cupboards, ceiling, and sections of the walls were covered with a thin layer of grease. The last time he had been here, two, maybe three years before, the apartment had been much cleaner, the air fresh. Now, the sharp odor of sausage, combined with the cigarette smoke, made him slightly queasy. The glass in front of him didn't look too clean either, but he knew if Magret came back and poured Scotch into it, he would drink.

Magret returned with a half-empty bottle and a full glass. She poured him half a glass, sat across the table with hers and set the bottle between them.

"I'm out of ice," she said.

"Doesn't matter." Cale sipped at the tepid Scotch, watching her. She had been attractive once, still could be again, he thought, but she'd let herself go to hell, and Cale felt vaguely guilty about it, though he knew it was not his fault; the guilt he felt about Tracy somehow carried over.

"I want to know where Tracy is," he said. "I need to get in touch with her."

"Fuck you." She said it quietly, staring at him. She took cigarettes from her sweater pocket, lit one while shaking her head. "Fuck you," she repeated, just as quietly, just as calmly.

Cale remained silent a long time. He did not know what to say. Magret continued to stare at him, eyelids drooping, smoking her cigarette and occasionally drinking from her glass. When the glass was half empty, she refilled it, added a bit more to his, though he had hardly touched it.

"You've stayed in touch with her, haven't you?" he finally asked. "You know where she is."

Magret didn't answer at first; she looked away, toward one of the windows, and her expression seemed to soften. She inhaled deeply on her cigarette, held it a few moments, then slowly blew out a long stream of smoke. He wondered if she was going to cry.

"You're chasing ghosts," she said. Voice soft, barely audible.

"I need to see her again. I need to talk to her."

She turned back to him, jabbed at the air with her cigarette. "You *had* your fucking chance." Shook her head and pounded once on the table. "You could have been with her right now, preparing to go with her, to be a part of the whole thing with her. With her. But you chose not to. You turned it down. You told her no."

"No," Cale said. "I couldn't decide. I was going to accept, I was . . . but . . . but it was too late."

Magret laughed quietly, shaking her head. "My ass. She told me. You *chose* not to. You rejected her." She crushed out her cigarette, ground it over and over into the ashtray. "*I* wanted to go with her. I *would* have gone, but the whole goddamn space program is still homophobic. No same-sex pairs. No 'dykes or poofs'." She stared at him. "You wouldn't do it, but I loved her, Cale, and I would have paired with her if they had allowed it." She laughed again. "Why the hell not? My leg's already half artificial, why not go all the way, throw in an arm, whatever else? I would have been with her."

"It wouldn't have mattered," Cale said. "She wanted me."

"Yes, but she would have paired with me rather than go solo, I know she would have."

Cale shook his head. "No," he insisted. "She wasn't that way."

Magret pounded at the table, bloodshot eyes glaring at him. "She *would* have, you bastard."

"No." Christ, he thought, why did he keep insisting? Why was he trying to hurt her?

Magret didn't respond this time. She drank some more of the Scotch and turned away toward the window again.

"I'm sorry," Cale said. "Maybe she would have."

Magret shook her head. "No." She barely got the word out. "Probably not." Still shaking her head. "Does it really matter? For either of us? She's gone solo, that's all." She looked back at him. "You know, I lost her too."

"But you've stayed in touch with her."

"Sure." She lit another cigarette, her fingers trembling

slightly. "Sure, but that just makes it harder. Don't you understand that?"

He hesitated, then nodded. That was why he'd left her, why he'd kept himself isolated all these months; but cutting himself off from Tracy hadn't resolved anything. The pain was still there, with the hollow feeling of important things still unsaid.

"Yes," he said. "I understand, but now I need to talk to her."

Magret sighed heavily, then slowly nodded several times. She got up from the table and left the kitchen, the limp far more pronounced now, her right leg almost dragging along the floor. Again, feeling uneasy, Cale could not keep from staring.

He was tired. His eyes burned, and he was starting to feel the effects of the Scotch, but he drank more anyway. The toilet at the other end of the apartment flushed, then a couple of minutes later Magret came back into the kitchen. She handed him a folded piece of paper, then sat across from him again, refilled both of their glasses. Cale opened the paper. The address was a department number at Kennedy Space Center in Florida, of course, and there were two phone numbers with call-through codes. He refolded the paper, tucked it into his shirt pocket.

"Stay with me a while," Magret said. "You're my only connection to the way she was."

"What do you mean, the way she *was*?"

"What I said before, that you're chasing ghosts. She's someone else now. Something else. Tracy's gone."

"What are you talking about?"

Magret shook her head, barely able to keep her eyes open; she drank more of the Scotch, dripping a little down her chin.

"I can't tell you, go find out for yourself. But stay for a while, please, just a little?"

He nodded. "Sure."

Cale lit a fresh cigarette for her, emptied the Scotch bottle into her glass. They sat in the kitchen for a long time without speaking. Cale opened the two windows to let in the cold, fresh air, and the sounds of the city came in as well. He listened to them—to a neighbor screaming at her kids; to a yelping puppy; to another neighbor playing loud ether-jazz on a stereo; to the cold rain.

When Magret passed out, Cale picked her up, staggering a little under her weight, and carried her into her bedroom where he gently laid her across the single bed, covered her with a blanket, and left.

Cale did not go directly to Florida. Instead, he flew to San Francisco, where he and Tracy had lived for nine years, and where he had last seen and talked to her.

He arrived at dawn, took a cab to their flat in the Inner Sunset, wondering if it was still theirs. Their names were still on the mailbox, and Cale rang the doorbell. When there was no answer, he tried his key in the porch door. The key worked, and the door opened into the staired hall leading up two flights to the top floor flat. The hall was quiet; the air, though cool, smelled musty, unused. He closed the door and started up.

At the top of the stairs, Cale stood for a minute and looked into the flat through the front door's glass windows. Overflowing bookcases still lined the hall, and at the far end, lit by the rising sun, he could see the old gray-topped 1950s kitchen table, the stainless steel legs shining with the light.

There was no movement at all from within, which seemed somehow wrong to him. Then he remembered Dexter, their sleek gray tomcat who would normally have padded along the hall to meet him at the door. Cale wondered what Tracy had done with him. Taken Dexter to Florida?

A second key unlocked the door, and he stepped inside. With so many large windows, the flat was bright, and very quiet. Cale walked along the hall, floorboards creaking, and glanced into the rooms as he passed them. Most of the apartment was as it had been when he'd left, but he did notice blank spots in the bookcases, bare areas on furniture and wall shelves. Later, if he felt like it, he would try to figure out what she had taken with her.

He went through the kitchen (dust on the old gas stove was highlighted in the sun) and out into the covered utility room, then opened the back door and stepped onto the narrow outside porch. Wooden stairs descended from porch to porch and finally to the cement yard and the trash cans. Cale heard a scrabbling sound from below, followed by a rapid, ascending cluster of thumps, and Dexter appeared, running up the stairs. Dexter leaped onto the porch railing, meowed once, and rubbed his head against Cale's arm.

Cale smiled, scratched the gray cat's ears. "Where've you been, old boy? Who's been taking care of you?" Dexter purred loudly with eyes half closed, but there was no other answer.

Cale remained on the porch with Dexter a long time, talking quietly to the old gray cat in the gradually warming sun.

A week later, Cale sat in the kitchen with the phone against his ear, waiting for the final transfers to occur. It had taken three days of calls, security checks (absurd, since he'd once worked for them), line clearances, and general stalling, but they finally granted him line access to Tracy's private apartment in Florida, and now they were switching him through. A tinny click sounded, then several pops, and finally her voice came through, clear and clean.

"Hello, Cale?"

The ache rose in his chest, and he stopped breathing for a few moments, listening to the silence.

"Hello, Tracy."

A longer silence followed (he thought it was longer; his sense of time seemed to be distorted). Cale did not really know what to say, and probably Tracy didn't either.

"How are you, Cale? Are you at home?"

"Yes. I'm fine. You?"

"I'm okay. How about Dexter? I asked Peg downstairs to take care of him."

"Sure, Dexter's fine too." He breathed in deeply, held it, then slowly exhaled. "I need to see you, Tracy."

"I'm not so sure it's a good idea."

"Maybe not. I want to see you anyway. After the last time . . . I don't know. I don't want to leave it there. I need to see you one more time before you're gone."

Another long silence passed between them. Cale watched Dexter lethargically rolling an unshelled macadamia nut around the kitchen floor, half-heartedly pouncing on it when it threatened to roll too far away.

"All right," Tracy finally said. "I'll talk to the people here, work something out, then get back to you." She paused, then, "I do want to see you again, Cale. I'm . . . I'm glad you called."

Cale nodded to himself. "Yeah." He paused. "I guess I'll talk to you soon, then."

"Yes. Couple of days, maybe."

He hesitated again, then said, "Tracy?"

"Yes?"

There was a final long silence, and Cale realized he just

couldn't say anything more to her, not over the phone.

"Talk to you," he said. "Good-bye, Tracy."

"Good-bye, Cale."

He broke the connection, but kept the phone to his ear, listening to nothing at all.

Cale had run all his credit lines to the limit, and now the checking account was empty as well. He went to their bank and closed out two CDs, stuffed the bundles of twenties and hundreds into his pockets. Tracy had called, told him when he could come, and he went to a nearby travel agency (Escape, Ltd.) where he booked a flight to Florida, paid with cash.

He wandered about the Inner Sunset, looking in the windows of shops and restaurants. Half of the businesses that had existed when he and Tracy had moved here had turned over, acquired new owners, new names, new product lines. The vitamin store was gone now, replaced by a boutique selling high-tech, electronic clothing.

Cale sat at an outdoor table at one of the Irving Street cafés, sipped at a cappuccino, and thought about the money in his pockets. When this was all over he would have to go back to work. He had no idea what he would do, but he would not go back to work for NASA. They probably wouldn't take him back anyway, not with the way he'd walked out. Cale wondered if he'd left like that to try to sabotage Tracy's chance of getting a slot. Maybe. Probably.

It didn't matter anymore. What mattered now was seeing Tracy again, and in three days he would.

Three days. It seemed like a long, long time.

Tracy's apartment complex was isolated, not another building within a mile or two. Cale assumed it was near the Space Center, but he didn't know the area and he couldn't be sure. The building was two-storied and surrounded by lush vegetation and electrified fencing. He had been picked up at the terminal and brought out here in a small car driven by a talkative man wearing a light suit. As Cale stepped out of the car in front of the security huts, he realized he could not remember a single thing the driver had said to him.

The air was warm, humid, and the sun was bright in the thinning overcast; Cale put on his dark glasses, and the world turned yellow again. The change in color did not soothe him.

Getting through security took a half hour of identification checks, body searches, passes through detection equipment. Eventually they cleared him, gave him Tracy's apartment number—17, on the second floor—and warned him against entering any of the other apartments.

The complex was rectangular, four connected buildings enclosing a long plaza of trees, dense green growth, and spectacularly flowering plants. The apartment doors all opened onto the interior plaza. Cale climbed cement steps to the second floor landing that ran along all the buildings. From that height he could see a large swimming pool in the center of the plaza, accessed by several paths that wound through the lush vegetation. The water in the pool, discolored by his sunglasses, sparkled at him with flashing scales.

Cale walked slowly along, checking apartment numbers, glancing discreetly into windows as he passed. He stopped in front of a rust-colored door with the number "17" tacked onto it, the numerals of black-painted metal. Cale hesitated a long time, almost turned away, then firmly knocked. Almost immediately, Tracy's voice called out from within.

"Come in, Cale. The door's unlocked."

Cale hesitated again, then took the doorknob in his hand, turned it, pushed the door open. He removed the sunglasses, stepped into the tiled entry, and closed the door. The first thing he noticed was the profusion of plants. They hung from the ceiling, jutted from wall shelves, grew in pots atop floor stands. Tracy had never cared much for plants before.

"I'm in here, Cale."

He followed her voice through a doorway at the far end of the entry, ducked to avoid the full leaves of a hanging fern, and stepped into a large, open room filled with more plants and bright light. Then he saw her.

Tracy stood in the light streaming down through a large skylight above her, the metal surfaces of her right arm and leg shining brilliantly at him. She wore only a pair of red shorts, a white T-shirt, and her one natural foot was bare. Her black hair was cut extremely short, no more than half an inch long, and it would not lay flat.

"Hello, Cale."

"Tracy."

She looked down at his feet, smiled. "You and your spotless white deck shoes. You haven't changed."

"Magret says *you've* changed."

She looked up at him, smile fading. "Look at me." She held out her shining metal arm, silently rotated it before him, the fingers twisting and curling like beautiful steel serpents. "Of course I've changed."

Cale nodded, but didn't know how else to respond. After a long, strained and awkward silence, Tracy crossed her arms (metal over flesh), gripped her T-shirt, and pulled it off over her head, revealing her small breasts, both intact, and a wide strip of flexible metal plating that ran the length of her right side, connecting arm to leg without a break. She remained motionless for a minute, then put her hands on the waistband of her shorts.

"Do you want to see more?"

Hints of more metal were visible around her waist and under the left leg of her shorts. "I don't know," he said.

Tracy breathed deeply once, released the waistband. "Probably not." She slipped the T-shirt back on, smiled again, softly. "I'm still me, Cale."

Cale nodded, but still said nothing.

"Listen," Tracy said. "Can I get you something to drink? Or eat?"

"Do you still eat and drink?" He smiled to let her know he was kidding, but from the look on her face he hadn't smiled soon enough. "I'm sorry," he said. "It was just a joke. Really. And a beer would be great, if you have some."

Tracy scratched at her left thigh, managed a kind of smile. "I bought some Dos Equis for you. I'll be right back."

She turned away and walked out to the entry. Cale watched her, her movements smooth and natural as if she'd been born with a metal arm and leg, lived with them all her life. Then, just before she turned the corner he looked up, saw that the metal plating curled along her shoulder and upper back, then divided into half a dozen finger-like extensions that snaked up her neck and spread out along the back of her skull and then seemed to embed themselves deep beneath her scalp. Jesus. What had she done to herself? She turned the corner and was gone.

Cale felt his heart crashing up against the interior of his chest, pumping up through his throat, and he sat down in a stuffed chair, sank back in it. Directly above him a thick spider plant trailed about thirty or forty smaller plants from its shoots; some of the smaller plants were blooming with tiny, delicate white flowers. He wondered if he should get up and leave before Tracy came back. He remained seated, waiting for her.

She returned a few minutes later, carrying a glass of orange juice in her left hand, a bottle of Dos Equis in her right. Tracy held out the beer and Cale took it from the metal fingers. He noticed now that the metal surfaces of the fingers, the arm and leg, were irregular, marked with male and female jacks, couplings, grooved slots. Tracy sat in the couch opposite his chair.

"I half expected you to be gone when I came back out just now," she said.

"I thought about it," he admitted.

"You've run away twice before."

Cale drank from his beer, tilted his head back so he could gaze out the skylight. The sky was clear now, a bright pale blue, the sun out of sight. He lowered his head to look at her again.

"That's why I'm here," he said. "No more."

Tracy nodded. They sat for a long time without speaking. Cale watched her closely. He didn't know what he was looking for—something that would indicate she was still basically the same person, or something that would indicate she wasn't. They sat and looked at each other and drank until Tracy finally broke the silence.

"Why don't we go for a walk? Maybe that'll make it easier to talk. Something."

"Where to?"

She smiled. "The plaza. They won't let us go anywhere else, not together."

"Sure."

Tracy left her glass on an end table, but Cale took his beer with him. At the front door, Cale stopped.

"Is everyone who lives here cyborged?" he asked.

"No. Just a few of us."

"And you don't mind going out like this? Without anything to cover the arm and leg?"

"Why hide it? This is what I am now. I'm not ashamed of it." She paused, held the door open for him. "Are you?"

"No." He stepped outside and Tracy closed the door behind them.

They walked along the landing in silence, descended the nearest flight of cement steps, started along a gravel path weaving through short dense trees and thickets of flowering plants. Insect and bird sounds became noticeable, loud in the silence that hung between them; there were no human sounds other than their own breathing and the crunch of gravel with each of their footsteps.

The path opened out onto a wide patio next to the swimming pool; half a dozen metal tables and twice as many chairs were scattered about, all empty. The place had a deserted feel. As they walked past one of the umbrellaed tables, Cale sat down, quietly set his beer bottle on the metal surface. Tracy walked on, then noticed she was alone, and stopped. She turned back to look at him, but said nothing.

"I guess I don't feel like walking," he said.

Tracy came back to the table, sat in a chair across from him. The right half of her body was in the sun, and it reflected brightly at him. He thought about putting on his dark glasses, but didn't.

"Why is this so fucking hard?" she asked.

"I don't know." He shrugged. "Maybe because we both wish things could have been different, and there's no way they ever can be now." He breathed deeply once. "What we wanted wasn't the same to begin with." He turned the beer bottle so the label faced away from him; the metal foil in the label had been reflecting the sunlight into his eyes. "I guess it was hopeless from the start." Tracy said nothing; Cale went on. "And now you'll be going to the stars, plugged into one of those big starships, running a part of it."

"I'll *be* a part of it," she said. She stared at him, chewing on her lower lip, something Cale had never seen her do before. "I really wanted you to go with me," she said. "But when you took off like that . . . I had to do this, with or without you. You just didn't understand that, did you?"

He shook his head. "No. I didn't think you would do it alone, go solo. But I guess I understand now." He looked down at her right arm, which lay on the table, cold, unreal. "I just could not let them do that to me."

"And then you ran again, left me."

He turned away from her, looked out at the pool. "I couldn't watch it happen to you." There was a long silence, then he finally turned back to her. "What's it like?"

Tracy quietly laughed, breaking the tension for the moment, and shook her head. "Don't you realize that's an impossible question to answer? I'm not even going to try." She reached across the table, picked up the beer bottle, and drank, grimacing. "It's warm." She put the bottle back on the table, pushed it across to him. "It's all yours." She leaned back in her chair, apparently more relaxed. "Tell me, how's Magret? She writes a lot, once in a while we talk on the phone, but I haven't seen her in a long time."

"She looks like shit," Cale said. "She's let herself go completely to hell. I don't know. Unrequited love."

Tracy shook her head. "It's more complex than that."

"Yes, probably. She says . . . she says you're a ghost. She says you're someone else."

Tracy shrugged, an odd gesture both because it seemed inappropriate, and because the metal shoulder did not move quite as much as the natural one did. She seemed to be tightening up again, and she looked away from him. She crossed her arms over her chest, held herself tightly.

"She thinks I've become . . . inhuman."

"Have you?"

Tracy swung her head around sharply, glared at him. "Of course not." Her voice took on a hard, coarse edge. "It's crucial that we remain human." She held up her left hand and arm. "That's why I still have one natural arm, one natural leg, both breasts. Shit, they could have cyborged almost everything except my head, but . . ." She opened her natural hand, looked at the spread fingers, then looked up at Cale. "I'm different now, yes, very different, but I am still *human*, dammit!" With that she raised her right hand, the metal fingers clenched into a fist, and banged it down, badly denting the metal tabletop. Tracy stared at the dent for a minute, then pushed away from the table, the chair scraping along the cement. "I *am* still human," she whispered. "I am."

Without looking at him, Tracy got up and hurried away along the gravel path, disappearing into the vegetation. A few moments later he heard the alternating metal and flesh footsteps ascending the cement steps, then saw her walking quickly along the landing until she reached her apartment. She glanced down at him for a moment, then went inside.

Once again Cale considered leaving. He sat and finished the beer, not caring that it was warm, tossed the bottle into a trash can at the edge of the patio, then started back up to the apartment.

The front door was ajar, and Cale pushed it open. He stepped inside, closed the door, and listened. The apartment seemed unnaturally quiet. He moved silently through it, searching for Tracy. There were no sounds, and the only smell was the damp earth from the plants in every room.

He found her in the bedroom. She sat on the floor beside the bed with her back against the wall, just below a window and a shelf of small plants. A set of stereo headphones rested on her head, covered her ears, and her right hand was encased to the wrist in a black metal box on a shelf next to the stereo amplifier. Cale could hear a faint, regular thumping of bass leaking out of the headphones.

Tracy looked up at him as he stepped into the room. He stopped, still several feet away from her, and waited. Her upper body moved regularly with her breathing.

"I *am*," she whispered, firm and pleading at the same time. She leaned forward, her mobility restricted with her hand encased in the dark metal box. There were half a dozen lights on the exterior of the box, two now blinking, and several dials. Tracy removed the headphones with her left hand (the thumping bass grew a little louder), reached for the amplifier. She kept her gaze on him.

"Listen," she said. "Listen to my heartbeat."

She touched a disk on the amp, and a regular thumping emerged from large speakers in the corners of the room.

Ba-thump . . . ba-thump . . . ba-thump . . .

"Listen," she repeated.

Cale listened. Tracy turned up the volume control, and the thumping pounded through the room, reverberating in his ears. He did not doubt for a moment that it was Tracy's heartbeat. It pounded all about him, strong and regular, perhaps a bit too fast.

"Listen!" she called out again, and turned up the volume once more.

Cale stared at Tracy as the sound of her heartbeat crashed through the room, rattling the windows and the mirror on the closet door, shaking the leaves of plants, shaking the clay pots, pounding through his head, vibrating his skull, and knocking petals from bright flowers.

She looked almost inhuman to him, with her metal leg and her metal arm, the hand encased in more metal, but as he watched her natural fist clenching and unclenching, watched her face twist with anguish and her left toes digging into the carpet, and watched the tears stream down her face, Cale knew she was, truly, as human as he was.

"*Listen!*" she cried.

He listened.

*   *   *

Cale stayed with her through the night. She still wore the red shorts, and they lay beside each other in the large bed, not speaking, not touching. The ceiling fan rotated slowly, hardly stirring the air, and Cale spent much of the night watching it, hypnotized. He did not sleep.

Toward dawn, as Tracy slept beside him on her left side, Cale brushed his fingers along the cool metal surface of her thigh, up along her side, her shoulder, then out across the extension of metal that curled along her upper back; he hesitated at the base of her neck, then slowly traced the extensions fanning out across the back of her skull. He watched her breathe slowly, deeply, watched the pulse of the carotid in her neck. Magret was wrong. Tracy was still there, inside that body, that mind. A little lost and confused, maybe. Changed and still changing, but Tracy nevertheless. Cale leaned forward and whispered into her ear.

"Yes, Tracy, you are."

In the morning they drank coffee while they waited to hear from Security that his ride back to the terminal had arrived. Cale had told her he had a mid-morning flight back to San Francisco, which wasn't true, but he was afraid to stay much longer, and he thought Tracy, too, was glad he would be leaving soon. It had been important, for both of them, that he stay the night, but much longer. . . .

They sat at the kitchen table, the sun coming in through the window, fragmented by the leaves of the ferns hanging from the ceiling. Cale felt very much at ease, but distant as well, and becoming more so as the morning went on.

"Do you know what ship you'll be on?" he asked.

"I'm slotted for both *Endeavor* and *Challenger II*, but I'll prob-ably end up on *Endeavor*. We'll be the first ones out." She paused, breathed deeply once. "It'll be better then, slotted in. They'll be monitoring me, hooked into my bloodstream, they'll control the mood swings, pump me with a little of this, a little of that." She tried to smile, eventually succeeded with a quiet laugh. "I'll be fine, really." Another pause. "And you, Cale, will you be all right?"

He nodded once, then again. "Yes."

The phone rang. Tracy let it go for several rings, then got up and answered it. She listened a moment, said, "All right," then hung up. "Your ride's here," she said.

He stood up from the table, and they walked side by side to

the front door. Tracy put her arms around him and they embraced, and though he felt the metal digging into the flesh of his back, Cale really did not mind.

On his way out to the security huts, Cale detoured through the plaza to the patio and tossed his yellow-tinted sunglasses into the trash can. He would not need them anymore.

Cale climbed the wooden ladder leading up to the roof above their flat, and started across the gravel. A minute later Dexter, via the roofs of adjacent buildings, appeared and scampered along at his side.

Cale reached the far edge of the roof and sat, dangling his legs. He had wanted to watch the sunset, but the fog was starting to blow in, and would probably block out the sun before it set on its own.

Dexter crawled onto his lap, stretched and dug claws into his pants. Cale put his arm around the gray cat and scratched Dexter's head and chin, behind his ears.

"Well, Tracy's gone, old boy. She won't be coming back, but I'll be staying for a while. I'm not going anywhere."

Dexter started purring, pushed his head against Cale's hand. Cale looked at the hand, then at his other hand, holding both up and flexing his fingers. He put a finger to his throat, felt the steady pulse of blood. Listen.

Cale sat without moving, watching the fog obscure the cool white disk of the sun . . . and listened.

Just Drive, She Said

NIGHT.

Ahead of us, the road ended at a washed-out bridge, but we were driving for it at eighty-five miles an hour. Moonlight lit the barricades, the ruins of the bridge dangling over muddy water below.

"Jesus!" I said, trying to look at her. She pressed the gun harder into my temple.

"Just drive," she said.

I drove.

It wasn't even my car.

It was my sister's, an ugly-brown Mazda RX–7 that drove fast and smooth. I'd borrowed it for a few days, and Friday night I drove to a nearby liquor store to pick up some wine—something to get me through another empty weekend.

I was inside for fifteen or twenty minutes. With three bottles of wine in hand, I walked back to the car. I unlocked the door, opened it, and the overhead light went on.

A woman sat in the passenger seat pointing a gun at me. She didn't move, silent and intense, and I thought she was trying to decide whether or not to shoot me.

"Get inside and close the door," she finally said.

I wasn't going to do anything stupid. I got in, closed the door, and the light went off.

The woman took the wine from me with one hand, and with the other jabbed the gun into my ribs.

"Start the engine," she said.

As I did, strange lights went on in the middle of the dash. The tape deck was gone, replaced by a larger, glistening piece of electronics with dozens of buttons, dials, and readouts. Amber and green lights flickered across the thing, the displays showing figures that were probably letters or numbers, though nothing I recognized.

"What the hell is that?" I asked.

"A probability wave console. Generator, tuner, and amplifier."

Jesus, hijacked by a lunatic.

She jabbed me again with the gun, and said, "Let's go."

"This isn't my car," I told her.

"You think I give a shit?"

No, guess not. "My sister's waiting for me," I said, without much hope.

"Want me to repeat what I just said?"

I shook my head. "Where to?"

"Just go right and drive a while," she said.

The gun was still in my ribs, so I did what she asked.

Her hair was short and dark, and she was wearing blue jeans, a gray sweatshirt, and dark boots. Slim, but strong-looking. She didn't look crazy, I thought, but then what did crazy look like?

As I drove along, she fiddled with the console, and a stream of figures moved across the largest display. She glanced up, nodded toward a wrecked Toyota ahead of us on the side of the road, and said, "That used to be my car." We passed the wreck, and she returned her attention to the console.

A blue light began to blink frantically on the side of the console.

"Goddammit," the woman said. "How the hell did she find me so soon?" She pushed another button and a small screen emerged from the top of the console. A glowing map appeared on the screen, with two different blinking lights a few inches apart.

"Turn right at the next corner," she said, "and hit the gas. Move this crate."

I turned and accelerated. Traffic was light, but I still had to pay attention to other cars.

"Faster," the woman said.

"What about the police?" I asked. Which was a stupid question. I *wanted* the police.

"Fuck 'em," she said. "Just move it."

So I stepped on the gas. I was weaving in and out of traffic now, getting nervous. But whenever I started to slow down she jabbed the gun into my ribs and said, "Keep moving."

She had me make a series of turns, wheels squealing with each one, then we were on a long, open road with hardly any traffic. I was pretty sure the river was ahead of us somewhere.

"Now floor it," she said. I hesitated, and she moved the gun from my ribs to my head. "Floor it, goddamn you!"

I floored it.

Which was how, a few moments later, we were headed straight for barricades and a ruined bridge at eighty-five miles an hour.

I should have hit the brakes. What was she going to do, shoot me? But I kept my foot on the gas, the steering wheel straight.

The woman punched a few more buttons. Green lights flashed, bright patterned circles. Just before we reached the barricades, she jammed a switch on the front of the console.

Everything lurched sideways. At least, that's how it felt, lurched so hard I felt sick. But we were still on the road, still moving straight ahead at eighty-five. Except now the barricades were gone, and stretching out ahead of us, spanning the river and glistening with bright lights, was a whole, undamaged bridge.

We shot across it over the river, came down on the other side, and kept going. I braked through a long, sweeping turn, barely keeping the car on the road, then we were driving along the river road.

I couldn't see much in the dark. It wasn't a part of the city I knew well, but I had been through it a few times, and something seemed out of place.

"Just keep going," the woman said. She was watching a display on the console, a rolling series of figures that made me think of a time counter.

I drove along the river road, trying to figure out what seemed different, but unable to pinpoint anything. About fifteen minutes after we'd crossed the bridge, the console display stopped changing, and flashed a single figure.

"All right," the woman said. "Bring the speed back up."

The gun was gone from my head, but I wasn't about to argue. I accelerated until we were back up near eighty. The woman punched buttons, then again jammed the big switch on the front of the console.

We lurched sideways without moving again, and this time I thought I was really going to be sick. Everything in my vision began to tilt, and I had a hell of a time keeping the car on the road. I hit the brakes and brought the car to a stop, no longer caring what she would do to me.

I left the engine running, put my head on the steering wheel, and breathed slowly, deeply, until the spinning stopped. I straightened and looked at the woman. She now held the gun in her lap.

"Are you all right?" she asked.

"Sure," I said. "Terrific."

"We won't have to go so hard now," she said. "Just coast along at twenty, twenty-five miles an hour."

"Does that mean I start driving again?"

She nodded.

I looked down at the gun in her lap, and nodded back. "Give me another minute or two, will you?" I held up my hand, which was shaking. "I can't drive like this."

"All right."

I sat there, trying to relax, trying to cut down the shakes. The street was nearly deserted; only a few cars drove by, and there were no pedestrians. The cars looked odd, but there wasn't enough light for me to figure out why. Then I leaned forward over the steering wheel and looked at the front end of the Mazda. It was still an ugly brown, but the nose had become more elongated, sharper. The retractable headlights were gone, replaced by conventional stationary lights.

"What the hell is going on?" I asked.

"If it was daylight, you'd see even stranger things," she said.

Which made me look more closely at our surroundings. The nearby streetlight was mounted on an unusually thick metal pole, and gave off a sharp, emerald glow I'd never seen before. The lights in the buildings were brighter, harsher than I would have expected.

"Let's go," the woman said.

I breathed deeply a few more times. Then I put the car into gear, let out the clutch, and swung back onto the road.

We drove slowly, and I kept searching for changes in my surroundings, but it was too dark to see much. The woman directed me through several turns, then onto a freeway.

On the freeway there *were* differences I could identify. The overhead signs were blue rather than green, lit from below by rose-tinted lights. And the street and city names were completely unfamiliar—definitely not English. I didn't think I could pronounce half of them.

"You going to tell me what the *hell* is happening here?"

"Just look for a motel," she said.

"And how am I supposed to recognize one?"

She smiled. "Spelled just the same here as where you're from. It's practically a trans-universal word."

We drove on, and I wanted something to break the silence, to ground me. "Will that thing play music?"

The woman just laughed and shook her head, and I wondered what was so funny.

She was right, though, about a motel. From a mile away I saw a bright glowing sign:

MOTEL

As we got closer, I could make out other words, but none of them made sense. There were numbers as well, but there were too many digits, and a strange hooked symbol instead of a dollar sign.

"Hope you can pay for this," I said. "My money's not going to be much good here."

She smiled. "You'd be surprised."

I pulled off the freeway, drove into the motel parking lot, and the woman pointed out the office at the end of the building. She made me go in with her. At the desk, she talked to a crusty old man who wore a black helmet, face covered by a smoky visor. What they spoke sounded like a mix of foreign languages—a few words close to English, others like German, a few like French.

The woman paid with large, brightly colored bills, and the man gave her a narrow cylinder that hung by a chain from a plastic ball. We walked back to the car in silence, then she directed me to drive around the back of the building, where we parked in front of a tan door. The woman handed the wine bottles to me, took two duffel bags out from behind the seats, then made sure I locked the car. She inserted the cylinder into a narrow opening where it hummed, then clicked; the door swung open, and we stepped inside.

There was a table with two padded chairs, a television set,

a radio, and a double bed. The woman set the duffel bags on the floor, and I put the wine bottles on the table; the labels had changed, and were now unreadable. I looked at her.

"There's only one bed."

"We'll manage," she said. "Let's go get something to eat, I'm hungry."

We went to a coffee shop next to the motel, where the woman ordered for both of us. I ended up with something that looked and tasted a lot like a Denny's chicken fried steak and mashed potatoes.

After we ate, the woman said she needed a drink. I figured I could use one too, so we went to the attached lounge and sat at a table in the back corner, empty tables all around us. She asked me what I liked to drink, and I told her Scotch. She ordered from the waiter, and when my drink came it did taste an awful lot like Scotch—cheap Scotch, but Scotch nevertheless. The woman was drinking something clear over ice.

"A trans-universal," the woman said. "Alcohol, coffee, and tobacco. Hotels and motels are close, along with guns and cars, but alcohol, coffee, and tobacco are almost everywhere."

Right. We drank. One drink, two drinks. Then a third. I was feeling it. We didn't talk, but we had another drink. I didn't know about her, but I was getting smashed.

"What's your name?" I asked. Drunk, I was feeling reckless, and it seemed like a reckless question.

"It would sound like garbage." She paused. "Call me Victoria." Another pause. "What's *your* name?"

"Robert."

"Robert." She nodded. "Robert, do you have any idea what's been happening to you?"

I shook my head.

"Of course not. Ever heard of parallel universes?"

"Sure. As an idea, not something that actually exists."

"They exist. We've been moving from one to another." She signaled for two more drinks, then looked at me for a minute before going on. "The console in the car? It generates probability waves that slip us from one universe to another."

The drinks came, and she drank half of hers immediately. It was a crazy idea, but how *else* had I come to this place? We sat for a while in silence, drinking. Actually, I kind of *liked* the idea of traveling between universes. It beat hell out of sitting alone in an empty apartment all weekend.

"Wait a second," I said. "How the hell do you know how to speak from one place to another? You can't *know* all these languages."

She shook her head. "I don't." She tapped at the base of her skull. "But *this* does. Batch of microchips planted in my head." Then she stretched out her arms. "Robert, I'm wired. I've got a built-in receiver running through my whole body. Every time I shift universes, my body pulls in all the radio and television signals, whatever's out there, and the batch in my head does the rest. In ten or fifteen minutes, I've got enough of the language to get by. That's how I picked up your slang. And each time I shift places, I shift languages. Or I can lock onto one, like I have with yours." She paused. "I like being able to talk to you."

I looked at her for a minute.

"Why? Why are you traveling between universes? And who the hell is after you?"

She didn't answer. She returned my gaze for a while, stood, then said, "Let's get back to the room."

Without thinking, I opened my wallet to leave a tip. My paper money had changed from green to the brightly colored bills I'd seen Victoria use.

"Just like the car," Victoria said. "Anything that's not alive." She took two small bills from my wallet, left them on the table.

I felt a lot drunker as we walked back to the motel. Or maybe it was just overload. I felt I was moving through water. Or mud. It seemed like a long trip across the parking lot, but we finally reached our room and went inside.

I dropped into one of the chairs. Victoria sat on the bed with her back against the wall. Someone in the room above us kept dropping things onto the floor.

"When I first opened the car door and saw you," I said, "it looked like you were trying to decide whether or not to shoot me."

Victoria shook her head slightly and smiled. "I would never have shot you."

"Maybe you shouldn't tell me that. Maybe I'll just take off."

"Yeah? Where the hell are you going to go?"

I shrugged.

"No," she said. "I was trying to decide whether or not to take you with me."

"Why did you? Hostage?"

She shook her head again, the smile gone. "I've been lonely," she said. "I just wanted the company."

I didn't say anything. She pushed up from the bed. "I'm going to take a shower." She turned away from me and walked into the bathroom, closed the door.

Find the gun, I thought. But only for a moment. I didn't really care where the gun was, I didn't want to have anything to do with it. What I did instead was undress and get into bed. I was beat, still half drunk, and I needed the sleep.

But I *couldn't* sleep. I lay wide awake, waiting for her to return. It had been a long time since I'd been involved with anyone, and that had been a woman who spent all her time on speed of one kind or another; I'd begun to feel like I was moving in slow motion whenever I was with her. Now I felt as if *I* had been on speed most of the evening. I closed my eyes, but that didn't help. I waited.

I opened my eyes to the covers being pulled away, and Victoria standing over me, naked and wet from the shower. She was a completely normal woman, whatever universe she'd come from.

She crawled across the bed on all fours, dripping onto my skin as she leaned over me. She blew air across my belly, through the hair between my legs. She moved down toward my thighs, and straddled me.

"I'm too drunk," I said.

She looked down at my crotch. "No you're not," she said.

"I'm too tired."

"No you're not."

"I don't even know what you are," I said.

"What do you think I am?" She moved forward, lifted slightly, then lowered herself onto me, warm and moist. She smiled. "Just drive," she said.

I drove.

She wouldn't talk about where we were going, or why. I had the feeling she didn't have any particular destination in mind, that she was just shifting from one universe to another at random, trying to lose her pursuer. For a few days, it seemed to work.

I got used to the changes. Or rather, to the *idea* of change. Each day we made at least one shift, usually two. Once we made three, which was a mistake—I got sick all over the front seat and nearly ran the car into a concrete channel on the side of the road used by people on cable-powered skateboards. After that, we shared the driving, and stuck to two shifts a day.

Everything changed—the car, our clothes, money. Language changed, occasionally becoming so close to English that I could understand it again, but usually becoming completely unintelligible. And the world around us changed.

Once we emerged into a domed city, buildings reaching to the dome itself and through it, jutting into the open sky above. Another city was a maze of narrow roadways with hundreds of footbridges above the streets, connecting the stone buildings in a vast, chaotic network of bent and twisted metal. And once we came out onto a cracked and potholed concrete road in the middle of a dry, gutted wasteland, flat ruins for miles in all directions, no signs at all of life. We shifted out of there as soon as we could.

We spent several hours a day on the road. Sometimes we shifted at lower speeds, which was easier on me, but which, she said, made for smaller jumps that were easier to track. And though she could make a second shift as soon as fifteen or twenty minutes after the first, Victoria liked to put as much actual distance between shifts as possible. Left a tougher trail to follow, she said.

We spent much of the time driving in silence, but we did talk a little. I talked about my own world, my universe, my life— which wasn't much. I was in charge of the Documents Department of a large corporate law firm. I liked the job itself, but working for asshole attorneys all day long had become almost unbearable. And my personal life was hardly fulfilling. But I talked about it all, and once in a while Victoria would talk about what it was like traveling between universes.

"Do you ever stop running?" I asked once. "I mean, how long can you keep it up? Don't you ever get a chance to just stop for a while?"

Victoria nodded. "When I've made enough shifts over a long period of time, it gives me distance. I get a few days, a couple of weeks. I'll just stay in one place for a while, relax, or maybe do something to pick up some money. But eventually I have to leave, start shifting again."

"You can't lose them?"

She shook her head and tapped the console. "These damn things leave a trail in the wake of the probability waves. Make enough shifts and you can make the trail faint, but a good hunter will always be able to pick it up eventually.''

Hunter. And I was traveling with the hunted.

Victoria did talk about bringing me back to my own universe. First couple of times she mentioned it I didn't say anything. I was thinking about it. But I liked the idea of staying with her.

"I don't want to go back," I finally said to her.

It was dusk. Victoria was driving through the outskirts of a haze-filled city, blue flashes of light bursting silently and sporadically high above us. The streets were nearly deserted.

"You don't know what the hell you're talking about," she said. "You can't just stick around for a while and then change your mind, get a plane flight *home.*"

"I realize that."

"You realize shit." She turned onto a busier street. Lights were coming on in buildings, and the blue flashes were increasing in frequency. "Just look for a goddamn motel, all right?"

Neither of us said anything for a while. The street seemed to be headed for the city center, and it got busier and more crowded, brighter and louder. A couple of miles along, Victoria pulled into the parking lot of a run-down motel set back in the concrete pilings of an overpass. She drove into a slot, switched off the engine, and turned to me.

"Look," she said. "The farther we get away from your universe, the harder it'll be to get back. We get far enough away, it'll be impossible. You'll be stuck out here somewhere, no way back. And traveling with me isn't the safest thing you can do. I've had people hunting me for two years. Some day they're going to catch up with me. You aren't going to want to be around when they do." She paused. "I've been on my own for years, and that's the way I want it. I like your company, but I'm not about to make this permanent. You're holding me up, for Christ's sake. You can't handle more than two shifts a day. On my own, I can do five or six before it hits me that hard." She paused again. "You understand what I'm saying?"

"I'll get used to it," I said.

"Not soon enough for me."

"I don't want to go back."

"Christ." She turned away from me, opened the door, and went to check in.

Three more days. Traveling, shifting, no resolution, no final decision. Then, one morning, driving slowly through the heart of a city, we shifted, and dropped into the middle of a war.

We went from bright afternoon sunshine to gray skies darkened by clouds of ash. From laughter and shouts and purring traffic to screams and sirens and gunfire. From busy but orderly streets filled with calm pedestrians and cyclists to chaos, people running from shelter to shelter, and vehicles burning on the roads.

I saw the crater in front of us just in time, swerved, and jolted up a curb, knocking over a metal canister that spilled fuming liquid across the sidewalk. I got the car back on the road, but half a block ahead of us was a barricade manned by armed soldiers. Huge guns were aimed directly at us.

I hit the brakes and made a half-accidental U-turn, downshifted and punched the gas. Gunshots exploded, something hit the car, but we were still going.

"Shift us the hell out of here!" I screamed at her.

"I can't, you fucking moron! It's too damn soon!"

I turned down the first side street, nearly losing control of the car, then, seeing more barricades up ahead, swung into an alley that dead-ended in a heap of trash.

Victoria was out of the car before it stopped, shoving aside the trash—blocks of foam rubber, huge wads of paper, and other lightweight bundles. I drove the car into the opening she'd made, half burying the car in the mound. I got out, locked the doors, and helped her finish hiding the car with the foam blocks and wadded paper.

No one seemed to have followed us. I wondered if we should have just stayed in the car, but Victoria was already crawling through a broken window into one of the buildings lining the alley. I followed her inside.

The building was dark, and nearly silent; the only sounds came from outside, muffled by the brick walls. There was enough light coming in through the grimy, cracked windows for us to make our way. I followed Victoria through jumbles of complex machinery.

"Where are we going?" I whispered.

"I want to get above ground level. I'll feel safer. Then we can find a window where we can keep an eye on the car."

She found a stairway, and we went up. The doorway to the second floor was scarred and warped, the door blown off its hinges. We went through it, and came out in a maze of clear-walled cubicles filled with cracked glass cylinders.

We made our way through the maze, the floor covered with huge chunks of broken glass and twisted coils of wire. Every step made loud crunching sounds. Eventually we reached a window looking down on the alley, only to see half a dozen people dressed in fatigues and carrying weapons. At first I thought they were searching the alley, but it soon became clear that they were actually making camp for the night. The car looked to be safe, but we had no way to get to it.

The soldiers erected a structure that was half tent, half lean-to against the brick building across the way, and started a fire inside a squat metal cylinder.

We watched the soldiers and the fire for a while, but it was obvious they weren't going to leave, so we set up for the night ourselves. We cleared a space to sleep in, scrounged some scraps of cloth and some torn cushions to make a bed. Then we tried to sleep.

I didn't sleep much. Sporadic gunfire sounded throughout the night, and bursts of bright color regularly lit up the window, reflecting shards of light from the broken glass and the cubicle walls.

I was glad when dawn came. The sky outside was overcast, a gradually brightening gray. I went to the window. Below, the soldiers were breaking camp. One of them extinguished the cylinder fire while the others broke down the lean-to and packed it away.

"It looks like they're leaving," I said.

Victoria joined me at the window. We watched the soldiers pack, and about a half hour later they gathered together, talked for a few minutes, then marched halfheartedly out of the alley. They turned left onto the main street, and were soon gone from sight.

"Let's wait a while," Victoria said. "Make sure they don't come back for anything."

The soldiers didn't come back, but a few minutes later a woman appeared at the mouth of the alley. She was quite tall, with long, light hair tied into a double tail, and wearing a dark green, form-fitting coverall. She hesitated, looking down the alley, glancing in all directions.

"Jesus H. Christ," Victoria said, her voice hardly more than a whisper.

I realized then that this had to be her pursuer.

The woman started into the alley, walking slowly, looking up and down the walls of the buildings.

"What happens if she finds the car?"

"She'll find it," Victoria said.

The woman was two-thirds of the way down the alley, almost directly beneath us, when a shout brought her to a halt. She turned. At the mouth of the alley was a group of soldiers; maybe the same group that had camped overnight.

One of the soldiers called out something, and the woman responded. I couldn't make out what they were saying, it wasn't loud enough, but I wouldn't have understood a word anyway. Victoria just shrugged when I asked her.

The woman took a few steps toward the soldiers, then stopped. The soldiers came into the alley, marched down it, and surrounded her. She gestured at the street, then at one of the buildings. I could see her smiling. One of the soldiers jabbed at her shoulder. The woman kept smiling. Another soldier shrugged, pointed up at the sky.

Suddenly one of the soldiers raised a handgun, put it against the woman's temple, and fired.

The woman's head jerked—*I* jerked—and she crumpled to the ground, blood running onto the gravel and pavement. Victoria made a sharp, quiet sound and gripped my arm. My own hands gripped the windowsill, nails digging into wood.

The soldiers didn't touch the woman. They looked down at her, but they didn't search her, didn't move her, nothing. They stood around for a few minutes, smoking cigarettes, then walked out of the alley.

Victoria and I stood at the window in silence, looking down at the woman's body, the dark spreading pool of blood.

"Did you want her dead?" I finally asked. Hoping the answer would be no.

Victoria shook her head.

"Would you have killed her if she'd caught up to you?"

She hesitated, then shrugged. She was pale, the first time I'd ever seen her when she didn't seem completely self-assured. I didn't feel too good myself.

"That's it," she said eventually. "You're going back."

I didn't say a word. I still didn't plan to go back, but I didn't think it was the time to argue.

We waited a long time. Two hours, maybe three. The soldiers never returned. The dead woman lay undisturbed, her feet in the shafts of sunlight that broke through the clouds and the jagged building roofs.

Eventually we went downstairs and crawled back out through the broken window. We crossed the alley to the dead woman. Victoria knelt beside her, went through the coverall pockets and removed a block of keys and a wad of money. She murmured a few words in a language I'd never heard, touched the woman on her chest, shoulders, and throat, then gently closed the woman's eyes. She stood.

"Let's go," she said. "You drive."

We dug out the car, got in. I started the engine and backed slowly down the alley while Victoria played around with the console.

"That way." She pointed down the street as we emerged from the alley. "Go slow."

The street was a mess, but now there were people out on the sidewalks who didn't look like soldiers, and a few other vehicles drove slowly in either direction. We'd gone a couple of blocks when Victoria pointed to a driveway leading through a hedge. I pulled into the driveway, drove through the opening in the hedge, and stopped just behind another car.

"Get this thing turned around so we can pull out in a hurry if we have to."

I did, and left the engine idling.

"Wait here." Victoria got out, walked up to the other car, produced the block of keys she'd taken from the dead woman, and opened the front door. She ducked inside, seemed to do something at the dashboard—another console, I figured.

While she was in the other car, I dug through her bags until I found the gun. I checked to make sure I could work the damn thing, then tucked it between my seat and door.

Victoria left the other car, walked back, and got in beside me. She didn't say anything at first. Instead, she did things with the Mazda's console, working intently for several minutes. Finally she finished and turned to me.

"You're going back," she said. "I am *not* going to be responsible for you being killed."

"No—" I started, but she cut me off, sharp and quick.

"No, nothing," she said. "This isn't the end of it. There'll be someone else after me before long." She paused. "You're going back. I've programmed this thing to make all the shifts, reverse the route we took here."

"It'll take me back?" I asked. "To *my* universe?"

"Close enough so you won't know the difference. Two shifts a day until you're home." She gave me a wad of money. "This should be plenty to get you back. Pretend to be deaf and dumb and illiterate, for Christ's sake, and you'll probably be fine."

"What about you?"

"I'll be taking that," she said, pointing to the car in front of us. "The console in it looks to be working just fine." She turned back to me. "You pull out, and get up to speed as fast as you can. It'll make the first shift as soon as you hit thirty."

"I'd just as soon stay with you," I said.

She got out of the car without answering, shut the door, and came around to the driver's side. I rolled down the window.

"I mean it," I said.

She sighed. "You want me to threaten you with the gun again?"

I gave her a half smile. She leaned through the window and kissed me. Then she pulled back, stepped away from the car. "Go," she said.

I nodded. I put the car in reverse and backed up a few feet. Victoria walked over to the other car, and I stopped. I took the gun, picked what looked to be the most vulnerable spot of the console, and jammed the gun barrel against it. I closed my eyes and pulled the trigger.

I got off six or seven shots, metal flying everywhere, before Victoria grabbed my arm. She screamed something at me that sounded a lot like, "Asshole!"

I opened my eyes. The console was a mess. I looked at Victoria, who stared at me through the open window. I held out the gun, and she took it.

"You're fucking crazy," she said.

I got out of the car, stood beside her. "Want me to drive?"

She didn't answer. We walked to the other car, and I got in behind the wheel, Victoria beside me. I started the engine, put it in gear, and backed around the Mazda. I shifted gears, moved through the hedge, then stopped at the edge of the street. I looked at Victoria, who was shaking her head, but smiling now.

"Do I have to say it?" she asked.

I shook my head. I let out the clutch, swung the car out onto the street, and drove.

In the Season of the Rains

I STILL SEARCH THE NIGHT SKIES WHEN IT RAINS, HOPING to see . . .

It's been a lot of years since my tour ended. Most of them have been all right. But there are times when I think about Scolini, and wonder where he is. And there are times when I wish I'd gone with him.

First there was the heat, wet and heavy and solid around us. Then there was the stifling, lush growth of the jungle, choking the air with its humid breath. And finally, there was the rain. Monsoon season had just begun. The rains came, and did not seem to leave. Even though they stopped during the day, the air was so humid, and we sweated so heavily, we hardly noticed the difference.

Scolini was reading a novel then, *Lord of Light*, by Roger Zelazny. " 'It was in the season of the rains . . . It was well into the time of the great wetness . . .' " That's how the book started, and that's how it was in the jungle. Scolini used to quote those lines over and over at us as we humped through the paddies and over the dikes and into the dense trees and brush and tall grass, weapons turning hot and slick in our hands, the heat leaching water and energy and life from us.

"Fuck you, Scolini," Spider called. "No more."

" 'It was well into the time of the great *wetness'!*" Scolini yelled back.

"I'm gonna pound your face into the fucking great wetness you don't shut the fuck up." Loud, coarse grumbling from the Wizard.

I said nothing. I didn't care, and neither did anyone else, really. It had been a bad week, and we'd been out in the bush too long. Bitching was a way to stay awake, stay alert, and stay alive.

" 'It was in the days of the rains that their prayers went up,' " Scolini intoned. He paused, gazed up through the dense foliage as though searching for something. "Except there's nothing to pray to." He spat violently, and lapsed into silence.

It didn't rain all afternoon, but we never dried out, and the sun boiled up a constant, steamy heat from the jungle. We found the mines and the booby traps on the trails, though, and no one was killed or injured that day—just miserable. Near dusk we came across a silent, deserted village, half a dozen empty, rotting hootches, a ville that wasn't even on the maps. No signs of locals, no signs of VC. Relief and disappointment collided. We were sick of being shot at, picked off by mines, with no way to strike back.

We dug in for the night. Scolini and I carved our foxhole deep in the grass and mud and clay, then ate C-rations as the rain started in again with the falling darkness. The wind kicked up, whipped the rain in under our ponchos.

"I want out of this hellhole," Scolini said.

I didn't answer. What was I supposed to say? Most of us wanted out. But there was a desperate intensity to his voice, and a strange distance, as if he were already partially gone. Still, I thought, he was new, just two months in-country, and I'd probably been the same myself, once.

He went on guard, leaving me alone in the darkness. I sat in the wet foxhole, unable to sleep. Waking dreams came and went, mingling with the reality around me until I couldn't distinguish between the two. It didn't matter. I was used to it now, and it no longer bothered me much.

What still bothered me, though, was that I could not remember what Megan looked like. We were the same age when I left,

talking about marriage, but now I felt I must be at least ten, fifteen years older than she, and I could not call up the image of
her face. I thought she had light brown hair, but was it long or
short, straight or curly or wavy? Hazel eyes, probably, but that's
what my own were, and maybe I was confusing hers with mine.
Her mouth, her nose and chin, all the rest was a blank.

I was still trying to call up a picture of her face, and still fail-
ing, when Scolini slid down into the foxhole, scattering mud
everywhere.

"Fuckin' *a*, Sahara, you're not gonna believe what I saw out
there!" His voice was a hissed whisper, broken by heavy
panting.

"Try me."

"I don't know, man, a flying saucer, a spaceship, something
like that."

"You've been reading too much of that science fiction."

"No, no, I *saw* it, man, a fucking spaceship. Just above the
trees, kind of silent and shimmering, a weird shape, a blue-
green glowing, and pulsing into black, like it was shifting in and
out of existence."

"You drop that acid you've been saving?"

"No, goddammit! I'm telling you, Sahara, it's for real." He
grabbed his helmet with both hands and slammed it into the
mud. "Shit, I saw the fuckin' thing, I *saw* it."

"Basketball ship," I tried. "Maybe something doing recon,
I don't know."

Scolini didn't answer. He picked up his helmet, dumped out
the mud and water, then held it out to let the rain wash it clean.
Distant mortar fire was barely audible, muffled by the rain.
Scolini stood and put on his helmet. He was the only one who
wore the damn thing.

"Gotta get back out," he finally said. "I'm still supposed to
be on watch."

"Hey, Scolini . . ." I started. But he was already climbing out
of the foxhole, and a moment later he was gone.

We were supposed to check out another ville in the afternoon,
but we had to get through the morning first. The rain stopped
just after sunrise, and damp, sweltering heat rode in on us again.
The clay trail was slick and littered with mines which we located
and exploded, one after another. All morning we were harassed
by sniper fire. No one was hit, but nerves were shot.

Just after midday, during a lull, we stopped to eat, and Scolini pulled out *Lord of Light* again. It was his second or third time through, and the book was falling apart in the dampness. He read silently for a few minutes, then quoted to us again: " 'A light rain was falling upon the building, the lotus and the jungle at the foot of the mountains. For six days he had offered many kilowatts of prayer, but the static kept him from being heard On High.' "

"Ain't that the fucking truth," said Fishbone. Scolini nodded, then resumed reading to himself.

"Hey, Rocket Man," Wizard said.

Scolini looked up. "Who, me?"

Wizard grinned. "Yeah, you with the outer space books. You want to keep reading that stuff out loud, that's just fine. Maybe the dinks'll shoot at you instead of me."

We all laughed, and Scolini smiled. He put the book away, and we started back onto the trail.

The afternoon was worse than the morning. The heat baked us, and sniper fire was continuous. Fishbone missed a trip wire, triggered a booby-trapped grenade. Somehow he saw it, or heard it roll out into the trail, yelled, and everyone dove for cover. Fishbone got a foot full of metal, but it wasn't going to kill him, and he grinned and laughed waiting for the dustoff, knowing he was going home.

"Hey, Scolini," I said. "There's your way out." I pointed at Fishbone's foot.

"I've thought about it," he said, serious. "Too goddamn risky. End up like Bristol." He shook his head and gazed into the sky, far away again.

As we neared the ville, the jungle went silent on us. Spider was on point, and slowed us to a crawl. We waited for the ambush, and were surprised when it didn't come. Hot and tense, we crept forward.

The ville was quiet in the heat. Pigs snuffled through the mud, and a dog whined. Old women chewed betel nut, squatting in the shade of the hootches, and grinned at us with dark, red-stained teeth. A baby cried, and we marched in.

The village search was rapid and thorough. We cleared out the hootches, herded all the old men, the women and children into a clearing. Interrogations were brief, repetitive, and fruitless.

We found tunnels. The lieutenant conferred with two sergeants, trying to decide whether to search or blow. Someone else made the decision for them.

"Fire in the hole!" a voice cried out. A few seconds later, two muffled explosions shook the air, then two more. "Fire in the hole!" again, and two more paired explosions.

When the lieutenant walked over to the tunnel mouths to see who'd dropped the grenades, there was no one around. He stood in silence, staring at the ground.

Three men dragged a young woman into an empty hootch, and I walked away so I wouldn't hear it, so I wouldn't see them when they came out.

We continued to search the hootches, tearing baskets apart, smashing pottery, knocking over rice-filled urns and spilling the rice out through the doorways. A dog yelped when somebody kicked it, and someone else knifed a squealing pig. Chickens squawked, and I thought I could hear the cries of a woman.

Crazy Carl was with the villagers; he started slapping the old men with his open palm, and screamed into their faces. Wizard marched a pig past them, then blew it away with his shotgun. Two old women started to laugh, thinking it was supposed to be funny, but when they saw the look on Wizard's face, they stopped. The lieutenant huddled in conference with the two sergeants, standing in the shade, letting things go, trying not to notice, which was fine with everyone.

I spotted Scolini in the brush, squatting with his back against a tree. He'd covered his ears with his hands, and his eyes were closed. I walked over to him, knelt at his side. Behind me, the noise continued unabated—the splintering of wood, the smashing of crockery, the smacking of Crazy Carl's hands, the grunting and squealing and whining and crying of people and animals, one indistinguishable from the other.

I tapped Scolini on the shoulder, and he jerked back, grabbing for his rifle, eyes snapping open. When he saw it was me, he settled back with a long, drawn out shudder.

"I've had it," he said.

We shared a cigarette and listened to the operation winding down. As the noise level dropped, the heat seemed to grow, the air became thick, stagnant and hard to breathe. Before long, we were ready to move out. Incredibly, the Zippo lighters did not appear, and the thatched roofs did not go up in flames.

But as we marched out of the ville, someone took out two of the hootches with a white phosphorous grenade. I stood at the

edge of the jungle, Scolini at my side, the sudden heat sucking
our breath away, and we watched the hootches burn to the
ground in beautiful, delicate flames and clouds of white smoke.

We marched on for another hour, up and down the lower
mountain slopes, and finally dug in for the night. An atmosphere of peace hung in the air, and no one seemed to mind the
rain that started falling at dusk. I gave in to a watering mouth
and aching cheeks, and opened my last can of peaches. I offered
some to Scolini, but he silently refused. He fixed himself a cup
of coffee instead, smoked a final cigarette for the day.

We huddled together in the rain, keeping each other warm,
not talking. Just after dark I went out on guard, but when I came
back, Scolini was gone. The foxhole was cold, and I sat under
the poncho, wet and shivering, wondering where the hell he'd
gone, and wondering if he'd ever come back. The rain continued, the night went on, and I could not sleep.

When Scolini dropped into the foxhole long after midnight,
I knew there would be another story. He was breathing heavily,
and even in the darkness I could see a flush to his skin.

"Christ," he said after a few minutes, then nothing more.

"Don't tell me you saw flying saucers again."

"No. I mean yes, but more than that. Sahara, I saw them,
Jesus Christ, they were . . . they were *aliens*. It *is* a spaceship,
they're from another goddamn world."

"Scolini, it's probably a trick, a helicopter disguised as a—"

He shook his head vigorously, cutting me off. "They weren't
human, Sahara, they weren't human. No fucking way it was a
disguise, man, they were . . ." He shuddered, and shook his
head. "It was weird, Sahara, I'm telling you, it was too fuckin'
weird."

"So tell me, Scolini."

We crouched under our ponchos, the rain still falling, and he
started. "I'm sitting here, watching and listening, I get these
funny feelings. Like some kind of strange vibrations going
through me. I know it sounds crazy, but they were there, shaking inside me, telling me things."

"Like what?"

"Like I had to go back to the ville, the one we hit."

"You didn't."

"I did. I crawled out of this damn hole and started back along
the trail. I don't know, somehow I knew it'd be clear, nothing

new planted, I could just head on down it and I'd be okay. And I was. Made my way mostly by feel. The vibes were still inside me, and I felt like I was in tune with the jungle, with whatever was out there.''

He paused, and blew into his hands a few times. I wanted to tell him he was losing his goddamn mind, but I couldn't. I said nothing, and he went on.

''The village was silent, not even the animals made a sound. Spooky, Sahara, real spooky. So I didn't go in. I stayed in the trees, and I circled the ville, watching for movement, listening hard. Nothing except the rain. No fires. Everyone asleep or dead. Then I saw them.

''Four of them came out from between the huts, glowing like the ship I saw last night. They were taller than anyone I've ever seen—seven, seven and a half feet—and thin, like they had no meat on their bones. Two legs, and I guess two arms, long rubbery things with something like hands attached. They were pale, with dark spots and patches of hair all over their bodies, and long heads with huge dark eyes, but I couldn't tell if there was any mouth or nose or ears, only more of the splotches and chunks of hair. There was the blue-green glow around them, just like the ship, and it pulsed, sometimes going into black so that for a second they would disappear, then shift back. The rain didn't seem to touch them.

''It was only after a couple of minutes I realized they weren't alone. Three of the villagers were with them, walking just behind them as they moved away from the ville. One, I think, was the woman those shits took into the hut today, and the other two were old men. They were following the aliens, willingly it looked like, unless they were drugged or something. But they looked all right, and they followed the aliens into the jungle.

''I stayed back a ways, hoping they wouldn't see me, and kept pace. Most of the time it was easy. I couldn't see the villagers, but I could keep that glow in sight, even in the thickest parts of the trees.

''I don't know how long I followed them. No one noticed me. Finally the glow stopped moving, and I edged in closer. A clearing had been burned out of the jungle, probably by the ship. I could still smell smoke, and the rain made a hissing sound. The ship was on the ground, shimmering and glowing, the same one, or the same kind. Big, like twenty feet high, fifty or sixty feet across. It glowed so much I couldn't really see its shape, I don't know, kind of like a giant claymore mine.

"The four aliens and the villagers stood next to it without moving. All of a sudden a hole sort of melted away in the side of the ship, then *pop! pop! pop!*, the aliens and villagers were just sucked inside, *pop! pop! pop!* Instantaneous. Then the hole closed. A minute later the ship started up, the ground shook a little, and I heard the hollowest sound, more popping in my ears, and the ship rose, pulsing in and out, color into black into color.

"I don't know what happened, next thing I knew I was out in the clearing, under the ship and yelling up at it, screaming at them to come back, yelling and waving. But the ship didn't stop, it kept going up, and up, and when it got above the trees, it hung there for a minute, then shot forward and disappeared."

Scolini stopped, and was quiet for a long time. The rain became heavier, blew in under the ponchos, but it didn't seem to bother him. Finally he spoke again. "Shit, Sahara, I wanted to go with them. I wanted them to come back, and take me away."

In the morning, the heat returned. The peace of the night before had become exhaustion, bodies trying desperately to shut down. We slogged through the jungle, and took sporadic sniper fire, but no one seemed to care. The lieutenant was trying to get us a resupply, but got no promises.

Scolini was distant, preoccupied all morning. He didn't read, he didn't quote anything to us, he didn't say a word. His movements were lethargic and careless, and he kept gazing up at the sky and into the treetops, paying no attention to the trail. I tried talking to him, told him he'd get killed that way, but he didn't answer me.

Midday, Spider was on point as usual, and he brought us to a halt. Word came down the line that there was a clearing ahead, and bodies. Word came down it was bad. Bad was not the right word.

One by one we entered the clearing, and there was no way not to see them. Hanging from the trees, facing us as we emerged from the jungle, were the half-dressed, mutilated corpses of three Marines.

They had been dead a long time, and the worst was the most visible—their sexual organs had been cut off and stuffed into their mouths.

That was the first thing we all saw, the one thing none of us could ignore. Much more had been done to them, and the evidence was there if you could keep looking. I couldn't, and I turned away, seeing nothing more. But it was too late, I'd already seen them, and that first image has never left me. It's usually what brings on the nightmares.

Watson was on his hands and knees, retching. The Wizard and Spider stood side by side in front of the limp bodies, their gazes to the ground. Spider had his knife out, as though preparing to cut them down. Crazy Carl had wandered to the edge of the clearing and stared into the jungle, cursing. "Jesus Christ, they're fucking animals, Jesus Christ, they're fucking animals, Jesus Christ. . . !" It was a litany he kept repeating without pause, louder each time until he was screaming it at the sky. The lieutenant started yelling at him, telling him to can it, ordering him to help Spider cut down the bodies.

And Scolini . . . Scolini was the only one who looked at them without turning away. He stood in the center of the clearing, his stare fixed on the three bodies. His face was dead, without expression. He didn't blink. When he finally moved, he walked slowly to the trees, climbed up into them, and out along the thick branches, and cut down the bodies without a word.

So we got our resupply after all. The helicopters brought in beer, Coke, and ice, food and cigarettes, ammunition and mail, and they took what was left of the bodies back with them. We were through for the day.

I sat with Scolini in the shade of a tall, thick bush. I was on my third cigarette and my second Coke, rereading the one piece of mail I'd received—a letter from Megan. The words in her letter carried no meaning. There was no picture enclosed, and her face became even less distinct. Scolini was sucking on ice, staring into the trees. He hadn't opened any of his mail.

"Sahara, what would you do if some alien beings offered to take you away in their ship?"

"Run like hell," I said. "Call in the gunships." I tried laughing, didn't quite make it. I'd hoped he wouldn't mention the aliens again.

"It would be a way out of here," he said.

"I've got a way out. A nice safe airplane back to the World."

"If you make it 'til then."

"I've only got a month and a half. Forty-six days. I'll make it."

"I won't." He bit down on the ice, cracking it. "I've got ten fucking months. No way I'll make it out of here with my body and mind both intact." He shook his head. "Look at you. Your heart's dead. You don't feel a fuckin' thing anymore." He sighed. "I'm sorry." For a minute he seemed very far away. "After today, you know what's going to happen in the next ville we hit? It's going to make yesterday look like a picnic."

I couldn't argue with him, but I didn't really want to think about it.

"I'm going after them," Scolini said.

"Who?"

"The aliens."

"They're not real, Scolini."

"They're real. And I'm going to find them. I'm going to find them and make them take me away from here. I'm leaving this goddamn war, Sahara, and I'm not coming back."

I knew he would go, and I knew I couldn't stop him, so when night fell and Scolini headed silently back down the trail, I went along. I didn't believe we'd find anything, but I wanted to be with him when he realized that, with him when he lost it all and freaked. I wanted to bring him back alive. And, I don't know, maybe I wanted to believe there *was* something out there that would take us away from the war.

The rain was light, but the darkness was complete. Scolini took us off the trails almost immediately, and we forced our way slowly through the lush jungle growth. It was crazy, two idiots wandering aimlessly through the jungle at night, but I couldn't say anything to him. Somehow we were quiet enough so we didn't get shot at by anyone. Maybe the rain helped. Maybe it was Scolini's vibes.

"Where the hell we going?" I asked.

"I'm tracking," he said. "I can hear them, just a taste. We're doing all right."

I could hear nothing but the rain above, water dripping from the leaves, animal noises, and my heartbeat. I could see nothing but Scolini's dark form just in front of me. "We're going to get wasted," I said.

"By who?"

"VC. Booby traps. Our own guys. The jungle. Maybe even your goddamn aliens."

Scolini laughed. "Shit, not a chance." Then, "There! See it? Now it's gone."

"See what?"

"The flash. The glow."

I'd seen nothing, and I didn't answer. We pushed on. My eyes adjusted to the darkness, and now I could see the leaves and branches ahead of me, and the ground at my feet. The moon was nearly full, and once in a while there'd be a break in the clouds and dull silver light would trickle down through the canopy for a brief moment before the darkness returned.

Every few minutes Scolini would hiss "There!" or "Hear that?", and follow with "We're getting closer, Sahara. I'm beginning to feel them." Each time I saw and heard nothing, and before long I was convinced Scolini had gone completely mad.

We moved through areas where mosquitoes overwhelmed us, pockets of jungle so thick we had to crawl. We waded through a river that might have been the one we'd forded that morning. We waded through other rivers of wet, chest-high grass. Several times we crossed trails that would have made the going easier, but Scolini ignored them and pushed back into the jungle.

Hours passed, felt like days. Exhaustion pressed in on me along with the trees and the rain and the darkness, and I just wanted to sleep. I itched everywhere, and I felt as if my flesh was dotted with tiny burning wounds. My clothes were soaked with sweat and rain, clinging to me. My breath came in hard, aching gasps, but Scolini pressed on, stronger and more confident, seeing flashes and glows more often as we continued, homing in on inaudible sounds.

After a while, though, I was beginning to see the flashes myself. "There," Scolini would say, and just in the corner of my vision I'd spot a shimmer of color. Sometimes I caught a glimpse before he said a word. When I told him I was seeing the flashes, he picked up the pace, rejuvenated. Soon I even began to hear what Scolini heard: a brief, hollow vibration, a fluttering in my ears.

But what was it we were seeing? Glimpses of a spaceship somewhere deep in the jungle, or groups of aliens moving through the trees? And the sounds, were they the result of alien machines and technology? Or was it all hallucination? I thought of Wizard, who had once said the entire war was a consensus hallucination. I was beginning to think Scolini wasn't so crazy, and that it didn't matter what was real.

Sometime after midnight, Scolini stopped, and pointed through the dense foliage. In the distance shimmered a dim, blue-green glow, fragmented by leaves and branches and tree trunks. It was more than a flash, more than an uncertain glimpse, and it remained in sight, motionless.

"There it is." Scolini's voice was a hushed whisper. "Our way out."

"You're serious," I said. "About going away with them, whatever they are?"

"Of course. Aren't you?"

"I didn't even believe in the goddamn things." I still didn't know what I was seeing, but I was certain it was, in some sense, real.

"Then why the hell are you here?"

"I don't know."

Scolini started to laugh. "Oh, shit, man." He grabbed my arm. "Hey, it doesn't matter. You're here now, and there they are. Let's go." He pulled at me and headed for the shimmering glow.

The timing was too damn good. They must have sensed us coming. As Scolini pushed through the trees, and I followed, a heavier vibration shook the jungle floor.

"Christ, Sahara, they're leaving!" He surged forward, crashing through the trees and grass and bushes. I followed, but couldn't match his pace, and he emerged into the clearing before I did.

The ship lifted slowly from the ground, and Scolini staggered toward it, arms outstretched. "Don't go!" he shouted. "Take us with you, goddammit!"

I reached the edge of the clearing and stopped, watching him, staring at the ship, which rose only an inch every few seconds. As big as Scolini had said, it was encased in a blurred, blue-green shell of light that pulsed regularly. Its outline was indistinct, fuzzy with the glow.

The ship rose to chest level and stopped, silently vibrating the air around us. Scolini yelled, leaped upward, and tried to grab onto it. His hands disappeared within the glow for a moment, he hung a foot or two above the earth, then a dark, swirling hole opened in the side of the ship, and Scolini was sucked inside. His helmet flew off, ejected away from the ship, and tumbled to the ground. The hole collapsed, the ship's glow solidified, and Scolini was gone.

I stepped out of the trees and approached the ship. It hovered, still not rising, as if waiting for me. I stared at it, watched it pulse as it loomed above. Scolini was inside, and I felt certain if I jumped at the ship it would take me as well. But what were they doing to him? What would they do to me?

I took two, three steps back, afraid another hole would open in the side of the ship. I wanted out, just like everyone else, but not this way. This was crazy, wasn't it?

I didn't move, and the ship remained motionless, nearly silent. Every ten or fifteen seconds it flickered to black for just an instant, then the color returned. I felt my heartbeat slow to match the rhythm of the colored pulse, felt it hesitate each time the ship went to black. I didn't know what to do; I could not approach the ship, and I could not back away. Once I leaned slightly forward, and a spot of black started to form within the glow, but I jerked backward and the spot disappeared. Finally, after what seemed like more than an hour, I took two more steps back, and the ship began to rise once more.

I watched, unmoving, as the huge, glowing craft rose above the treetops and hovered for several moments. It shifted colors, tailing momentarily to indigo, then slipped back to blue-green and shot forward, vanishing into the west.

The rain had stopped. I picked up Scolini's helmet, put it on, and gazed up into the cloud-covered sky. I waited a long time, watching for colored glows, listening for the hollow vibrations in my ears, but there was nothing. The ship did not return. The wind picked up, cold and damp, and once again it began to rain.

I never saw him again. Nor did anyone else. He was listed MIA, a status that never changed.

Maybe the aliens took Scolini for a long ride, then dropped him off somewhere else in the jungle where he later died. Maybe they kept him, studied and experimented on him, tortured and killed him. But maybe he found a way to talk with the aliens, explained to them what he wanted, and they took him away to a better place.

It's been a lot of years since my tour ended. Most of them have been all right. But there are times that haven't been. Scolini was wrong about one thing. My heart isn't dead; it is just encased in a protective shell, preserving what still survives. Sometimes that shell cracks, or begins to melt away, and then come the bad times—when hallucinations overwhelm me and I see rice paddies in my bathtub and body bags in mail trucks; when I get the shakes and can't hold down any food; and when the nightmares start with the three dead Marines, and get so bad I wake up screaming in the hot darkness, afraid to go back to sleep.

Times when I think about Scolini, and wonder where he is.

Times when I wish I'd gone with him.

And when it rains, I still search the night skies, hoping to see. . . .

The Open Boat

ALL OF THEM KNEW THE COLOR OF THE SKY. THEY DID not look out at it anymore, but they knew—black, unending black, blacker than night. No stars; nothing.

They drifted in a nonsector of the nonuniverse. That's what Jackal had called it just a while ago—a nonsector of the nonuniverse. He was the amateur astrophysicist, he was the one who was supposed to know. Sara pictured herself in an open boat, rising and falling with ocean swells. The reality, of course, was nothing like that.

They were not in a boat, exactly, though it was, in theory, the interstellar equivalent of a lifeboat, and it was not open, though the canopies could be retracted from viewing ports so they could look out at the blackness all around them. But no one did that anymore.

There were three men and two women, though one of the men, Hallic, was hardly more than a boy, really, eighteen, nineteen years old. The boy was catatonic, sat against the wall without moving, without speaking, eyes open and rarely blinking. There was Jackal, who did not seem to be anything like his name—he was quiet, his movements slow and deliberate with an almost surreal economy. There was Cass, a strong, lanky woman who could not seem to stop moving about their cramped quarters. And there was Bertrand, a tall man dressed in clothes more fit for a trek through the mountains than for a starship voyage. And finally there was Sara: disillusioned sound-sculptor and despairing social critic; that was how she had often described herself. But she didn't say anything like that to the others. Neither of those labels seemed particularly relevant in their present circumstances.

The lifeboat hovered completely without motion, held in stasis, moored outside reality.

The lifeboat: two cabins, one in which they slept (there were bunks for six and a tiny bathroom), one in which they ate, read, talked, did everything else. According to the lifeboat manual, which Cass had found in a wall cubicle, there was food, water, and air for months, perhaps years, assuming all the recyclers remained functional. They had all tried reading the manual during the first couple of days, but only Jackal understood much of it. He appeared to know a lot that was not in the manual. The boat, he explained, was programmed to shift back into the real universe at some randomly determined time, at which point an automatic beacon would begin broadcasting. There was no control over where they would appear, but there was a ninety-seven percent probability that they would reappear within the Milky Way.

Sara did not find that particularly reassuring.

None of them knew what had happened to the main ship. For the jump into subspace—nonuniverse, Jackal insisted—all passengers entered the lifeboats. If the jump had gone well, they would have remained in the lifeboats for an hour or two, then, after the jump back into real space, they would have returned to their regular cabins.

Apparently the jump had not gone well.

Sara had felt a strange, hollow vibration, a queasy loss of gravity followed by a brief, jolting acceleration, then nothing. She had felt nothing from the lifeboat since.

The vibration, the drop, and acceleration—that was the lifeboat being jettisoned from the main ship, Jackal had later explained. It was a kind of secondary subspace/subspace jump, each of the 350 lifeboats given a different set of vectors. The theory was, Jackal went on, that this way all the lifeboats would reappear in different parts of the galaxy, and at least some of them might be rescued.

The more Jackal knew, the less reassured Sara felt. She began to wish he'd know nothing.

Sara knelt beside the boy, brushed fingers across his cheek. He did not move.

Bertrand did push-ups, sit-ups, jumping jacks. Cass paced relentlessly back and forth, from one corner to another. Jackal sat on one of the wall benches and rolled his head, neck bones popping and cracking. Hallic did nothing. Sara watched, doing little more than the boy.

Following the realization that the jump had gone wrong, and that they were in trouble, they had spent the first two or three days making what Sara now saw were futile attempts at forging a united front against their circumstances. Striving for a sense of community, camaraderie. Pulling together to find a way out, a way to survive.

Actually, not all of them. The boy, Hallic, had said almost nothing, speaking only when directly questioned. But even that had not lasted through the first day—he soon withdrew completely, stopped speaking or moving, and they had heard nothing from him since.

As for the others, Sara thought, well, they *had* tried. They had talked about their occupations, where they had come from, where they were going. Families, friends, even enemies. They read and reread the lifeboat manual, discussed options (there weren't any). But none of their discussion had any real value in the end, none of it meant anything. None of it brought them together. None of it could help them.

They soon gave up trying. There was nothing, absolutely nothing they could do, and they knew it.

Sara sat on her own bench (tiny territories had been wordlessly staked out within hours), trying to gauge the passage of time. No sun, no moon, no clock (Sara had no wristwatch, and would not look at Jackal's). She took a small pleasure in the way time seemed to shift, sometimes moving slowly, sometimes quickly, and always catching her by surprise.

"It's time to feed him again," Cass said. She wasn't looking at the boy, but Sara knew who she meant.

The boy was naked from the waist down. They had undressed him that much to make the trips to the toilet easier; his body, once seated, seemed to know what to do.

"How long before we drop back into real space?" Bertrand asked. He had already asked the question a dozen times, and Jackal had ceased trying to answer.

Sara punched for a foodpac, took it to the boy. She sat beside him, held the open packet to his mouth and squeezed. As the thick, gluey substance moved into his mouth, the boy chewed, then swallowed. Sara fed him the rest of the packet, then Cass brought a second, and two bulbs of juice. When he was done, Sara washed his face.

"He has a better appetite than I do," Cass said. She looked at Sara, tried to smile, then shrugged.

"How *long?*" Bertrand asked.

There were pens but no paper. Sara discovered seven blank sheets in the back of the lifeboat manual, and tore them out. She wanted to write, but didn't know if she should try writing a story, or start a journal.

If she wrote a story, she could title it "The Open Boat." She had long ago read a story with that title, a story about people in a lifeboat. She closed her eyes and tried to remember exactly how the story had begun. Something about no one knowing the color of the sky. Sara opened her eyes, looked at the closed canopies. Here, they all knew the color of the sky, and wished they didn't.

She set aside the paper and pen. Maybe later.

Sara wondered if there were other lifeboats nearby. When she asked, Jackal said that "nearby" was a meaningless word in the nonuniverse. She went to one of the viewing port canopies.

"If we opened all the canopies," she said, "maybe we could see the lights of another lifeboat."

Jackal snorted. "You really have no conception of what the nonuniverse is all about, do you?"

Sara turned to look at him. "No, I don't," she said. "Do you?"

They slept in shifts—to give themselves privacy to sleep, and a little privacy while awake. Cass and Sara had one shift, Bertrand and Jackal another. A third shift was completely open. The boy slept wherever he was, with no apparent regularity. Jackal programmed his wristwatch to sound off for each shift.

Bertrand did push-ups, sit-ups, jumping jacks. Cass paced up and down, back and forth. Jackal cracked his neck. The boy did nothing. Sara tried to write.

Day . . . she began. She glanced up at Jackal. Crack. "How many days has it been since the jump?" she asked.

"Days don't have any meaning in the nonuniverse," he replied.

"How many days?" she asked again.

Jackal looked at her. Then he looked at his wristwatch. "Six and a half," he said.

Day Seven:, Sara wrote. *I would like to strangle Jackal.*

"We are in God's maw," Cass said. Then she laughed.

"We need to stay in shape," Bertrand said. "Physically. Mentally. Here and when we get back into real space. We don't want to be insane when we're rescued."

Cass stopped pacing, looked at him. "Doctor," she said, "will I be able to play the violin after the operation?"

Jackal laughed. Bertrand looked at Cass, confused. Sara smiled.

"I don't understand," Bertrand finally said.

"It's an old joke," Cass said.

"A *very* old joke," Jackal said.

Sara stopped smiling, watching them. Bertrand breathed in deeply, then started doing more push-ups.

"Oh Christ," Jackal whispered.

"So why do we have gravity?" Cass asked. "Why aren't we floating around in here?"

"I don't know," Jackal said. "It's an unexplained side-effect of a jump into the nonuniverse."

Cass grinned. *"You* don't *know?"*

Jackal glared at her. "No one knows."

Day Ten: The lifeboat is too small for us. Perhaps it would be different, easier, if we had known each other before this trip, if we had been friends. Perhaps not. Sleep is the best time for me, even with so many strange dreams. Last night ("Night has no meaning in the non-universe," Jackal would say) I dreamed I was performing in an underground grotto, thousands of people in the audience. I was part of an ensemble, with four other sound-sculptors. But when we began to perform the first piece, I found I had forgotten how. I stood on the stage and made awkward, miming motions, shaping no sound at all, hoping no one would notice. Then I woke up.

"How long before we drop back into real space?" Bertrand asked.

Sara looked at Jackal, who returned her gaze for a moment then looked away. He did not answer.

At first, Bertrand's constant questioning had been annoying, then almost amusing, but now it had become awkward, raising the tension in the cabin.

"Shut up," Cass said. "Just shut the hell up."

It had been far too long, Sara knew. They all knew. Except, perhaps, for Bertrand. She had read the manual, and though it was not very specific, it was clear that the random program to drop the lifeboat back into real space should have activated within a few days at most. Something had gone wrong. There was, as far as she could tell, no backup procedure that would allow them to activate it manually.

"Is it really an unreasonable question?" Bertrand asked. It was the first time he had pursued the matter beyond the initial question.

Jackal cracked his neck, then stood and approached Bertrand. When he spoke, his voice was soft and even. "Reasonable or not, you ask that question one more time, and I will smash your head against the wall."

"I think *he* has the right idea," Cass said. She was looking at the boy.

Sara jerked out of a doze, sat up. A strange, hollow feeling had come upon her, a heavy unease laced with vertigo. It moved through her like a slowly, slowly breaking wave. She lost her sense of time, and couldn't tell how long it was lasting. A few seconds? A few minutes? An hour?

Then it was gone.

She looked around the room, wondering if the others, too, had felt it. They were *all* looking at one another.

"What the *hell* was that?" Cass finally asked.

"It's the nonuniverse leaking through the walls," Jackal replied. "Leaking into us. The walls are breaking down."

"Will it change us?" Sara asked.

Jackal looked at her and snorted. "What do you think?"

Bertrand did push-ups, sit-ups. Jackal cracked his neck. Sara thought about going to bed, thinking she might be tired. She thought her shift might be on. No one could be sure anymore, not since all the wristwatches had ceased to function. Cass apparently was already asleep. She hadn't been in the front cabin for a while.

Sara went to the door, pressed the plate, and the door slid aside. The cabin was dark, and she palmed up the light.

Cass sat on a lower bunk, next to the catatonic boy, her head buried in her hands. The boy was naked from the waist down, as always, but now was disturbingly aroused. Cass looked up at Sara, her face streaked with tears, her skin flushed. "Leave me alone!" she shouted. "Just leave me the hell alone!"

Sara backed out and closed the door. She turned, looked at Jackal and Bertrand. Jackal just shrugged. Bertrand, as usual, appeared confused.

Sara returned to her chair, picked up pen and journal. She sat and stared at it for a long time.

Day Thirteen: Thirteen? It's an arbitrary number. No one has any idea anymore what day it is. All I can do is number these entries consecutively.

I've been thinking about a story, "The Open Boat." It's about four men in a lifeboat from a sinking ship. Working together, cooperating with each other, enduring, they row the lifeboat through a storm, against heavy waves, strong currents and tides, eventually reaching shore, and safety. One dies, I think, but the others live. I think about the story, but I find no comfort in it. There is nothing in it that applies here.

Sara went to one of the viewing ports and retracted the canopy. She looked out into the unending black, seeing nothing. She wondered if, when the canopy was retracted, the light from inside the lifeboat traveled out through the viewing port and into the black, into the nonuniverse. If it did, what happened to it out there? If not, what stopped it? She decided she would not ask Jackal.

*   *   *

"We're not going to be rescued," Bertrand said. He looked surprised, as if the thought had just occurred to him.

Jackal snorted.

"Brilliant observation," Cass said.

Sara watched Bertrand and, for some reason she did not completely understand, felt tremendous pity for the man.

Day Seventeen: The waves are coming more frequently now. The non-universe leaking through. Not all the time, but once every few hours, perhaps. It's getting hard to tell time, so I can't be sure. It's getting hard to do anything now, even think. But the waves are coming. Do they mean anything? No one knows.

"Close that damn thing." Cass's voice, harsh and dry.

Sara was standing at one of the viewing ports again, the canopy retracted. She turned to look at Cass, who stood in the doorway between the two cabins. There were large, dark patches under her eyes.

"I said close it."

Sara turned back to the port, looked out once more, then closed the canopy.

Bertrand did a few sit-ups, then stopped. Sara could not remember the last time she had seen him do a push-up or a jumping jack. Cass no longer paced the front room; she sat, hardly moving, gazing at nothing. Jackal still cracked his neck, but the sounds were growing louder, and Sara wondered if something was going to break soon. Sara picked up her journal. She stared at it, but could not think of a single thing to write.

Sara got up and walked through the two cabins, taking inventory. Bertrand standing in the corner, arms outstretched. Jackal on his bench, rereading the lifeboat manual. The boy on his back in a bottom bunk, eyes open, staring at the bunk above him. Cass in an upper bunk, curled up tight, asleep. Sara returned to her seat. They were all still here.

"How long before we drop back into real space?"

Sara looked up, wondering what Jackal would do to Bertrand. But then, as she saw Bertrand asleep in the corner, a real fear dug into her. It was Jackal who had asked the question.

*   *   *

Sara picked up her journal, glanced through it. The last words written were *Day Nineteen*. There was no entry.

She wondered how long ago that had been. When she thought about it, she was surprised she had been able to keep up with the entries as long as she had.

Sara flipped back to the first page, stared at it without reading any of the words. She thought about reading all the entries, first to last. Instead, she dropped the journal to the floor.

There were no mirrors in the lifeboat, no polished metal surfaces to act as a substitute. Sara wasn't sure she remembered what she looked like. She approached one of the viewing ports and retracted the canopy, certain she would be able to see herself in the port glass. But there was nothing there, not even a glint of light, as if the nonuniverse outside sucked away her reflection, returning nothing.

"The second law," Jackal whispered.

"The second law?" Sara said. "Second law of what?"

But Jackal did not answer. He did not even look at her. The second law, Sara thought. Of thermodynamics? She couldn't think of anything else. Was that the one about entropy? Or inertia? She wasn't sure. She wasn't sure if it even mattered. They weren't in the universe anymore. Did the second law of thermodynamics apply here? Did *anything* apply here?

Sara was fairly sure she was not sleeping anymore. She still dreamed, but she did so while awake, her eyes open. The visual aspects of her dreams overlaid her surroundings, so that she saw both at the same time. And sometimes, when a wave of the nonuniverse moved through her while she dreamed, a third reality joined the other two, each remaining distinct, yet connecting with one another, forming new and wonderful patterns, opening new worlds to her. And when that happened, she wished for it to never stop.

Inventory. Sara was losing track of everything. It was slower, harder each time. Bertrand. Jackal. Cass. Hallic. Herself. Everyone was still here.

Sara realized she had not eaten in a long time. And nothing

to drink. For days. Weeks, perhaps. She could not remember when she had last eaten. She could not remember when she had last used the toilet. She could not remember when she had last seen *any* of them eat or drink. Perhaps they no longer needed food or water to live.

It occurred to her then that they would never starve, never die of thirst, no matter how long they were stranded. They could go on forever.

Panic swept through her. She wanted to ask Jackal if it was possible, but when she opened her mouth, no sound emerged. Just as quickly as it had come, the panic left her.

She could not remember the last time any of them had spoken.

Inventory. One, two, three men. A woman. Herself. Was that everyone?

Sara stood at the viewing port, the canopy retracted. She stared out into the emptiness, the unending black. She had not moved in a long time, not even to look around the cabin. She no longer knew if the others were still here with her.

For a long time she had wondered when it would end. Not anymore. She knew, now.

It did not end. Ever.

Ever.

Lunar Triptych: Embracing the Night

SIDE PANEL

"YOU MUST NOT EMBRACE THE NIGHT," KARYN SAID. Carter did not understand. In part, she was telling him to stay on Earth, to stay off the shuttles; but there was little chance of spaceflight for him, or anyone, in the near future, and they had been through all that before. So what was she trying to tell him now?

Carter stepped out onto the apartment balcony and looked up into the night sky. He left the sliding door open so Karyn could follow, but he knew she would stay inside. For seven and a half weeks now Karyn had not once left the apartment unless the sun was out, the sky clear and blue without a trace of cloud.

Far to the west, across the open plaza and just above the lowest building of the apartment complex, Carter could see the lights of the gantry blinking in the warm night air, flickering like the stars overhead. He sat in the chair nearest the railing where he could look down at the smallest of the plaza's three pools, five stories directly below him. Although it was close to midnight, a lone figure swam steadily back and forth, in and out of the cone of light from the underwater lamp. The swimmer—a woman, he thought—did not slow or miss a beat, even when making the smooth flip-turns at each end of the pool. Perfectly at home in the water, even though not born to it.

Maybe that was the analogy he needed for his testimony at the Congressional hearings, Carter thought. That there were people, like the swimmer, always at home in the water, while others never were. The same should be true of outer space, he believed, and he could see no reason for halting manned space exploration because of those who could *not* go into space. The answer was to go on with those who could.

Carter's hand reached to his empty shirt pocket, a reflex action that remained even after four years. Right now he wished he still smoked. His hands wanted something to do.

"Are you coming to bed?" Karyn asked.

Carter turned to look through the open doorway at her. Fair-haired, fair-skinned, she was already between the white sheets, wrapped in a heavy flannel nightgown and propped against the headboard, the white spread pulled up over her bent knees. One of the two lamps on the stand beside her was lit, and she reached over to switch on the other.

Karyn would not even sleep in the dark anymore. At night there was at least one light on in each room of the apartment, illuminating her nocturnal wanderings which were growing more frequent; she rarely slept the night through now. Two weeks earlier, when she had only a single lamp on the night-stand, the bulb had gone out at three in the morning, plunging the room into darkness. Karyn had jerked up convulsively, instantly awake and screaming. Her screams had continued until Carter managed to retrieve the living room lamp and plug it in, returning light to the bedroom. Now Karyn slept with two lamps next to her, spare bulbs in easy reach.

Carter turned back to look down at the pool, but the swimmer had emerged from the water and now sat in a lounge chair, looking up at him, wearing dark sunglasses. He felt certain it was the same woman he had seen around the complex lately, often enough so it seemed she was following him. With black hair, and always wearing the sunglasses, she only appeared at night. Maybe she thought the darkness and the sunglasses gave her some kind of protection. She never spoke to him, but when he encountered her she watched him continuously, her head turning to follow wherever he went, and he wished that just once he could see her eyes.

He watched the woman a few moments longer, her face still directed up toward him, glanced once more at the gantry lights in the distance, then stood and went inside.

"You *are* going to testify tomorrow, aren't you?" Karyn asked as he got into bed next to her.

"Yes."

She sighed heavily, shook her head. "It doesn't much matter," she said. "Your testimony won't help anyway, it's too late now, the verdict's almost in."

"Probably so."

There was a long silence, and they lay beside each other without touching. Carter could not remember the last time they had made love. It had been back in their house in Massachusetts, that was all he knew. Not once since they had moved out here and into this apartment.

"The eternal night," Karyn whispered. "We aren't meant to join it."

Carter rolled onto his side and looked at her. This was new, like what she had said earlier. She was beginning to sound like a newly converted mystic.

"Can't you see the pattern, Carter? All the problems, the accidents, the mechanical failures, the nervous breakdowns, and now the collapse of the Mars Expedition. They'll go on, growing worse all the time until we stop trying, until we realize we belong here, only on Earth. Until we stop trying to leave."

Carter did not know what to say. He had heard the same ideas before; they had all heard them, more often in recent weeks. Voiced by what NASA liked to call the "lunatic fringe." For a while it had been a kind of in-joke. Luna, lunatic. But with the Congressional hearings nearly concluded, and the effective demise of NASA practically a foregone conclusion, the joke had quickly paled.

He turned over and looked out through the glass door, unable to see much of the night with the two lamps burning brightly behind him. He tried to sleep, but his eyes remained open, and he began to wish he had sunglasses of his own to shade his eyes as he searched for sleep, for signs of the night sky.

CENTER PANEL

Two nights after the Congressional hearings had ended, there was an enormous outdoor party at the apartment complex, celebrating the end of NASA and manned exploration of space. Residents and invited guests only were permitted, but still Carter guessed there were nearly six hundred people milling around the main pool and through the lush plaza lit by a hundred burning torches, dancing on the large cement patios to the loud music of a local rock band. The music was techno-punk, complete with rainbowed lasers blazing forth from the instruments. Carter stood at the balcony railing, watching, and wondered how all these people, many of whom would soon be losing their jobs, could be so happy.

He turned and looked into the bedroom through the screen door, at Karyn who sat in a corner chair reading.

"You want to go down to the party?" he asked, knowing she wouldn't. "This ought to be your victory celebration."

She looked up at him, but didn't respond. Carter shrugged and opened the screen door, stepped inside. "I'm going down," he said. He slid the door shut and started toward the hall.

"Wait," she said. "Before you go . . ."

Carter stopped, turned and leaned against the wall, watching her.

"I've lost you, Carter."

Yes, he thought, a long time ago, though he had not really known it, or known why. "Do you really want me?" he asked.

"Not anymore. We've become too . . . different."

No, we've always been different, we just never saw it. But he did not say anything.

"I wanted to wait until the hearings were finished," she said. "Until you were done. I've already talked to an attorney. I told him I didn't think there would be any problems, any fighting. That it would be an amicable divorce."

He looked at her for a long time without speaking, then nodded once. "All right," he said.

"I want the house."

He nodded again. "It's yours." He paused for a moment, then added, "The kids, too."

She turned away from him, her fingers trembling for a moment before she clasped her hands together. They had no children.

"I'm sorry," he said, meaning it.

She breathed deeply twice. "You can have the car." Another pause, another deep breath. "I'm leaving tomorrow morning. Will you drive me to the train station?"

"Of course."

She looked back at him. "What will you do now, Carter? Your job won't last much longer."

He shrugged. "I really don't know."

Karyn nodded, returned her attention to her book, and said no more. So simple, Carter thought. He turned away from her and walked out.

At the edge of the plaza, Carter hesitated a moment, then pushed into the crowd. He welcomed the press of people, the feel of bodies in motion and close contact, flesh touching flesh. He breathed deeply, inhaling the aroma of sweat and smoke and pot, alcohol and perfume, the gas-like smell of the torches. The babble of the crowd was almost as loud as the band, and he relished the noise. He felt lost and anonymous, and was content.

Carter passed one of the open bars and squeezed up to the counter, where he ordered Scotch on the rocks. Drink in hand, he pushed back into the crowd. As he neared the elevated stage, the music and singing from the band became more distinct. Surprisingly, some of the lyrics were intelligible, though shouted rapidly, almost erupting from the singer's mouth. He caught the words "silver" and "light" and "sucking illusions," and the word "night" repeated several times, but he could never quite make any sense of what he heard.

A hand gripped his shoulder, pulled him around. Carter found himself staring into dark sunglasses reflecting torchlight directly back at him. The woman.

She smiled, hooked her arm through his, and led him through the crowd. He didn't resist, too curious. She was dressed in a short, dark jumper, her legs bare, her feet in white ballet slippers. As they passed another of the bars, Carter quickly finished his drink and set the empty glass on the counter.

The woman led the way toward the lobby of the south building. The security guard, recognizing them, let them through without a word. When the door closed behind them, a heavy quiet filled the lobby.

They stood in front of the elevator doors, waiting. Her glasses were so dark and mirrored he could not see her eyes, only a doubled, distorted version of himself reflected back at him.

"My name is Carter," he said.

"I know. Carter Strang. I'm Nicole."

"How do you know me?"

The elevator opened, Nicole smiled, and they stepped inside. Nicole touched the sixth floor circle, which lit up a pale orange. She leaned back against the elevator wall, looking at him. The elevator began to rise.

"I know you," she said. "You've shot up. To the stations, to Luna."

She made it sound like a drug trip. Maybe that was how she saw it.

"I follow all the astronauts," she went on. "All who leave this prison and sail up into the night."

Carter started to protest, then said nothing. He never thought of himself as an astronaut. He was a psychologist for NASA, and had made seven previous trips off Earth—four tours of the stations and three trips to Luna. But people like Nicole saw them all as astronauts, and it would not matter what he said to her about it.

The elevator stopped at the sixth floor and the doors slid apart. Carter hesitated before leaving the elevator; he was beginning to realize what she was. But something, simple curiosity perhaps, continued to draw him, and he followed her along the hall.

"I watched the hearings on TV," Nicole said. "I watched when you talked. They didn't listen to you, but *I* did, and I understood what you were trying to tell them."

Carter wasn't so sure he had understood himself, and almost asked her to explain it to him, but he didn't. At the fifth door on the right, Nicole stopped and inserted a key. Before she turned it she reached out with her other hand and took his arm.

"Quickly please," she said. She turned the key and opened the door just enough to reach inside. Carter could see that the interior of the apartment was brightly lit, but only for a moment. Nicole's hand touched a switch, the apartment went dark, and she pulled him inside, closing the door behind them.

Points of fluorescent light, thousands of them like stars in the night sky, were everywhere. Walls, ceiling, furniture, even the floor sparkled with the tiny pinpoints of silver. Although he did not recognize any constellations, Carter would not have been surprised to see one.

There was enough light from all the fluorescent dots to barely make out furniture outlines, to see Nicole just a foot away. She faced him and slowly removed her sunglasses. He had expected her eyes to be something special, shining with a strange, dazzling light, but they appeared to be quite ordinary. In the darkness he could not make out their color.

"What you were saying was so right," she said. "About some people being at home in the water, and some being terrified of it no matter how well they swam, and that that's how it is with space—some people can't handle it, but that some people *can*. Some people might even be more at home in space than on Earth. *I* understand. I believe you're right, because that's where *I* belong, out in deep space among all the stars."

She took his hand and gently guided him along the short hall into the bedroom. He knew he should leave, perhaps should never have come in at all, but he was still too curious.

The bedroom was like the rest of the apartment, dark and filled with stars. Carter had trouble maintaining his balance, his referents hazy, almost invisible—he felt cast adrift, loose and without moorings.

In front of the sliding glass door that led out onto the balcony was a telescope. It was directed slightly downward and to the east. Carter walked unsteadily to it and looked into the eyepiece.

As he expected, the telescope was trained on the balcony of his apartment. He could see the bright glow emanating from the bedroom, and wondered if Karyn was still reading, or sleeping . . . or packing to leave the next morning.

"Come here," Nicole whispered.

Carter turned toward her, shaking his head. It was time to go.

Nicole reached for him, a dark phantom, and he backed away, jostling the telescope. He turned from her and, still disoriented, staggered out of the bedroom. His lungs seemed to tighten, cutting his breath, and he bumped into walls twice moving along the hallway.

"Carter, come back," Nicole called, little more than a whisper.

He stumbled through the front room, crashed into a chair, then found the front door and opened it. He stepped out into the light of the hall, closed the door quickly behind him and leaned against it, breathing heavily.

The terrible thing was, he *did* want to go back to her, despite the dizziness, despite the fear. But he couldn't. Not yet.

After a minute or two his breathing was almost back to normal, his balance steady. Surprised that Nicole had not followed him, but relieved, Carter pushed away from the door and started slowly down the hall.

Emerging from the elevator and into the lobby, Carter saw a vaguely familiar man dressed in a dark suit seated in one of the chairs near the street entrance. The man stood—he was tall and large with sandy, gray-streaked hair—and casually approached. His tie was loose, top shirt button undone.

"Carter Strang? I'm William Knopfler, with the Defense Department." He put out his hand. "We've met once before."

"I think twice, actually," Carter said. They shook hands. "And I believe I saw you at the hearings."

"I was extremely interested in what you had to say."

"No one else was."

Knopfler smiled. "Let's go for a walk. I'd like to talk to you."

"What about?"

"A job. You're probably going to need one soon." The smile didn't falter.

Carter gave Knopfler a half smile in return, and nodded.

Knopfler led the way out through the street entrance, into warm fresh air and relative quiet. The sounds of the party were muted, distant, and street traffic was light, just an occasional car or truck driving slowly past. They walked along the sidewalk around the complex, silent at first, but eventually Knopfler began to speak.

"What interested me was your idea about people having an ingrained affinity, established either by genetics or early life, for a specific environment. Also the converse, that people have ingrained antipathies to different environments. Of particular interest was the notion that these affinities and antipathies, especially subtle and complex variants thereof—things much more delicate and specific, for example, than simple claustrophobia—can be detected and identified through more refined, precise, and extensive procedures than currently exist."

Knopfler paused, and Carter felt he was waiting for a response. He looked up at the sky, but though there were no clouds, the stars were dimmed by the rising glow of the city lights.

"As you say, it's just a notion." Carter shrugged. "I've

never really had the opportunity to develop anything along those lines. And as the committee chairperson pointed out so emphatically, I do not really have any empirical evidence to support my ideas. A notion, yes. Nothing more."

"Just a gut feeling?" Knopfler offered.

"I suppose."

They passed a break in the buildings, where a gate led into the plaza, and for a few moments the noise increased, then gradually faded again.

"Several of my colleagues and I give your ideas much credence, however, and we would like you to work for us."

"Why? Manned space flight will be effectively defunct, at least for the next few years. Unless you're looking at long term . . ."

Knopfler shook his head. "We aren't interested in space flight. We're not interested in space at all, not from a human standpoint." He paused to light a cigarette, but did not offer one to Carter. "We have recently developed new high-tech fighting suits for our infantry. You may have heard something about them."

"Something, yes."

"They are completely self-enclosed, self-contained, computer-monitored, and designed to be worn around the clock for days at a time, even weeks. We've done extensive testing in labs, on domestic bases and training grounds, testing both the suits and the soldiers, and now we've begun field testing in the jungles of Guatemala." Knopfler paused, inhaled on his cigarette. "Frankly, we've had a few problems not unlike those encountered by the Mars Expedition. The Rigger syndrome, some have started to call it. The men we've sent into the field, none of them have claustrophobia, all of them have spent at least two continuous weeks during training inside the suits without once breaking the body or helmet seals, and all with no adverse effects, no panic reactions, nothing like that. And yet, some of them, within hours of being dropped into the jungle inside their suits, have . . . fallen apart. Panic reactions, auditory and visual hallucinations, complete breakdowns. Nothing like a majority, just a few here and there. But a significant number. I'm sure you can understand that we cannot afford that happening in actual military operations."

Knopfler stopped, apparently finished, and they continued their circuit of the complex in silence for some time.

"And what is it you want from me?" Carter finally asked.

"We want you to develop a testing and evaluation program along the lines of what you suggested for the space program, capable of identifying those who will thrive in the fighting suits under various conditions—jungle, desert, mountains, snow, urban centers—and those who will not. We offer you a position with complete freedom, choice of staff, whatever facilities you require. There will be large financial and technical resources at your disposal. You will be allowed essentially to do whatever you want, explore any lines of research you wish, within reason." Knopfler smiled. "What more could you ask for?"

"Why have you come here to talk to me?" Carter asked. "Why tonight?"

"We've tried reaching you at your office. You haven't shown there since the hearings. We are under some time pressure, pressure to produce success. The problems in the field have, on occasion, been serious. We have had . . . a few deaths. As you are more aware than most, money is becoming difficult for everyone, and mistakes and failures are not much tolerated. We, too, are in danger of losing funding for this program, and we'd like your assistance as soon as possible. In fact, if you accept, we will want you to fly to Guatemala immediately."

They had completed the circuit and now stopped, once again at the street entrance to the south building. Knopfler dropped his cigarette to the cement, crushed it with a brief twisting motion of his shoe.

"I'll need time to think about it," Carter said.

"Of course. I don't expect an answer tonight. But tomorrow would be best."

Carter nodded. The entire proposition seemed absurd to him, but he could not tell Knopfler that.

Knopfler handed him a white card with only his name and two telephone numbers. "Any time, day or night."

Carter nodded again, pocketed the card. They shook hands, then Knopfler turned and strode down the street without another word. Carter remained in front of the building and listened to the crisp, regular footsteps retreat into the night.

Carter walked through the hushed quiet of the lobby, then opened the door to the blast of sound from the party still going strong. He continued along a short stretch of empty cobblestone, and pushed his way back into the throng.

If anything, there were more people now than before, and Carter could hardly move of his own accord. Instead, he let the flow and surge of the crowd guide him randomly about the plaza, and he was reminded of film clips he'd seen of Carnival in Rio. The band had cranked up the amps another notch or two, but still only barely managed to overcome the shouts and laughter of the crowd.

Somehow he ended up with a drink in his hand, Scotch fortunately, and he sipped at it as he was bumped and shoved along. Near the main pool, the crush eased, then broke up completely leaving a perimeter of relatively clear space around the pool's edge. People sat in pool chairs, lay on chaise longues, talking and drinking and laughing. Carter squeezed free of the crowd and wandered among the chairs until he spotted an empty one and sat in it. Next to him, two people squirmed about inside a sleeping bag, only the tips of their heads visible.

A roar welled up to his right, and when Carter turned to look, he saw a giant ball, ten or twelve feet in diameter, bouncing slowly up and down along a jungle of upraised hands. The ball was gray, with patterns and words he could not yet distinguish. It looked like the kind of giant inflated ball he had first seen as a kid at an Earth Day Festival, a hippie holdover celebration his mother had taken him to once. Then, the large, stitched leather ball filled with air had been called an Earth Ball, and had been painted with swirls and slashes of bright colors. But as this gray Earth Ball rolled and bobbed closer, Carter saw that it had been painted with craters and maria to resemble the moon. Graffiti had been added, slogans of the protesters who had marched outside the gates of the launch fields day after day for the last few months—NO MORE $$ FOR $PACE; YANKEE STAY HOME; STOP ASKING FOR THE MOON!

The people lost control of the ball, and it began rolling over them toward the pool, gradually picking up speed though hands shot into the air to try to stop it. Near the edge of the crowd a few people were knocked to the ground by the weight and momentum of the ball as it struck them and tumbled to the ground. It bounced across several chairs, jolting people and spilling drinks, then rolled into the pool with a splash. A cheer erupted as the large, gray ball floated serenely about the pool.

Carter finished his drink, set the glass under his chair, and was about to get up when a gunshot sounded from nearby. A few cries cut the air, then gradually transformed into laughter and more cheers as air hissed out of the new hole in the ball. Carter remained in the chair and watched the Moon Ball slowly deflate until it was just a limp, bulging mass floating listlessly across the surface of the water.

Carter got up from the chair and slowly worked his way toward his building, searching the faces around him for a pair of dark sunglasses. Why did he want to find her again? What was it about her that both frightened and intrigued him? Why did flashes of her apartment—the telescope, the vast array of bright dots, the star-covered bed—keep rising in his mind?

He entered his building, nodded to the security guard. Instead of going to the elevators, Carter approached the stairwell, opened the door. He stepped through, let the door slam shut behind him, and began climbing.

The stairwell was quiet, the air hollow and warm, the cement walls echoing each of his footsteps. For a moment he felt as if he was walking along the hushed, hollow corridors of one of the stations—*Luther King, Lagrange, Challenger.*

Challenger. The space program had hardly stuttered following the *Challenger* disaster with its seven deaths, had hardly missed a beat, had in some ways emerged stronger than ever. Carter had been a teenager at the time, and it hadn't fazed him either, hadn't dulled his own fascination with space, his own dream of one day traveling to the stars.

But now the program was not going to survive the Mars Expedition. No deaths, but the aborted mission had capped a decade of other space-related injuries and deaths, of mishaps and unexplained mechanical failures, equipment breakdowns, mistakes in judgement, rumors of deliberate sabotage, all of which seemed to increase steadily each year, leading to growing dissatisfaction among the public, graver doubts in Congress, and eventually to the massive protests and demonstrations. When the Mars Expedition had aborted, one more colossal failure, the program had no more support to fall back on. It was doomed the day *Explorer* turned back.

At the top floor, Carter rested a minute, then continued up the final flight of steps to the roof. He unlocked the door with his apartment key, and stepped out.

The air was warm, and the moon was bright above him, nearly full. The noise of the party rose from the plaza and drifted over the edge of the roof, but it was hushed, more like the surf of an empty beach.

Half a dozen pool chairs were scattered about, but otherwise the roof was deserted. Carter walked to the nearest chair and sat, feeling suddenly very tired. He adjusted the arms so he lay halfway back and could look directly at the moon and stars above him. Once again his hand moved to his empty shirt pocket, fumbled at it before returning to his side.

Luna. The last time he'd been there was to assist in the debriefing of the *Explorer* crew. He still vividly remembered the sight of Rigger emerging from *Explorer*, nearly catatonic, his eyes wide, staring but unseeing, his entire body trembling. And Carter would never forget that incredible sigh of despair that issued from Rigger just before he collapsed to his knees, sobbing and shaking his head.

Luna. It was quickly moving out of reach, and now Knopfler wanted him to go to Guatemala to help better prepare men—not for the exploration of space, but for war on Earth.

Carter breathed in deeply, sat up, then stood. He walked across the roof, gravel crunching under his shoes. At the roof's edge he leaned against the low railing and gazed down at the crowd surging about the plaza. The deflated Moon Ball still floated in the main pool, motionless in one corner.

No, Knopfler did not understand him at all. He had made an offer of what he thought Carter wanted and needed, but the man clearly did not understand. Carter could not accept Knopfler's offer. If he did, if he went to Guatemala to work with the military, helping soldiers to fight in wars, he would ground himself to Earth in a way that would be irreversible. He would become so grounded that if the space program ever revived he would be completely useless to it, and that was something he could not accept.

No, Knopfler did not understand him. Neither did Karyn. No one really did, with the strange, possible exception of . . .

Carter pressed against the railing and looked straight down at the small swimming pool below him. It was empty, but a foot from the edge, seated in a chair and looking up at him through dark sunglasses, was Nicole.

They watched each other for several minutes without moving, then Nicole slowly stood up from the chair. She kept her gaze on him and, after another pause, started walking toward the building. Carter did not move, and even when she disappeared into the lobby he remained motionless at the edge of the roof, waiting for her to join him.

Carter heard the door open behind him, and he turned to watch Nicole step out onto the roof. Her ballet slippers were nearly silent on the gravel as she crossed the roof to stand at his side. Once again as he looked into her sunglasses he saw his doubled reflection, but now he caught a glimpse of her eyes as well.

"Will you come now?" she asked.

Carter said nothing for a long time, though he already knew what his answer would be. He looked up at the moon, a sense of loss aching in his chest at the thought that he might never return to it. Maybe someday, somehow, if he could avoid closing off his options. . . .

He turned back to face Nicole. "Yes, I'll come now."

They walked side by side across the roof to the door, went through it, and began their descent. Neither spoke, and Carter's chest tightened as he listened to their regular, echoing footsteps in the hollow air—his firm and sharp, hers like whispers. He was still somewhat afraid of Nicole, afraid of returning to her apartment, but he knew he would go through with it now, that it had become as important to him as it was to her.

They emerged from the stairs into the lobby, passed through it and out onto the street. Still silent, they circled around to Nicole's building, and entered. Just as they had descended from the roof by way of the stairs, they now ascended echoing stairs to the sixth floor. When they came out into the hallway they rested for a few minutes, breathing heavily. Doubts rose again, and Carter thought of withdrawing to the stairwell, descending again, but when Nicole started down the hall toward her apartment, he followed.

Entering her apartment went as it had before—Nicole unlocked the door, cracked it open to reach inside and turn off the lights, then pulled him quickly inside, closing the door and locking it behind them.

Stars again. Though he had already seen the apartment, the sheer number of silver pinpoints managed to once again overwhelm him with a sense of vast, open space, of star-filled skies of deepest night.

As before, Nicole led him through the hall and into the bedroom, into a bright, new galaxy. This time the curtains had been pulled over the sliding glass doors so that now everything in the room was completely covered with stars.

His disorientation returned, tinged with a slight panic that threatened to grow, panic at the sensation of being cut loose from Earth and drifting without moorings through the unending night of space. Carter stood at the center of the room, swaying, unable to move.

Nicole knelt at the foot of the bed and reached for something on the floor. Four enormous globes of stars in the corners of the room, and one above him (how was it he had not noticed them before?), began to slowly rotate. More disturbing, they rotated in different directions, some laterally, some vertically, and all at varying rates.

The panic stepped up a notch, and Carter tried to move toward the bedroom door, searching for escape, but before he completed his first step he lost all sense of orientation. Vertigo overwhelmed him. All the points of light in the room began moving, even those he knew were stationary, and he started to fall.

He felt cool hands supporting him, guiding him, but it took a moment to realize they were Nicole's. He tried to look down at the floor, to focus on the sensation of his feet touching firm ground as an anchor to steady himself, but it was hopeless. Still supported by Nicole, he stumbled, his knees gave out, and he felt himself drifting downward and twisting to the side, felt the soft give of a mattress under his body.

Carter knew he was on his back on the bed, but was aware of little else. The stars continued to spin about him, and he felt as if the bed itself was spinning. He closed his eyes, but nothing changed. The vertigo only worsened, and the panic struck with full force, swelling in his chest and throat.

But Carter, rather than fight it, accepted the panic. He let it blossom into fear, then let the fear spread evenly throughout his body, out along his limbs to hands and feet where it smoothly leaked out of him and dissipated into the night, leaving him drained, but unafraid.

He opened his eyes again, the stars everywhere, still whirling and dancing, but the vertigo disappeared, and he began to sense the regular patterns of the stars' movement, the rhythms of their dance, and began to sense his own growing harmony with their graceful motions across the sky.

But where was the moon? For some inexplicable reason he felt he should be seeing it, that its presence was somehow crucial. Then it struck him.

I am on the moon. I have returned.

Nicole's face loomed above. Naked now, wearing only the dark glasses which reflected the stars at him, she straddled him and her hands moved to his shirt, delicately working the buttons loose, running her cool fingers along his chest and down toward his belly. Carter felt his body respond to her touch, and he brushed his fingertips lightly across the dark reflecting lenses, her soft nose, her firm mouth. Yes, he thought, this is where I belong, here among the stars. Nicole breathed in sharply and kissed his hands, pressed her hips against his.

With the blood now rushing through him, Carter reached out to embrace her, and to embrace the night as the stars continued to spin and dance in delicate, bright patterns all around them.

SIDE PANEL

Early the next morning, Carter drove Karyn to the train station, the trip endured in silence. They had nothing to say to each other anymore, and he did not stay to see her off. That part of his life was over.

On the way back to the apartment he filled the car with gas, checked water and oil, brake and transmission fluids, put air in the tires. He cleaned all the windows, bought a map of the United States. On impulse, he stopped at a bookstore and bought maps of Canada and Mexico as well.

Carter spent the day packing whatever remained in the apartment, filling boxes and bags and suitcases, sorting through it all and deciding what he would take with him, what he would leave behind.

Knopfler called twice during the day, and Carter finally promised him an answer the following morning. By then he would be gone, and Knopfler would get no answer at all.

He would go to the mountains or the desert, that much he knew. Somewhere he could really see the stars, the moon, and the clear, black skies of night. He would be ready when the space program revived, ready if not to go into space himself, then to prepare others who would.

Night fell, and Carter loaded the car with everything he planned to take with him. Back in the apartment, he sat one more time on the balcony, the apartment dark for the first time in months. The night air was warm, the plaza below nearly empty, quiet. Someone had pulled the deflated Moon Ball out of the pool and draped it over a chaise longue.

Carter gazed up at the night sky, but though it was free of clouds, the stars above seemed dull and lifeless. The lights of the city sent up too much glow, and there were too many stars he knew should have been visible but which he could not see. Even the moon, which was rising, remained hidden, blocked from view by the brick and cement of the apartment building. This is no place to be, he thought, this is no place to live.

He looked across the plaza to the south building. In a sixth floor window he caught a glint of light, probably from the telescope. So, she was still watching him. After tonight, though, he would be gone, and she would be watching a deserted balcony, a dark and empty room.

At midnight he locked the apartment and walked out to the parking lot. Nicole stood next to his car with a single suitcase and the telescope. The building lights reflected at him from her dark glasses. Carter breathed in deeply.

All right, he thought. For now.

They squeezed the suitcase into the trunk, then packed the telescope in the back seat. He secured the lens cover, and they wrapped the telescope carefully in thick blankets, wedged it tightly into the luggage for protection.

They left under clear skies. Mountains or desert, he would decide later. He drove north, away from the city and the rows of amber street lamps, and on the freeway the moon blazed down upon them, lighting the way.

Celebrate the Bullet

WENDY WAS TAKING PICTURES OF A MIDNIGHT BEACH party.

It wasn't much of a party, actually—five people she knew (all of them younger than she was), and one guy none of them knew, who had been walking along the beach and joined them. A fire burned inside a ring of charred stones, and a few feet from it, propped on a driftwood log, was a thirty-inch color TV that Tony had brought, power cable snaking down to a big battery pack on the sand. On the screen, without sound, was an old Japanese monster movie about a giant mutant turtle that flew and breathed fire.

Wendy kept back from the fire, fiddling with her camera while the others drank beer and talked. The only one who seemed to be watching the TV was the guy they didn't know. Hicks, he had said his name was; he had been carrying two six-packs and so had been immediately invited to the party.

Fog threatened to roll in from the sea, and the wind kicked up. Wendy zipped up her jacket, resumed adjusting her camera. She was using fast black-and-white film, no flash, making what she knew would be good guesses with the time exposures. She sat on the sand, set the camera on her knee for support, and took a picture of all six people, the fire, and the TV, the flickering image of the screen at a severe angle. Then she got up and backed farther away, looked up at the moon slicing through the incoming fog, and wondered if she could get it into a picture along with everything else.

"This movie SUCKS!" It was Hicks, and he sounded so angry everyone else stopped talking; the beach became suddenly quiet, the only sound the rolling hiss of the waves on the sloping sand.

"It's only a movie," Avra said. She laughed.

But Hicks sat there shaking his head. "I've had it," he said, and he pulled a gun from inside his jacket.

The gun was big, obviously real, and Wendy's chest tightened, catching her breath. Christ, she hated guns, even just looking at them. They scared the hell out of her, especially since most people really had no idea how to handle them.

Hicks raised the gun, holding it with both hands, and aimed it at the television set.

Tony scrambled to his feet, spilling beer onto the edges of the fire with a sizzling hiss. "Hey!" Tony said. "Hey, come on, man, don't fuck around! I paid a hundred and fifty bucks for that TV!"

Hicks turned to Tony without moving the gun. "A hundred and fifty? Must have been stolen, then. That's a good TV."

"Shit, who cares if it was stolen?" Tony was holding up his hands, palms out toward Hicks. "It's a lot of money, man, so just freeze down a bit, all right? All right?"

Hicks nodded, turned back to the TV, and fired.

The explosion of the gun, loud and sudden in Wendy's ears, was followed almost immediately by another, much softer explosion as the bullet ripped into the TV and the picture tube burst into bright crackling light and shattering glass.

Tony grabbed the sides of his head, grimacing. "Oh, Jesus, you motherfucker! You out of your goddamn mind or. . . ?"

Tony stopped as Hicks brought the gun around, aimed it directly at Tony's chest.

"Oh, hey, man," Tony said, backing away. "Don't *fuck* with me like this. *Jesus!*"

The gun went off again, louder this time as Tony jerked back and sprawled face up on the sand. More sand scattered as the others scrambled to their feet and started running. Tony, on the other hand, wasn't moving at all.

Wendy, too, remained motionless for a few moments, in a kind of stunned paralysis. Her chest ached as she watched Hicks rise to his feet, walk over to Tony, and hold out the gun again, this time aimed down at Tony's face. Wendy turned and broke into a run as the shot sounded.

Her feet sank in the soft sand as she ran up the slope, and her breath quickly became ragged and harsh. The slope steepened into sandbanks leading up to the road, and Wendy scrambled up on hands and knees, pulling herself along by grabbing tufts of the long grass that grew out of the sand. There were no more gunshots, no sounds at all except her own painful breath.

The sand leveled out. Wendy stepped over the knee-high wire and wood fence and ran out onto the Great Highway, which was empty of traffic; distant approaching headlights were visible, but more than half a mile away. She stopped for a moment and looked back out over the beach, but saw no one coming. Down near the water, the fire continued to burn, flames whipping in the breeze; a few feet from the fire lay Tony's dark, motionless form. Wendy turned away and hurried across the black pavement, down another sandbank, and headed for the motel and restaurant down the road near the end of Golden Gate Park.

In front of the restaurant stood a pair of empty phone booths. Wendy stepped into one, kept the door open and watched the road. She picked up the receiver and dialed 911.

Over the phone, Wendy told the cops what had happened, and provided them with a description of Hicks, but she had refused to give her name. Later she might go to them, see if she could help any further, but she would have to think damn hard about it. With half a dozen arrests on obscenity and various other charges because of her photography, Wendy couldn't imagine going to the police voluntarily.

She remained in the phone booth looking up at the Great Highway, half expecting to see Hicks (if that really was his name) appear on the road above her, gun in hand. Two cars drove slowly past, headed south, then another headed north, but no one appeared on foot, and Wendy wondered what had happened to the others.

She stepped out of the phone booth and slowly climbed the bank back up to the road. Wendy still had time to go back to the beach before the cops arrived. It was crazy, she told herself, but she knew she would go as long as it looked safe, though she didn't really want to admit *why*.

The fog had broken up almost completely, and the nearly full moon shone brightly down on the road, giving the asphalt a ragged, liquid sheen. Wendy crossed to the sandbanks, stepped over the low fence, and stood at the edge of a grass-covered drift.

The fire still burned, though low now, more glowing embers than flames; the orange glow, even from this distance, pulsed like an irregular heartbeat, fanned by the breeze. The beach, in both directions, was deserted. To the north she could see a few waving, flickering lights in the upper levels of the old Ocean Beach condo ruins; farther on, the remains of the Cliff House seemed to hover in the air like an apparition, dark ragged hulks of shadow on the jutting point of land, stone illuminated by the moon. All around Wendy, with the silver light of the moon and the darkness of the night, the world looked as if it had been created all in black and white except for the tiny spot of orange flame near the water's edge.

Wendy glanced once more in all directions, then started down the bank toward the fire. As she walked, she could make out the shape of Tony's body a few feet away from the fire, and the shape of the blasted TV. She conceived possible shots in her mind, considered the different camera angles, tried to calculate the effect of the moonlight. You're sick, Wendy, she told herself, you're *sick*. And she did feel sick, nausea rolling through her stomach and bringing acid up into her throat, but she knew it wouldn't stop her.

When she reached the fire, Wendy skirted the glowing embers and approached Tony's body. The blood, which at first glance seemed to be everywhere, looked more black than red— shiny where it had pooled on his chest and what was left of his face; duller where it had spread out and soaked into the sand. If she had not seen what had happened, she didn't think she would have recognized him.

Feeling still sicker now, Wendy brought the camera up and adjusted it with shaking fingers. A close-up of the body, the moon from behind and just to the side. Somehow she managed to make her mind work and concentrate on the photograph she was about to take, to stop her hands and fingers from shaking long enough to set the exposure, focus the lens, snap the picture.

Wendy moved around the body, the glowing fire, the shattered television set, taking one picture after another; between shots her hands shook, but each time she prepared a shot she steadied herself long enough to click the shutter. Before long, as she moved farther and farther away with each shot, Wendy began to cry. Tears streamed steadily down her face, salty to the taste when she licked them from the corners of her mouth.

But none of it—not the tears, not the nausea rolling through her, not even the self-disgust— stopped her from taking the pictures, and it wasn't until she heard the faint wail of approaching sirens that Wendy lowered the camera, snapped on the lens cover, and, still crying, ran back up the slope toward the moonlit road.

She woke once in the night, a clawing desperation bringing her slowly, painfully out of a dream she could not remember— nothing remained except a hollow feeling of dread. Wendy sat up in bed, sweating in the windowless, cinderblock room, the darkness heavy and cloying. Vibrations from machinery below her rumbled through the room. She leaned against the wall, pressed her face against the cold, trembling stone.

For a long time she remained motionless, eyes open though she could not see a thing, listening to the muted chug of machinery. Then she slipped back down between the sheets, pulled the blankets tight around her, and waited for sleep, almost hoping it wouldn't come.

In the morning, Wendy bought a newspaper and read through it in a coffee shop down the street from her rooms. A huge photograph of the second space station filled half of the front page. The station had just been officially completed after eleven years, three major accidents, and sixty-seven deaths. In the lower corner was a photo of the President seated at a monitor in Kennedy Space Center, headset on, congratulating the station commander.

As for killings or other deaths, there were plenty in the paper —a street person who had flipped out in the Financial District and attacked people with a large kitchen knife, killing a woman attorney and injuring half a dozen other people; a woman who had shot and killed her husband, their two dogs, then turned the weapon on herself; an eight-year-old boy who had been crushed to death when an abandoned building collapsed on him.

Nowhere, though, could she find anything about what had

happened on the beach. It had probably been too late to make the morning paper, but she had hoped there would be something anyway. Why? She didn't really know. She had seen far more than she would ever learn from a news account.

Around noon she called in sick to the print shop, bought an early edition of the afternoon paper, and read it on the cement porch of the building she lived in, the concrete vibrating slightly beneath her. Half the ground floor was a dry-cleaning operation, and the machines ran day and night. The other half was supposedly an upholstery shop, but machinery ran day and night inside it as well, far louder than the dry-cleaners, rumbling and chugging beneath her apartment; Wendy felt certain something else was being done in the shop, though she really didn't care what.

Her apartment was on the second floor, above the upholstery shop, part of a collection of illegal apartments and tiny offices. The apartment was small, but had three rooms including her darkroom, a stove and sink for a kitchen, a shower and toilet of her own, and a tiny wall heater that kept the worst chill out of the air—all she needed.

She found it—a short article in the second section, no picture. There wasn't much to it, two paragraphs stating that a body had been found out on Ocean Beach about one a.m., apparently shot to death (apparently?). No name was given. Police speculated the shooting was drug-related.

Wendy leaned against the stone wall, feeling the vibrations trembling through her, listening to the muted hisses and groans, and began slowly, methodically, tearing the newspaper to shreds.

She spent the afternoon in the darkroom, developing then printing the pictures from the night before. She didn't know what she expected—maybe shots of Hicks's face, details of his clothing, pictures she could take to the police (if she could bring herself to do that; if they would even listen to her)—but there was nothing like that. There *were* pictures of Hicks, but none that showed his face, none that could identify him in any way.

And then there were the pictures of Tony. She made small enlargements, to about 5 by 7, and clipped them up on the wall. First was a close-up of his face, taken early in the evening while Tony was building the fire—his features set in concentration, light and shadow from the flames in irregular patterns across his skin. Next was a shot of Tony and Avra laughing and throwing sand at one another just a few feet from the fire. Then came the series of pictures after Tony was dead: a close-up of what remained of his face; his sprawled body with the darker splotches of blood on the sand around his head; then several more shots from a gradually increasing distance until the last, which took in the dying embers of the fire, the shattered television set, scattered beer cans, Tony's body, the reflecting ocean in the background, and in the upper right corner, just barely in the picture, the shining silver light of the moon.

Wendy sat on her work stool, stared at the pictures mounted on the wall. The sick feelings of the night before were gone, replaced by a heavy numbing sensation. But something in the pictures slowly dug into her gut and into her heart, cutting away the numbness, and revealing the pain underneath. Something either in the photographs or in the circumstances surrounding them that was important, but Wendy did not know what it was.

Late that night, long after dark, Wendy went to the Bomb Shelter. The Bomb Shelter was half pub, half nightclub; half indoors, half outdoors. It had been built up hodge-podge around and under the ruins of a freeway overpass that had been accidentally blown up two years before by a performance art troupe. Seven people had been killed, including three of the four troupe members. The surviving performance artist had started building the Bomb Shelter as soon as he had been released from the hospital, and now ran the entire complex.

In the outdoor section, covered by sheets of canvas stretched high above the tables, a thin bearded man played an electric sitar on a platform that served as a stage. Most of the outdoor tables were empty, and his audience consisted of about ten people clustered around the platform and drinking; two of them were asleep or passed out, heads and arms on their tables.

It was too damn cold, and Wendy went inside. The interior of the Bomb Shelter was a series of makeshift chambers connected by narrow, dimly lit passages. Those walls not formed by the concrete remains of the freeway were built of wood, or brick and stone, patched sheetrock, old mattresses wedged between sheets of metal, wire-bound bundles of flattened cardboard. Each chamber held half a dozen tables, all with fat, flickering candles; speakers mounted in the ceiling corners emitted crystal clear ether jazz. Paintings and drawings and photographs hung on the walls, and desiccated plants grew from clay pots in the corners.

Nearly all the tables were occupied. In the second chamber, Wendy sat at a single empty table in the corner, and faced one of her own photographs that hung on the opposite wall. It was a large black and white close-up of Kit, almost in profile—her eyes partially closed, gazing downward, her cheek tight with a smile.

Wendy stared at the picture, her chest aching. She missed Kit. They had worked together on several art projects over a period of three or four years, but now Kit was dead. She had died a year before of "the white monkey," as she had put it. Kit had called it "the white monkey" because AIDS was still thought by some to have originated in African monkeys; also, since Kit had never had sex with anyone, male or female, she was certain she'd contracted AIDS during her needle freak days mainlining cocaine—yes, her "own personal white monkey."

No matter what you called it, though, Kit was dead. Kit and Will and Laskey from AIDS; Skipper and Marty, and now Tony, from bullets; Stoke several years ago, probably from bullets as well, in some damn Central American jungle; Sheridan and Manny and Bobo from street-sliced drugs; and Tracy, who was beaten to death by cops. All these people she knew, dead before they were thirty-five. Wendy was nearly forty now, and she knew it wasn't really that old, but Christ, sometimes she *felt* old.

She looked at the picture of Kit, tried to imagine what one of the close-ups of Tony's shattered face would look like up on the concrete wall.

Carla, one of the regular waitresses, came up to the table, smiling. "Wendy, how you doing? What can I get you?"

"Jack Daniels," Wendy said. "A bottle." Wendy pulled all her cash from her pockets, counted it. It would be enough. She couldn't afford it, but right now it didn't matter.

Carla's smile disappeared. "A bottle?"

Wendy nodded. "A bottle, a glass, and ice."

Carla nodded, moved slowly away, and Wendy was alone again.

She was going to get drunk. Wendy only got drunk two or three times a year, and this was going to be one of them. It would take a long time, because she would drink slowly, and because, though she rarely drank, she held her liquor well. But tonight she would get so smashed she would hardly remember a thing in the morning.

Carla came back with a bottle of Jack Daniels, a bucket of ice, and a glass. "Are you okay, Wendy?"

"I'm fine," Wendy said. She paid, and Carla left without another word.

Wendy put two pieces of ice in the glass, then filled it with Jack Daniels. She held the glass up, gestured with it toward Kit's picture, then drank.

She woke in darkness to a terrible pounding in the walls, a hammering at the floor beneath her. The bed shook with the vibrations, and for a moment Wendy thought some massive piece of machinery was going to break through the walls or floor, shattering cinderblock, destroying her room.

I'm still drunk, she told herself, but she soon realized that had nothing to do with the hammering sounds in the room, or the vibrations in the floor. Upholstery shop my ass, she thought.

Wendy rolled out of bed, got to her feet and staggered into the bathroom. She sat on the toilet and relieved herself, amazed that her bladder could hold so much without more pain.

In the bathroom the pounding was quieter, the vibration of the walls less violent. She remained seated for a few minutes, holding her head in her hands. Her mouth was dry, and her head felt stuffed with cotton. She didn't want to move.

Finally, Wendy stood and went to the sink, ran cold water and splashed it over her face. It didn't help much. She started back toward the bedroom, but the pounding was too loud and jarred her head. She grabbed the pillow and a blanket from the bed, and returned to the bathroom. Wendy wrapped herself in the blanket, stuffed the pillow into the back corner and lay down between the toilet and the wall, where the pounding was quietest. She slept.

She didn't have much of a hangover in the morning. The pounding had faded, and only the normal thrumming and vibrations remained. She felt almost rested.

After a quick shower, Wendy took a bus into the Mission District to see Libby. A low overcast obscured the sun, kept the morning a dark gray. She dozed against the scratched window, holding her shirt over her nose to filter out the stink from the woman lying on the seat in front of her.

Libby lived in a three-room cottage on a quiet dead-end street that always smelled of anise, especially on hot days. Wendy stepped up onto the small porch, rang the doorbell, then stood back so Libby could get a good look at her through the peephole. A few moments later she heard the deadbolts being thrown, the two chains being unhooked, then the knob turned and the door opened.

"Wendy." Libby stood in the open door, smiling, her arms held out. They embraced, then went inside, Libby shutting and locking the door behind them.

As usual, books and magazines and newspapers were piled and scattered all over the front room; those stacked on or near Libby's worktable dealt primarily with genetics and quantum mechanics. On the PC monitor, a toroid-shaped diagram shifted jerkily from one position to another.

"Sorry if I'm interrupting," Wendy said.

Libby shook her head. "I was about to go out in the garden, take a break while this program runs. C'mon out, I've got a fresh pot of coffee in the Chemex."

They walked into the kitchen, where Wendy picked up two glass mugs and the Chemex and Libby picked up her shotgun, then walked out into the back yard garden. Wendy hated the shotgun, it always made her nervous, but there was no way she could complain about it. A year and a half before, Libby's sister Diedre, who had shared the cottage with Libby, had been stabbed to death while sunbathing in the garden. Libby had bought the shotgun the following week.

They sat in two deck chairs facing the garden. Wendy set the coffee and mugs on the wooden table between them, poured the coffee while Libby propped the shotgun against the redwood planter box beside her. Above, the overcast was burning off, and the sun broke through, bringing out the colors of the garden. Tall, thick green shrubs lined the back fence, and a path of coarse gravel curled through lush beds of flowers and herbs —irises, hydrangeas, oregano, parsley maybe, and a lot of others Wendy didn't know.

Wendy sipped at the strong, hot coffee, then closed her eyes and leaned her head back, letting the warmth of the sun bathe her face. She could smell the oregano, and flower scents she couldn't identify, and a trace of anise from the street, and the coffee in her hands. She felt warm and peaceful, a pleasant lethargy suffusing her body.

"Something's eating at you," Libby said. "When you come over and start sitting back with your eyes closed and get quiet, that usually means something's bothering you. Something you want to get away from."

"This place always relaxes me," Wendy said. "Sitting out here in the garden with you. Sometimes I wish I could go somewhere like this permanently. Out of the city, away from people, away from the world."

"Wendy, what is it?"

Wendy didn't say anything for a long time, but eventually she opened her eyes, turned to face Libby. She told Libby what had happened to Tony. She told her about the pictures she took.

"You're a photographer," Libby said. "Taking photographs is what you do."

"Sure, but like that? Sometimes I think it's *all* I do, and sometimes I think I must be sick. No matter what happens in my life, no matter how awful, I take pictures of it. I'm beginning to think I can't even see the world around me in a normal way anymore." She paused, looked away, up at what was left of the overcast. "When I think of Tony now, I see an image of his ruined face. . . . Not as I *saw* it that night, but as it appears in the photograph I took. I wonder if I'm capable of seeing the world in any other way."

There was a long silence, then Libby said, "Want some amateur analysis?"

Wendy softly laughed. "Sure."

"The world is pretty fucked up, *people* are pretty fucked up. And it all seems to just be getting worse."

"I won't argue that."

"Okay. Things are getting worse, but on top of that a lot of the shit that goes down seems pretty irrational, meaningless. Pointless. Like some stranger shooting up a TV and then killing someone, apparently without reason. Like a young woman getting stabbed to death in her own back yard, again apparently without reason."

Libby paused and looked out at her garden. Wendy didn't say anything, and eventually Libby turned back to her and resumed.

"So a lot of it doesn't make sense. Causality is suspect, sort of like quantum mechanics on a social scale, let's say. How do people deal with a world like that? A lot of them retreat, either physically or mentally withdraw from the world. A lot of others ignore most of what they see, or learn how to *not* see what they don't want to see or what they can't deal with. Head in the sand.

"But not you, Wendy. You can't do that, you see the world around you, and maybe when you take photographs, what you're doing is giving the world some structure, enough so that you *can* see it for what it is and still live with it without going out of your mind." She paused, smiled. "Maybe. There, that's my lecture for the day."

Wendy watched Libby for a minute, then shrugged. "I guess it makes a kind of sense, though I don't know that it does me much good."

"Maybe make it easier to accept what you do."

Wendy shook her head. "Best thing might be to just stop taking photographs altogether."

"You serious?"

"I'm thinking about it."

Libby didn't say anything, just slowly shook her head. Wendy shrugged again, drank from her coffee, then closed her eyes once more and stretched out on the chair to take in the heat from the sun above.

It was midnight by the time she got off work at the print shop, and nearly one o'clock by the time she got home. The streets were quiet, and as she approached her building she could hear the faint sounds of machinery from the dry-cleaners and the so-called upholstery shop. Nothing unusual, nothing like the night before. Everything back to normal.

Wendy climbed the stairs to the second floor, walked down the quiet, dimly lit hall. She knew at least two other people lived on this floor, but there were no lights in door windows, no sounds to indicate anyone was here.

She unlocked her door, stepped into the apartment. Just as she closed the door, loud pounding sounds broke in again, and the floor began to shake beneath her. Pots and pans rattled quietly against the kitchen wall, and glasses clinked together in the cupboards. She checked the darkroom, and though her equipment was shaking somewhat, it looked safe enough.

Then she walked into the bedroom.

The floor shook with a steady hammering, as if a pile driver was driving something *up* against her floor from below, and everything in the room shuddered and rattled—books, pictures, homemade cassettes, the alarm clock. The nightstand lamp vibrated with each jolt, and threatened to tip off the stand.

Jesus Christ, what the *hell* was going on down there?

Wendy stood for a minute in the middle of the room, listening to the hammering sounds, watching the walls and waiting for them to begin crumbling around her. Then she grabbed the lamp, laid it on the bed, and backed out of the room. She stopped by the darkroom, picked up her camera and several rolls of film, and left the apartment.

As she moved along the hall and down the stairs, the noise and vibrations lessened. Outside, it was quiet again, only a faint thrumming punctuated regularly by muted thuds.

Blinds covered the upholstery shop windows; she couldn't see inside, but a kind of smoky, dim blue light leaked out from the edges and through tiny cracks. She stopped at the shop's front door, which had a dirty plastic sign in the wire-mesh window that said "CLOSED," and tried opening it, but the door was locked.

Wendy walked slowly along the building, checking the windows to see if any were open. At the entrance to the dark alley between her building and a large brick warehouse, she hesitated. She couldn't see much—shadows within shadows, dull reflections of ambient light on windows and damp metal, unidentifiable clumps along the alley floor, and two or three hints of the dark blue light leaking out around window blinds, barely discernible. She breathed in, and entered the alley.

Gravel, broken glass, and bits of other trash crunched under her shoes. Wendy moved slowly along the building wall, stepping carefully, and tried each of the windows. But none were open. Halfway down the alley she reached the dry-cleaners.

Wendy backtracked to the last upholstery shop window, which was already partially broken, a three-inch jagged hole in the upper section. The chugging sounds of machinery were slightly louder, emerging from the hole. She took a handkerchief from her pocket, wrapped it around the fingers of her left hand, then gripped the glass at the opening. She gently hit the glass with the heel of her right hand, then hit it again, harder each time until it quietly cracked. Two more hits and she was able to pull a piece away with her protected hand, enlarging the hole. She continued working at the hole, cracking the glass and pulling pieces away, letting only a few tiny shards fall into the building, the noise covered by the rumble of machinery inside.

When the hole was large enough, Wendy reached in and twisted free the lock, then withdrew her arm and used both hands to work open the window, raising it as far as it would go. Wendy climbed through and into the building.

She left the window open, made sure the blinds covered it,

then turned to look around her. Pale, dark blue light lit the interior of the large room, casting hundreds of shadows through a jungle of scaffolding, metal stools and workbenches, thrumming machinery, tanks and cylinders, and lengths of pipe crisscrossing through the air. Nothing pounded at the ceiling now, but there was a squat, silent piece of machinery mounted high up in the scaffolding, just a foot below the ceiling.

Though most of the machinery was running—some of it periodically releasing jets of steam—the place seemed deserted. The dim blue light provided just enough illumination so she could get around without running into anything, and Wendy began to work her way through the machinery. The floor was cluttered with plastic and metal debris and twisted lengths of electrical cord, but the metal workbenches were clear, covered only with layers of dust. Wendy couldn't identify most of the machinery, but none of it seemed to actually be *doing* anything except making noise and releasing bursts of steam. She was certain that none of it had anything to do with upholstery.

Near one rear corner of the room, Wendy was overcome by a stench much like that from the woman on the bus that morning. She stepped around a large piece of drilling equipment and stared down at the floor. Tucked between the wall and the machinery was a dark form wrapped in a thick coat and several scarves, swollen feet squeezed into a pair of faded pink tennis shoes. A snorting sound erupted from the figure, an arm twitched. Wendy held her breath and backed away, wondering how the person on the floor had gotten into the building.

She continued her search through the room. She spotted a dim glow against the back wall, behind a huge, long piece of machinery with a large metal funnel at one end. Wendy made her way to the machine, then around it. Between it and the cinderblock wall was an opening in the floor about four feet across.

Wendy approached the opening, and knelt at the edge where she felt a damp warm draft rising from below. A metal ladder, bolted to the rim, descended into what appeared to be an enormous, high-ceilinged chamber, the floor at least thirty feet below. The chamber, too, was lit by pale blue light, though slightly brighter. She could not see how far the chamber extended. But below her she could see a maze of portable dividers, cots, stacks of wooden crates, partially enclosed toilets, stone mounds, and a variety of other wooden barriers. A large number of people lay sleeping, either on cots or on the floor; a few wandered aimlessly through the maze. Two fires burned in metal barrels, each with several people sitting or lying around them.

She remained at the edge of the opening for several minutes, watching, listening to the steady pounding of machinery around her. Then she stretched out on the floor, got out her camera, and began taking pictures.

After she had taken a dozen pictures, Wendy secured her camera, rose to her knees, turned around; she backed over the edge of the opening, set her feet securely on the metal rungs, then started down the ladder.

As she descended, she saw that she was in one of the chamber's corners, just a few feet from the stone and concrete walls. The chamber was enormous, at least two hundred feet in length and width. Concrete projections, pipes, and spinning fans jutted down from the ceiling, which was dotted with dark blue light globes. Steam issued forth from ceiling vents, dissipating slowly as it floated down toward the floor. The air, though damp, was warm.

No one seemed to notice her as she climbed down the ladder, stopping occasionally to take a picture. The ladder ended about ten feet above the floor, but was within reach of a brick ledge protruding from the wall. Wendy stepped across the gap to the ledge, released the ladder and crouched against the wall. A couple of people looked up at her, but neither said a word.

She couldn't see as much of the chamber now, and only those people sleeping near her. Most seemed to be street people —men and women wrapped in thick old coats, baggy pants and layers of shirts and sweaters; most of the men wore dull black or brown leather shoes, most of the women wore tennis shoes. They were of all ages, except that there were no children. The pungent odor permeated the chamber, but she was already getting used to it.

Brick steps led to the floor and, after taking several more pictures, Wendy started down. But she stopped on the second step, staring at a gun beside her foot. It looked a lot like the gun Hicks had used. Next to the gun was a cartridge box, presumably ammunition for the gun. She bent over, reached forward to the touch the gun, then pulled back her hand before her fingers made contact. What was a gun doing here?

Wendy continued down the steps, and when she reached the floor she began to wander through the chamber. She moved slowly through the maze-like passages formed by sections of brick or stone walls, portable dividers of wood or sheet metal, tall mesh screens, empty bookcases and battered shelving units, stacks of wooden crates. The passages linked small square areas filled with cots and wooden benches, and usually no more than five or six people. Most of them were sleeping or lying motionless with open eyes, some in groups, but many alone. Though there were quite a few empty cots, at least half of the people slept on the floor—curled up against walls or in corners, sometimes under the cots, a few stretched out in the shelving units.

Nobody seemed to talk to anyone else, and the chamber was relatively quiet, but it was not silent. Aside from the hiss of steam from the ceiling vents, the people in the chamber snored or muttered in their sleep, cots creaked with movement, a toilet occasionally flushed, and every so often someone would quietly cry out.

But no one objected as she moved among the sleeping forms, discreetly taking pictures, changing film, taking more pictures; none of those awake even asked her what she was doing, as if they expected someone to be taking pictures, or had come to expect anything and anybody without question.

Her eyes continued to adjust to the dim light, and Wendy grew more and more disturbed as she began to make out even more details of her surroundings. Though most of the bookcases and shelves were empty, every so often she would see a hand-gun on a shelf, or in a chink of stone, or tucked between two crates, usually with a box or two of ammunition beside it. Occasionally there would be a knife or an ice pick or some other sharp instrument, but usually it was a gun. Then, looking more closely at the sleeping figures throughout the chamber, Wendy noticed that some of them had guns of their own, cradled to their chests or tucked between their legs, stuffed inside bundles of other belongings. What the hell was going on down here?

It was the same question she had asked herself earlier that night while standing in her room with the floor hammering away beneath her, but the question seemed much different now.

She proceeded more slowly through the chamber, the need to ask people about this place growing within her. But for some reason she was afraid to talk to any of them as they sat and stared silently at her or wordlessly passed her in the passage-ways. Wendy said nothing, asked no questions, and continued through the chamber.

A young man stepped in front of Wendy, startling her. He had come through a doorway in the concrete wall, now stood staring at her. Dressed in dark blue jeans, flannel shirt and leather boots, he looked different from the other people in the chamber—neater and cleaner, somehow. Healthier.

"Hello, Ms. Burke," he said softly.

"How do you know my name?" Wendy asked, her voice a whisper.

"I know your work," the man said. "I also know you live up above us, and I've been waiting the last couple of nights for you to show up."

Wendy looked at him, but didn't respond to the statement, trying to sort out the implications. She saw now that he was older than she had first thought. Wide streaks of gray ran through his dark hair, and there were lines around his eyes. She guessed he was in his late forties. "Who the hell are you?" she finally asked.

"My name is Dominic. Please, come this way, I'd like to talk to you, away from everyone." He retreated through the doorway and down a short hall which ended at a flight of stone steps leading upward in a tight spiral. Wendy stood in the doorway, hesitating, and Dominic turned back to her. "I won't do anything to hurt you," he said. "I just want to talk. And please, feel free to take as many pictures as you want." He turned and started up the steps.

Wendy hesitated a few more moments, but she knew there was no way she could leave now, not without some answers, and Dominic looked like her best shot at getting some. "Shit," she whispered to herself, then she hurried down the hall and followed him up the stairs.

The stairway spiraled around one and a half times, climbing steeply with high steps, then opened onto another short, dimly lit hall. Dominic waited for her to join him, then led the way into a small dark room illuminated only by the pale blue chamber light that fanned in through a large opening in the opposite wall. In front of the opening stood a small table and three chairs.

"Please, sit down," Dominic said.

"Christ, aren't you polite," Wendy replied. "You like the word 'please'?"

Dominic smiled, held his hand out toward the table. "Please," he said again.

Wendy crossed the room, sat in a chair next to the opening,

and looked out. The room was about fifteen feet above the chamber floor; she could see nearly the entire chamber now, almost as good a view as she'd had from the top of the ladder, which she could see hanging from the hole in the ceiling. She thought of Dominic's suggestion that she take pictures, but for some reason she did not want to right now.

She heard clinking sounds from the rear corner of the room, and Dominic approached with a tray holding a clear flask of coffee and two cups. He set the tray on the table, sat across from her. "Coffee?"

Wendy shook her head; Dominic poured a cup of coffee for himself, sipped at it.

"What *is* this place?" Wendy asked.

"A place for the homeless to sleep," Dominic answered.

"Yeah?"

"You sound skeptical."

"That surprise you?" Wendy asked. "This doesn't exactly look like a city shelter."

Dominic nodded once. "No, it doesn't, but then it's not a city shelter. This is a private institution. And it *is* a place for the homeless to sleep. We even provide a free evening meal. We have a large dining hall up at street level, in the warehouse next to your building. I'm surprised you haven't noticed all the people we bring in at the end of the day."

"I work nights," Wendy said. "I'm not around then."

"That's right, I hadn't thought of that." He paused, sipped his coffee. "We have several vans, and we go through the city as night comes on, offering a hot meal, a warm place to sleep. Then we bring them back here—street people, drifters, whoever doesn't have a place to stay. Anyone who wants to come. We serve them a meal, then bring them down here."

"Anyone?" Wendy interrupted. "I didn't see any children. Do you split up families, or just ignore them?"

Dominic slowly nodded, said, "Yes, that's true, there are no children." He leaned through the opening in the wall, gestured toward the far left. "You can't really see them, but there are a couple of big freight elevators down at that end, we bring everyone down in them." He looked at Wendy. "A lot of them would have a tough time going up and down stairs. Then they can sleep wherever they want. In the morning, back up in the elevators, coffee and donuts, and then we drive them back to the streets." He gave her an odd smile. "The city likes us, because we get people off the streets at night. They'd like us even better if we could keep them off the streets during the day as well, but they'll take what they can get."

Wendy didn't say anything at first; she stared at Dominic. Did he really expect her to buy this story? She didn't doubt that basically it was true, as far as it went. But there was obviously much more involved.

"A private shelter for the homeless," she finally said.

"Yes."

"And what about the guns?"

Dominic breathed in deeply, slowly let it out. "Yes, the guns. That's what it's really all about, isn't it?"

"Shit, you tell *me.*"

Dominic drank more coffee, then said, "Are you sure you don't want any?" When Wendy didn't respond, he refilled his cup, then resumed.

"I had a kind of lecture, or speech, all prepared about the terrible state of the world and, in particular, the terrible state of this country—greedy, rapacious corporations; corrupt, incompetent politicians; unethical financiers; an out-of-control military-industrial complex; an economy held together by frayed string and desperation; police state repression of radical thought. That kind of speech, with a few sayings thrown in that, despite being clichés, are now more true than ever before—'The rich get richer while the poor get poorer;' 'Politicians spend more time worrying about getting re-elected than doing their jobs.' You know . . ." He shrugged.

Dominic sipped at his coffee, looking out the window into the chamber. "Let's just take it as a given that the world's a mess, shall we?"

"Sure," Wendy said, wondering what the hell he was leading up to. "A given."

"From there, then," Dominic said. "People, organizations, are always trying to improve things—get rid of corruption, make the laws fairer, stop spending waste, and so on. The fact is, though, that things will *not* get any better until this whole society hits crisis and either collapses, or self-destructs. Until things get so bad that we're forced, for survival's sake, to work out better, more equitable systems. Until people are forced, by an undeniable threat to their existence, to change their attitudes and values, or at least their behavior." He waved across the window. "Here, we're trying to speed up that process."

"What are you talking about?"

Dominic turned to face her. "You won't like this."

"I don't like any of it now."

He nodded. "We're providing guns and other weapons to people so they will go back out into the city and use them, bring a little more chaos, a little more destruction, and maybe help bring this whole society down so it can be built up again from a fresh start."

Wendy looked at him in silence, unsure if he really meant what he was saying. "Are you serious?"

"Dead serious."

Stunned, Wendy shook her head. "You're out of your goddamn mind," she said, voice quiet but hard. "You're fucking crazy."

"I knew you wouldn't like it. Would you let me explain?"

"Be my goddamn guest."

Dominic sighed heavily, drank the rest of his coffee, put the empty cup on the tray. "You won't understand."

Wendy remained silent.

"The people we bring down here are outcasts, for one reason or another. They live within society, in the heart of the city and among people, but they're . . . outside, somehow. They don't belong. Some of them are furious, angry at the world because of the way they've been treated. Some are simply frustrated at lives gone bad. Some have given up. And some are psychotic." He paused. "These are the people who *should* be bringing the world down around them."

Dominic pushed back his chair, stood, and Wendy thought he was going to begin pacing the room, but he only leaned against the wall where he could both look at her and gaze out into the chamber.

"We don't actually *give* them the guns, or the ammunition. That's an important point. We don't encourage them to use them in a certain way, we don't encourage them to use them at all. In fact, we don't even acknowledge the guns. We make them available—in cubbyholes, on shelves, tucked away in corners, hanging from the side of a crate. But we do not mention them, and if asked about them by people who find them, we ignore the questions. The only thing we do is provide what we hope is a conducive atmosphere—the rumbling of machinery, the steam, the dim blue light. If people take the guns, fine. If not, that's all right, too. Plenty are gone every morning."

Wendy continued to remain silent, hardly believing what she was hearing, but she did not doubt that what Dominic was telling her was true, or at least what he believed to be true.

"We have no political agenda. There is no organization. We believe that if anything is to work, these people have to act willingly, and on their own, in their individual, random ways. What they do or don't do with the guns is up to them. Some *will* use the guns themselves, accidentally or otherwise. A lot of these people have good reason to become violent, given the opportunity . . . and the means. Others won't, but will sell the guns on the street to other people who will use them. One way or another, the guns get out onto the streets, the triggers get pulled, the bullets get fired and . . ." He didn't finish the sentence. "This isn't the only city with a shelter like this. They're all over the country."

Wendy sat up in her chair, thinking about Hicks and the gun he had used to kill Tony. Suddenly she was shaking with a surprising rage, and then she was out of the chair, around the table and grabbing Dominic by his shirt. "You fucking maniac!" she screamed into his face. "You're killing innocent people, for Christ's sake."

Dominic didn't resist. He simply said, "Quiet, please, they're trying to sleep down there."

Wendy stared at him, whispered "Jesus Christ," then released his shirt and backed away. She remained standing. "The other night," she began, "I was on the beach with some friends when this guy showed up, a *drifter*, as you might put it. He had a gun, which could easily have been provided right here, and he shot and killed a friend of mine. For nothing."

Dominic shook his head. "Whoever it was shot your friend probably didn't get the gun here." His voice was very soft. "The odds are against it."

Wendy put both hands on the table and stared at Dominic. "It doesn't matter, don't you understand that? The guns you're giving to these people are killing *someone*, they're killing somebody's friends, even if they're not mine."

Dominic didn't say anything at first, just returned her gaze. Then he said, "I know."

Wendy shook her head, suddenly very tired, and sat back down. "Christ," she said quietly. "How can you sleep nights?"

"I used to ask that question about a lot of people," Dominic said. "Certain politicians, military fanatics, corporate executives, TV evangelists, the last few presidents we've had. I could go on, but again I won't." He paused, sat across from her once again. "Fact is, sometimes I don't sleep. Sometimes I can't, sometimes I'm afraid to." He looked at her, shrugged.

"Then you have doubts? Second thoughts?"

"Constantly. But I've made a commitment, and I don't really know what else to do."

"Quit," Wendy said. "Get out, stop this whole thing, close it down, go to the police or whoever and get them all closed down."

Dominic shook his head. "I can't do that."

A sharp pain rose in Wendy's chest, and suddenly she was very much afraid. With all that Dominic had told her, what would keep *her* from going to the police?

"What am I doing here?" she asked. "You said you were waiting for me to show up. The pounding under my apartment? That was to get my attention?"

"Something like that."

"Why didn't you just ask me?"

"I wanted to know if you would come down on your own, find your way in." Dominic poured himself a fresh cup of coffee, emptying the flask. As he sipped the coffee, he looked at her over the rim of the cup. "Are you worried about whether or not I'll let you leave?"

Wendy hesitated, a knot tightening in her chest. "Yes."

Dominic shook his head. "Don't be. I'm not concerned that you'll go to the police, no matter what you think of all this. You *could*, but it wouldn't do you any good. If they were to get a search warrant and come in here, we'd know about it ahead of time, and they wouldn't find a single gun, they wouldn't find anything illegal. All they would find would be a dining hall and accommodations for all these people to sleep.

"But they won't come here with a search warrant, because they just would not believe you. You've been arrested what, six or seven times by the police because of your photography?"

"Six."

"You're a troublemaking, radical artist, see, and as I said, the city knows about this place, and the city is grateful for what we do. But aside from that, no matter who you were I can't imagine they would believe you. Because the bottom line is, this whole thing," and here he waved expansively at the opening in the wall, "the whole idea of what we're doing in here is *crazy*. It sounds too damn wacko, you want to know the truth, the product of some psychotic imagination, and so they won't believe it. Who in hell would?" He paused, shaking his head. "The fact is, it *is* crazy. I know that."

"Then why, for Christ's sake, are you doing this?"

"Because it's the only hope I have. It's the only thing I believe in anymore."

Neither of them spoke for a long time. Dominic sipped at his coffee and gazed out at the chamber. Wendy looked down at the people asleep below her, watched the flickering glow from the two barrel fires rising from behind the barriers.

"What am I doing here?" she asked again.

"I want you to take pictures," Dominic said.

"Why?"

"I'm not really sure. My colleagues were not happy with this whole idea, getting you down here. I convinced them, somehow." He paused. "I feel it's important, no matter how this all turns out, to have some kind of visual record." Dominic shook his head. "No, that's not right, I could get that with a Polaroid. You're a terrific photographer, Ms. Burke. I said earlier that I know your work. I think it's important to have your vision of this place where it will be seen. I know your history. No matter how much trouble you have with the police, you always get your work exhibited somewhere, and people see it. A lot of people. If you exhibited photographs that you take down here, no one who saw them would know what was really going on, of course, but the salient aspects would, I think, sink in, even if on a subliminal level. Now, if that were to happen, would that aid or obstruct the overall goals of what we're doing down here and in other cities? To convince them to allow you down here, I told my colleagues it would help, but frankly I don't know. And I suppose I don't really care. For reasons even I don't understand, I believe it's important." He drank the rest of his coffee, put the cup on the tray and pushed the tray away. "And that is what you are doing here."

Wendy turned away from Dominic and looked out again over the chamber. She felt numb, disoriented, and some of the fear still remained, though now it was unfocused, no longer connected to Dominic.

"I'm going now," she said.

Dominic nodded. "You can stay as long as you like, and you can always come back. You know how to get here, now."

Wendy stood, said, "I don't think I'll be back."

He nodded again. "Do you want me to take you out through the regular entrance? Through the dining hall?"

"No. I'll go back the way I came."

Wendy left the room, went down the spiral staircase, and emerged onto the chamber floor. The sounds were the same—the hiss of steam, the crackle of flames, muttering and snoring and creaking, the pervasive thrum of machinery—but it seemed louder now. She worked her way slowly through the chamber, her camera untouched at her side.

Near the back corner, she walked up the brick steps toward the ledge. She stopped when she saw the gun and ammo box on the upper step, thinking she should do something with it, but couldn't decide what, so she left the gun behind.

Standing on the ledge, she gazed out over the chamber once more, at the sleeping forms, the maze of walls and barriers, thinking of all those guns, thinking of Tony. Then she reached for the ladder, pulled herself up onto it, and started climbing.

Wendy came out onto the beach at dawn. The sun was not yet visible behind her, and the sky was a dark gray growing slowly lighter. Exhausted, she staggered down the dry sandy slope toward the water. It was low tide, and the water seemed far away.

She searched the beach, but there were no signs of what had happened three nights before—nothing remained of the shattered television set, the charred stones of the fire, the beer cans, the blood.

Wendy continued down the slope, struggling in the dry, sinking sand until she reached the wet hard pack near the water. With the tide so low, there were several fingers of rock and gravel exposed far down the slope, the gravel sounding like rolling marbles as the tips of the waves washed over it. Something shiny on the nearest split of rock caught her eye, and she walked over to it, skirting the waves as they hissed up the sand.

It was a gun. *The* gun? she wondered. Wendy stood at the edge of the jumble of rock and gravel and stared down at the weapon. It looked like the gun Hicks had used, but there was no way to know. No, that wasn't true, she could find out, she could take the gun to the police. *Ballistics,* she thought. For some reason, she liked that word.

But it really didn't matter whether or not it was the same

gun. The gun hadn't killed Tony, a bullet did. Or two bullets.

A wave came in, swirled an inch or two deep around her shoes, and Wendy looked away from the gun, out toward the ocean. Maybe it was time to stop taking pictures, she thought. Just stop. Time to leave the city, go somewhere quiet and isolated, some small town where she could have a garden like Libby's, but away from the city, away from people. Time to get *out*.

She fingered the exposed rolls of film in her jacket pocket, film that held the images of people sleeping in an underground chamber filled with hissing steam and pounding machinery, a place run by lunatics, a place littered with guns and bullets.

Yes, time to leave. She should take her camera, she told herself, and the film, and the gun at her feet, and heave them all out into the sea, as far as she could throw them. Let it all sink beneath the waves where it would disappear, at least for decades, maybe for centuries. And maybe forever. Then she could leave the city and do something else with her life.

But she didn't move. The sun was coming up over the city, and now reflected off the gun at her feet. She raised her camera, took off the lens cover, adjusted the exposure.

Wendy stepped back, aimed the camera at the gun, and focused. She waited until the next wave came in, washing over the gun and soaking her shoes, then, as the water slid back down the slope, exposing the gun once again, she snapped the picture.

Watching Lear Dream

AT NIGHT SAMUEL SAT BESIDE HIS OLD FRIEND LEAR and watched him dream. Lear's dreams manifested in the air above his prone and twisting figure, malformed creatures and almost familiar people and half-living machines that threatened to become fully substantial and take on strange and complicated lives of their own in this world. Samuel, too, had once dreamed dreams like these.

But now he kept watch over his old friend. Kept watch over Lear's dreams. And destroyed those dreams.

Samuel and Lear. They were the last of their kind.

Samuel acted as a gatekeeper, human Cerberus, guarding the natural world from the supernatural. Doing so, he kept Lear alive. Watching over him, preventing the old man's dreams from becoming primed realities loosed and wreaking havoc upon the world, he held back the executioner's axe. As long as Samuel kept Lear's dreams at bay, DivCom allowed Lear to live.

Lear had once been a DivCom hero. So, too, had Samuel, and the other twenty-seven like them. They had dreamed into existence strange and powerful creatures and superhuman beings, incredible living weapons and organic star-jumping ships, and then, in full control of their creations, directed them against the invading forces of an alien civilization that attacked them from somewhere near the heart of the Milky Way. And they had triumphed.

But the others were all dead now, most of them killed during the conflict, others by accident or old age; two by suicide. Only Samuel and Lear remained, and they were no longer needed, the conflict years ended, no other foreseen. They would have been useless even if needed—Samuel had no more dreams, and Lear had lost all control of his own. Neither was a hero anymore.

For years Samuel kept watch over Lear, fought Lear's dreams, and dispatched every one. For years.

Until the day Lear dreamed Teresa back to life.

DivCom had settled the two of them on a sparsely inhabited world, almost primitive, habitable but lacking exploitable resources. Set them up in a small house several kilometers upstream from a village that straddled a swiftly flowing river, which poured over stones and crashed around boulders as it came out of the dark and craggy mountains. Another hundred and fifty kilometers farther downstream, the river—much wider and slower by that point—emptied into a vast inland sea. Neither Samuel nor Lear had ever seen the inland sea, and Samuel was certain they never would. He and Lear would live out the rest of their lives in this house, never going much farther than the village. They would die here.

Three people stayed with them at the house: two men and a woman provided by DivCom to cook and clean and garden and maintain the house, to accompany Samuel and Lear on shopping trips into the village—for food and supplies, books and music, clothing and news capsules—and to go with them on those occasions when Lear felt the need to spend an afternoon or evening or both in the local tavern drinking himself into a stupor.

The day Lear dreamed Teresa back to life, Samuel was down by the river, dozing in the shade of a dense tree. The summer air was still and hot, but in the shade, so close to the river, it was cool. Samuel was half asleep, and he was almost dreaming.

A normal dream, a human dream, one that would never manifest in the air above him, never threaten to come to life.

Fragmented and incoherent, the dream images overlaid the thick and leafy branches above him: red and orange flames, a black vehicle on fire in the snow. . . . And then he realized Lear was inside the vehicle, screaming through the flames and the black smoke and Samuel knew Lear would be burned alive. . . .

The flames scattered, Lear's face dissolved, then coalesced into Carpentier staring down at him.

"Wake up!" Carpentier was saying. A member of the Div-Com contingent, he did most of the cooking and cleaning, a bit of gardening. Errand boy.

Samuel blinked, pushed at Carpentier's arm. "Go away," he said. He wanted his dream back, even the awful dream of Lear burning alive. Any dream.

"It's Lear," Carpentier said. "He's dreaming."

"Now?"

"Now." Nodding his head. "He wanted to take a nap." A shrug. "He's an old man."

Then so am I, thought Samuel. Yet it *was* somehow more true of Lear.

"Hurry!" Carpentier insisted.

But there was no hurry. Samuel got slowly to his feet, brushed leaves from his legs and arms. It was quite possible that Lear's dream creations would fade of their own accord, but even if they didn't, they would need to manifest for several hours before they became difficult to dispatch.

He followed Carpentier back to the house, his head swimming in the heat. Dust puffed up at his feet, and the electric buzz of insect-like creatures oscillated around him like a fan that provided no relief. Samuel walked slowly, eyes half closed, vision bleached, ignoring Carpentier's urgings. He was so tired, of everything.

When they reached the house, Carpentier remained outside with the others—Arturo Langley and Rashida Gamel, both of whom pretended to be occupied with outdoor chores. All three of DivCom's people were afraid of Lear's dreams.

Samuel climbed the creaking wooden steps and stood for a few moments in the shade of the large covered porch, readying himself for what he would have to do inside. The house was quiet, the air surrounding it still and just as quiet except for the electric buzz and the hesitant sounds of the DivCom people moving about. He didn't want to go in. He didn't want to do this anymore. But he opened the door and stepped inside.

Inside the house wasn't much cooler, though he could feel

the air moving about him, blown by the small, whirring fans in every room. He walked through the entry and down the hall, then stopped outside Lear's room and listened for sounds of the old man's dreaming. Nothing, really—the whisper of sheets, a faint huff of breath. Samuel entered.

He stopped, unable to move.

He had been prepared for almost anything but this.

Life-size, and almost life-like, she hovered in the air above the bed: Teresa.

Teresa had been Lear's wife. And Samuel had betrayed his old friend with her. Together, Samuel and Teresa had both betrayed him.

She was not yet aware of him. It would be an hour or two, maybe longer, before she became substantial enough. Samuel stood just inside Lear's door, watching her. She was talking to someone inside the dream, Lear probably, and her smile didn't seem a happy one; she looked as if she was about to cry.

She looked so young. No older than the day she had died, perhaps even younger, while Lear and Samuel had, of course, aged. She was wearing loose tan pants and a white short-sleeved shirt, leather sandals on feet still vague and blurred; long sandy hair shimmered around her face. Then she brought her hand up and tugged at her hair in a gesture so painfully familiar it made Samuel's heart ache.

He knew what he should do. He should dispatch her right now, before this all went too far. And if he couldn't bring himself to do that, then he should wake Lear, as dangerous as that could be for both of them, and hope his waking would destroy her. But he did neither.

He left the room, carefully closing the door. As he came out of the house he went over to Carpentier and Rashida; Arturo was off a ways, watching them.

"Stay out of the house," Samuel said. "This is going to be a difficult one."

Rashida opened her mouth, but Samuel cut her off before she could say a word. "Everything will be fine," he said. "I'll be back in a little while, when I'm prepared. Just stay out of the house."

Then he turned away from them and headed back toward the river.

*　　*　　*

He sat on the grassy riverbank, gazing into the swirling white and silver-blue water. The rapids were strong here, but he didn't think they were unnavigable. He wondered about a boat, a canoe, finding one somewhere nearby, maybe down in the village. Then he could risk the river, the rocks and the whirl-pools, the heat and the insects, and the DivCom people who would come after him once they realized he had gone, once they realized what he had left behind. He could take the boat all the way to the inland sea, and from there . . .

It wasn't Teresa. He knew that. A simulacrum, an imperfect, incomplete doppelganger. It was only a thing, unliving and in a way unreal, at least for now.

The last time he had seen Teresa she had been dying . . . and then dead. He and Lear had both been with her, waiting for her last breath, the last beat of her heart. She had died from a vicious bacterial infection, her pain and mind dulled by anal-gesics and tropo-opiates. Suffusing her face, though, was an expression that suggested to Samuel a real sense of peace—she was already gone from this world, and was content with that.

But now she was back.

Two hours later he returned to the house. The DivCom con-tingent was still outside, waiting for him. Carpentier ap-proached, but Samuel glared at the man until he backed away without a word.

Just outside Lear's room Samuel stopped and stared at his hands. They were trembling. He felt the trembling all through his body.

He opened the door. Lear was still asleep. Teresa sat on the edge of the bed, her gaze unfocused, but as Samuel entered the room she turned and looked at him, eyes widening.

"Samuel?" Her voice was warped and distorted, as if she was speaking through metallic water.

He didn't reply. Something about her silently snapped into focus, a solidification, a sharpening of resolution, and she was completely there.

"Samuel?" she said again. This time her voice was almost normal, almost Teresa's.

He still didn't reply. She stood and walked toward him, then reached out and touched his arm with warm dry fingers, and he shivered inside, his chest collapsing in on itself.

"Samuel," she said for the third time, but now there was no question.

Finally his volition returned, along with breath and pulse. "Yes," he said.

She touched him again and he stepped back.

"Do you know who you are?" he asked.

"Yes, of course. I'm Teresa. Don't you know who *you* are, Samuel?" And she smiled.

"Do you know *what* you are?"

Her smile faded, but she nodded. "I am one of Lear's dreams." She paused, breathing deeply. "But I am still Teresa."

Samuel shook his head, so slowly it seemed the room was moving from side to side. "No. You are only the Teresa that he imagines you are. Or were. Or the Teresa he wanted you to be."

This time it was her turn to shake her head. "You're wrong, Samuel. I am everything he knows about me, whether he liked it or not. He can't change his own knowledge of me."

"It's not that simple. Besides, there were so many things about you that he could never have known. That only you knew. Or I knew. Things that you can't know about yourself because he never knew them."

"Then help me, Samuel. Help me to *become* me. Tell me the things that you know, that Lear never knew."

He turned away from her. This was insane. He needed to bring her under control, and dispatch her before it became too difficult. Except that it was already too difficult.

"Samuel. What would you tell me about myself? What would you tell me that Lear doesn't know?"

He was looking across Lear's sleeping body and out the small window, gazing at the fruit trees behind the house. The reddish-orange fruit, in clusters of three or four tiny spheres, was almost ripe. Another few days and the bitterness would be gone and the fruit would be sweet, the thick juice cool and refreshing.

"You were his wife," Samuel said without looking at her. "He was your husband. But *I* loved you too."

"He knows that, Samuel."

Yes, he thought, of course he does. But there was so much more. He turned back to her. "But what he didn't know was that you loved me as well." He paused, his stomach folding, clutching at itself. "And we betrayed him."

"He knows that, too," she said.

"He *knows?*"

Teresa nodded. "*I* know, and so he must know."

Samuel was too stunned to reply. He looked again at Lear,

at the closed eyes and open mouth. His old friend.

"Come," Samuel said. He turned and walked out of the room, and Teresa followed.

He led the way to his own room. It seemed so stark and empty to him now. He hesitated for a few moments, then went to the small closet and opened the door.

"You'll have to stay in here until dark," he said. "They'll try to destroy you if they find out you're still . . ." What word? ". . . alive," he finished.

"They might not be able to," she said. And there was something hard and defiant in her voice.

"That's true," he replied. "But they'll try. And they'll kill me, and they'll kill Lear."

She stared at him, as though trying to decide something. "All right," she said, nodding. "And then what?"

"I don't know."

She let out a quiet but harsh laugh and shook her head, but didn't say anything more. They made a place for her to sit in the closet, a nest of his clothing. When she was settled in, he shut the closet door, then walked out of the house and onto the front porch. The three DivCom people were waiting for him.

"It's done," he said.

"Something's wrong." Lear spoke quietly, almost hushed. He looked and sounded confused.

"What?" Samuel asked.

Lear just shook his head. Somehow he looked even older this evening, old and frail and lost.

They were eating out on the front porch, the sky mottled with bits of dark crimson, remnants of a sunset long gone. Samuel could see the flickering lights of the village downslope in the distance, and he thought about the walk he'd never made in the dark before, the one he would have to make later this night.

"A dream I had," Lear finally said.

"What dream?" Breath catching.

Lear shook his head again. There was pain now in the pale blue eyes almost hidden beneath furrowed gray brows. "I can't remember. It's . . . it's . . ." The old man's mouth trembled and he blinked his eyes. "Gone," he eventually said, a strange grieving in his voice.

No, Samuel thought. But there was nothing he could say.

They remained on the porch, drinking coffee as complete darkness fell and the stars emerged bright and cool, both of the men lost and confused each in their own private way.

He should have been watching Lear. Lear slept again, tossing fitfully in the hot darkness of his room, more disturbed than usual. But no dreams formed in the air above him, and Samuel returned to his own room.

Teresa was waiting for him, the closet door already open, her eyes aglow in the night. He motioned for silence, and for her to follow him.

Carpentier and Arturo were sleeping, but Rashida was on watch, walking about both inside the house and out. Samuel had her route worked out, and just as Rashida was coming back inside he led Teresa out the back door and around the side of the house, into the small grove of fruit trees. The scent of the fruit hung delicately in the warm night air. The stars provided just enough light for them to make out their footing, and they moved quickly through the trees.

Once they were out of the grove they worked their way across a stretch of rocky ground to the road, which roughly followed the course of the river down to the village.

"Where are you taking me?" Teresa asked.

"There's a village downstream," he told her. "We'll find a room for you, a place to stay for a few days."

She didn't ask him any more questions, which surprised him, but he was grateful for that. He didn't think he would have had any more answers.

They walked in silence, but her presence enveloped him, as if there was some electrochemical quality to her that charged the air, penetrating his skin. And maybe there was, because of *what* she was.

As they approached the village, the nearly silent whisper of a breeze and the gurgling of water gave way to the sounds of humanity—voices, faint music, the rumble of motors and clink of glass, crackling, loud hissing—and trees and bushes were replaced by low, scattered buildings and vehicles and lights. A few people were out on the streets walking or pedaling wheeled carts and cycles, and occasionally a motorized vehicle went by, engine incredibly quiet.

The first place they tried, an inn, was full for the night, but farther on was a tavern where Lear liked to drink. Behind it, facing the river, were several night rooms. Samuel and Teresa went through the crowded, music-filled tavern and into the back office, where they talked to Marissa. There was a room available on the second floor, and Samuel paid for five nights with local money.

The room was surprisingly quiet, and overlooked the river; the moving water flashed up at them, scales of silver and amber and red. There was a floorbed, a table and chairs, private bath, a balcony. Teresa sat on the end of the bed, but when Samuel walked out onto the balcony, she got up and went with him.

He looked up at the night sky. Besides the stars there was only a tiny, distant moon high in the east, hardly more than a small bright coin in the sky. The only moon this world had. He'd been on worlds with large, almost brilliant moons that, when they were full, lit the night almost like day. He missed that. He missed the roar and the pressure of ships rising from a launch field taking him into space. He missed the sight of a vast, densely populated city at night as he descended over it, the combination of moving and stationary colored lights giving the impression of a living organism pulsing in the dark. He missed so much, but he especially missed the woman whose simulacrum stood beside him now.

She almost *smelled* like Teresa.

"Stay with me tonight, Samuel."

He turned to her, and her eyes were bright, almost glowing. Maybe they *were* glowing, some strange effect that resulted from her creation. How could he stay with her? She wasn't really Teresa, she wasn't really human.

"Stay with me," she said again.

How could he *not?* Samuel put his arms around her, feeling his breath catch and his heart hesitate, and pulled her tightly to him.

He slept lightly and fitfully, always at least partially aware of her presence beside him, even as he slept. And for the first time in years he dreamed intensely, dreams so vivid and overwhelming it seemed they would never end.

In the morning they ate breakfast at a small outdoor café on the river. Strong hot coffee, fresh rolls and fresh fruit, thick pieces of sweet cheese. The river was quieter in the early morning light, and comforting.

She wasn't Teresa. He knew that now even more than before. But she was close enough. If this went on for long, the differences would become unimportant. No, that wasn't right. The differences were already unimportant; eventually they would cease to exist for him.

"What do we do now?" she asked. She was smiling, as if it didn't matter what he answered. As if she already had something in mind.

"I don't know."

And now she laughed. There was something reckless about her. Teresa, too, had been reckless; it was one of the things that had attracted him to her. If it had been up to him to take the initiative, their affair would never have begun.

"I'd better get back," he told her. He handed her the rest of his local money. "Get what you need, clothes, food, whatever. If you need more money, I'll get it." It was easier to think about practical matters.

"When will you be back?" she asked.

"It won't be easy. Late afternoon, if I can."

She reached across the table, took his hand in hers, and gently rubbed his fingers while looking directly at him. Those eyes, still glowing even in the light of day. Samuel finally got up, reluctantly pulled his hand away, and left.

No one seemed to have noticed that he'd been gone all night. Rashida asked him where he'd been, and when he said he'd gone into the village for breakfast, that satisfied her.

Lear, apparently, had not dreamed anything new into existence during the night, but he still seemed disturbed and confused. "Walk with me," he said to Samuel.

They walked through the grove of fruit trees, side by side in silence for a while, two old friends with long lives between them. Samuel could already feel the guilt beginning to settle into him, and he knew that, just as before, the guilt would not stop him. Other things might, but not the guilt.

"I feel lost," Lear said. "Something's happened, and I don't know what it is. I feel as if a piece has been carved out of me and devoured." He looked at Samuel and smiled, shaking his head. "I know, I sound like a madman."

Samuel shrugged. He still didn't know what to say to his old friend. There was a wooden bench under the largest of the fruit trees, and Lear led the way to it. He dropped onto the bench with a heavy sigh, and Samuel sat beside him. Lear tipped his head back and gazed up through the leafy, fruit-filled branches, gazed up at tiny windows of aquamarine sky.

"I miss her," Lear said.

"Who?"

"Teresa. I still miss her after all these years." He lowered his gaze and looked off in the direction of the river, though they couldn't see it from here. "I've been thinking about her a lot."

Which was no surprise to Samuel. But he didn't say anything.

"Do *you* miss her?" Lear asked, turning to look at him.

Samuel wondered if guilt could appear on his face or in his eyes; would Lear even recognize it if it did?

"Sometimes," he said.

Lear nodded. He continued to stare at Samuel, as though waiting for him to say something, or perhaps trying to come to some decision. But Samuel said nothing, and eventually Lear just shook his head and looked away.

"I want to be alone," Lear said.

Samuel got up, feeling somehow even guiltier than ever, and walked away, leaving his old friend behind.

As he neared the village, Samuel had to fight the urge to break into a run. He was a young man again, heart and mind battling each other, love and betrayal rekindled, and somehow he didn't care that she wasn't really Teresa, that she was an organic dream creation of the man he was betraying once again. And he couldn't believe he was doing this.

When he arrived at the room, she wasn't there, and panic kicked in. He hurried into the tavern, but she wasn't there, either. Frantic, he ran out into the street, gaze jumping back and forth, whipping about in all directions, but there was still no sign of her anywhere.

He leaned against a wall and closed his eyes, forced himself to calm down and relax. She had to be somewhere nearby. The village wasn't that big, and she could take care of herself, probably better than he could. He opened his eyes and set off down the street, searching for her.

He found her across the river at the village airfield. She was sitting in the makeshift open air terminal, watching a small jumper plane preparing for takeoff. He sat beside her, and she took his hand in hers; her skin was warm and dry and her touch was almost electric.

"Let's go away," she said, not looking at him, still watching the plane. "We can take a jumper to Aleron City and the spaceport, then we get a ship off this world and start over again somewhere. Without Lear, without the DivCom people." She turned to him, eyes sparkling with her smile. "Just the two of us, Samuel."

He started to ask her if she was serious, but he knew she was. So he just shook his head, a strange fear growing inside him.

"I can't," he said. "They won't let me leave this place. They certainly won't let me leave this world."

"We'll find a way." Spoken with absolute certainty.

"It's not that simple."

"It is," she said. "If you want it. We'll find a way."

"What about Lear? They'll kill him."

"No they won't." But there wasn't the certainty in her voice this time, and she looked away from him. "They'll figure out something else. Drugs, maybe, to keep him from dreaming. Something like that."

Samuel shook his head.

"There's no other way," she said. "You have to realize that. How long will it be before they discover what's happened? Before someone finds out about me?" She turned back to him. "I love you, Samuel, and if you love me . . ." But she left it unfinished.

He looked into her eyes, deep into those dark and shining eyes, and had no answer for her.

He spent the days with Teresa, and the nights with Lear.

Leading two lives again, as he had so many years ago, and knowing that this time it couldn't go on for very long before something disastrous occurred. But knowing that didn't change a thing.

"Teresa is alive!" Lear staggered up the steps of the front porch, flushed and out of breath. He held onto the railing for support and said, "She's alive."

Samuel didn't respond. Fear caught his breath. Could Lear really have seen her?

Still breathing hard, his gray hair wild about his head, Lear pushed away from the railing and sat across the table from Samuel. Sweat rolled from his forehead, but his eyes glittered with life and madness. He picked up Samuel's iced drink, brought it to his mouth, and drained the entire glass. He set the glass down, dug out some ice and pressed it against his face.

"She was in the village," he finally said. "I saw her."

"It couldn't be," Samuel said. "Someone who looked like Teresa, that's all. Teresa's dead."

"No." Lear shook his head, adamant.

"We saw her die, remember? We were there."

"No," Lear said again. "I called out her name and she turned, and when she saw me her face lit up and she said my name. She knew me." He paused, confusion distorting his expression. "Then she suddenly seemed frightened, and she ran off into the crowds. I tried to follow, but I lost her."

"You're imagining things, my old friend." Samuel leaned forward and looked steadily into Lear's eyes. "We both lost her years ago." And immediately regretted saying it, knowing it was exactly the wrong thing to say.

Lear's expression darkened. He stood slowly, gaze never leaving Samuel. "Still the same," he said. "You can't stand it. You never had her to lose. She was mine. She's alive, 'old friend.' And you won't have her this time, either."

He turned away and hobbled down the porch steps, back into the heat and the sun, leaving Samuel alone and afraid.

"Why did you answer him?" Samuel asked.

They were sitting at the table inside her room, drinking coffee, watching and listening to the afternoon thundershower that did little to ease the day's heat.

"It was an automatic response," she answered, not looking at him. "My name being called out like that, I just reacted."

"No," he said. "You can't get away with that. He told me that you saw him, then called out his name."

Her head came around fast and she glared at him with angry defiance. "He's my husband."

"He's not . . ." But then Samuel stopped. What was the point? It didn't matter what he said to her, she would do and say and think as she wanted. And she refused to believe that she wasn't as much Teresa as the real Teresa had been. "He's old," Samuel said, "and his mind doesn't work right anymore, but he'll figure it out."

"Figure *what* out?" she asked, still defiant, daring him to say it.

"What you are."

And then a smile appeared, joining the defiance. "And what am I, Samuel?" When he didn't answer, she got up and went to him, took his hands in hers and pulled him to his feet, then led him to the bed. "*Who* am I, Samuel?"

"Teresa," he whispered, and wrapped his arms around her, breathing deeply of her scent which only intensified as he felt her lips on his neck and cheek, her hands gripping his shoulder and back. "Teresa."

Samuel sat out on the balcony, gaze only vaguely focused on the water rushing past below him, the swirl and spray almost hypnotic. Teresa was asleep in the room, and he thought he could feel that electric buzz of her presence even out here.

I'm losing control, he thought to himself. And then almost laughed aloud at the absurdity. He'd never really *had* any control over what was happening now. Not one bit since Lear had dreamed her back to life.

He looked into the room through the open doorway. Teresa, sprawled naked on top of the bed, seemed perfectly at ease, unconcerned about a thing. She would leave soon. With or without him, she would leave.

He returned his gaze to the river. The heat from the sun overhead baked all energy from his limbs. Which was, he thought, as it should be. There was nothing he could do but wait for it to happen.

He sat on the porch in the afternoon heat, a strip of sun on his bare ankles, almost burning his skin. He was drinking iced coffee and reading, and he was waiting for Lear to return from the village. He set the book down and gazed along the path that led to the road, but there were no signs of Lear.

Rashida Gamel came out of the house and stood next to the table, looking down on Samuel.

"I don't like this," she said.

"What?"

"Lear's excursions into the village. Something's going on, and I don't like it. Especially since he always insists on going alone."

Samuel shook his head. "But you always send Carpentier or

Arturo to follow him, don't you? You know where he goes, what he does. He's not trying to 'escape,' is he?''

"We don't know *what* he's doing. He seems to be searching for something. Or someone."

"Ask him," Samuel suggested.

"I have. He doesn't answer."

Samuel smiled, though he was certain that would annoy her. "He's an old man," he said. As if that would somehow explain it all.

Rashida frowned at him, but didn't say anything more. Something caught her attention and she looked toward the road. Samuel followed her gaze and saw Lear shuffling along the roadway, looking tired and dejected. Lear turned up the path, dust kicking up from his feet, and walked toward them. When he reached the porch he climbed the steps without once looking at Rashida or Samuel, then went into the house.

Rashida remained on the porch until Arturo appeared on the road. As he came up the path he looked at Rashida and shrugged, shaking his head. Then he, too, climbed the porch steps and went inside.

"I don't like it," Rashida said once again. Then she turned and followed the others into the house.

Half an hour later, Samuel was on the road to the village, and so preoccupied he hardly noticed his surroundings. Rashida worried him. Her suspicions would probably never be allayed, and he suspected it wouldn't be long before she had Arturo or Carpentier following *him* as well. And Lear worried him, with his foul moods and his own suspicions, his daily trips into the village searching for Teresa. Samuel had warned her, but he didn't trust her to be careful. Right now *everything* worried him, particularly since it seemed there was nothing he could do about any of it.

Dark, heavy clouds scudded in overhead, bringing with them a damp and electric feel to the air. There was a silent, generalized flash sheeting across the clouds, then a few seconds later came a crash of thunder that rumbled quickly away. A few seconds more, and the rain started.

He was on the outskirts of the village, and he broke into a halting trot, hugging the few scattered buildings, stopping for a few moments whenever there was complete shelter and catching his breath before plunging back into the rain. He found it all strangely exhilarating.

He was soaking wet by the time he reached the tavern, where he finally slowed to a walk as he went around back. As he climbed the stairs to the second floor, the rain let up a little, became a drizzle washing across his face; he stopped outside Teresa's door and, tilting his head back, opened his mouth to the water.

He was still standing like that when Teresa opened the door. She smiled. "Look at you," she said. Then she took his arm and gently pulled him inside.

In the bathroom, he took off all his clothes and hung them in the shower, then dried off with towels, wrapping one around his waist like a skirt. He looked at himself in the mirror, suddenly dismayed. *I'm an old man, too.* The hair on his chest was almost completely white, coarse and kinked; the outline of his ribcage was distinct; and the skin under his neck was beginning to sag. Deep lines fanned out from his eyes.

What did she see in him? He had no idea.

When he came out of the bathroom, Teresa had coffee ready, made in a small steamer she'd bought. She handed a cup to him and said, "We need to talk."

An ache mushroomed in his chest, then dropped into his gut, but he nodded. They went out onto the balcony, which was sheltered from the rain, and sat facing each other. Samuel drank from his coffee, then set it under the chair.

"What is it?" he asked her.

Teresa shook her head. "The same thing, Samuel. We can't keep this going. Lear coming into the village every day looking for me. You coming later, for just a few hours, then going back to keep watch over his dreams. It's time, Samuel."

He didn't answer. He knew she was right, but he still didn't know what to do. The choice was simple enough.

"I'm leaving," she said. "I *have* to, Samuel. I can't stay here any longer. Not in this town, not on this world. This isn't the life I want, the life I *need.* And I can't risk it any longer, that DivCom will find out about me. You said it before, they'll try to destroy me if they know." She paused. "So I'm leaving. I want you with me, Samuel. But if you choose to stay, I'll go without you."

He knew she wasn't bluffing, and he knew she was right to go. The risks were growing every day, and there was little they could do about them.

"What are you going to do, Samuel?"

Thunder cracked and rumbled, but he hadn't seen the lightning. The rain intensified again, becoming a darker, louder curtain between the balcony and the river.

"I don't know," he finally said.

"You have to decide," she told him. "Today. Before you leave." She drank slowly from her coffee, as though savoring it. "I won't be here tomorrow."

A simple choice. Go with Teresa, or stay with Lear.

What would DivCom do if he went? As long as they didn't know about Teresa, they might just let him go. But what would they do to Lear?

Samuel looked out through the pouring rain at the river gone almost completely gray, only hints of pale blue occasionally winking up at him from the water.

What did he owe Lear? What did he owe to this woman, this Teresa simulacrum who only existed because of what he hadn't done? And what did he owe to himself?

The front door opened and Lear staggered into the room. His hair was wet and wild about his head and his eyes were just as wild, shifting crazily from side to side until he saw Teresa and Samuel out on the balcony. Samuel stared at Lear through the open doorway as if the old man were an apparition, not quite believing Lear had found them, and yet not quite surprised either.

Lear slowly crossed the room and stopped in the doorway, looking back and forth between Teresa and Samuel. Teresa set her coffee at her feet and stood, gazing steadily at Lear. Samuel remained seated—not out of paralysis, but more out of a strange inertia, as though all of this no longer had much to do with him. This was between Lear and Teresa now.

"I knew you were alive," Lear said.

"Yes," Teresa replied. "I'm alive."

"All this time . . ." Lear shook his head as he spoke, and Samuel wondered what Lear meant—did he really think Teresa had been alive all these years? "All this time," Lear continued, "you were with him."

"Yes."

"Just like before."

"Yes."

Lear turned to Samuel. "I knew before," he said. "I knew, but I loved you almost as much as I loved her, and so I said . . . nothing. I let it go on, even though it was tearing me up inside. I let it go on because . . . because . . ." He shook his head again, then reared it backwards, letting out a loud, chopped laugh. He lowered his head and gazed out at the river. "Because I was a fool."

No one said anything for a long time. A faint flash washed across the gray-black clouds, and it was several seconds before a quiet rumble reached them.

"Storm's moving on," Lear said. Then he looked at Teresa. "I won't be a fool this time," he told her.

"You will always be a fool," Teresa said. And Samuel thought she was as mad as Lear.

"No," Lear responded. "Not this time." Then he cocked his head, staring as if he'd just noticed something about her for the first time.

Samuel grew suddenly afraid, and the fear shivered through him.

"I know what you are," Lear eventually said. He turned to Samuel. "You let her live."

Samuel didn't reply. He tried to stand, but now found himself unable to move. Everything was out of his control.

Turning back to Teresa, Lear said, "I won't let this happen again."

"You don't have any choice," she told him, that defiance in her voice, daring him.

"This time you're wrong," he said.

And then Samuel knew what Lear was going to do. The fear notched up inside him and he abruptly stood, knocking over his chair and kicking his coffee over the edge of the balcony. But it was too late.

Teresa, too, seemed to realize what Lear was going to do, and she stepped back, but there was nowhere for her to go.

Lear lunged and wrapped his arms around her. They crashed against the balcony railing, and for a moment Samuel thought the two of them were going over, but Lear managed to pull back from the railing while maintaining his hold on Teresa. She struggled in his arms, twisting and squirming, but he was too strong. If anything, Lear tightened his hold on her.

A glow appeared between Teresa and Lear, shimmering wherever their bodies made contact. As Samuel stepped forward, sparks began to arc out from the glow with tiny crackling sounds. He reached out to grab Lear, intending to pull him away from her, but he was knocked backward by a tremendous jolt, like energy fields explosively repelling each other.

He lost consciousness. Probably only for a few seconds. When he came to, he was on his back, staring up at the over-hang that sheltered the balcony from the worst of the storm; scattered raindrops blew in across his face.

He raised his head and saw Teresa still struggling, still without success. The glow intensified and the sparking increased. Lear held on, mouth open and teeth bared, his eyes almost luminescent within the shimmering glow that now sur-rounded the two of them.

Suddenly Teresa stopped struggling. She hung limply in Lear's arms, and turned to Samuel. She had that expression on her face once again, the one from the earlier time she was dying—acceptance and peace, a readiness to leave this world.

But Samuel wasn't ready for her to leave. He struggled to his feet and watched in a shattering grief as she turned back to Lear and embraced him. She screamed once, and burst into a cas-cading shower of sparks, like a human fireworks display. Lear, too, screamed, and arms flailing he fell backward into the room.

Silence. Silence and smoke and the stench of burned flesh. She was gone.

No, not silence. There was still the rain, spattering on the overhang, hissing into the river.

Samuel looked over at the spot where they had struggled, searching for signs of her—a piece of charred clothing, or a sandal, a ring, something . . . *anything*. But there was nothing, and he thought he could feel his heart coming apart.

When he finally could move again, he stepped into the room and looked down at Lear. The old man's flesh was singed in several places, but he had managed to pull himself to his hands and knees. He looked up at Samuel for a moment, then leaned back on his haunches, buried his face in his hands and began to sob.

Samuel walked past him without a word, went into the bath-room and put on his cold, damp clothes. Then he came out, crossed the room without looking at Lear, and stepped outside. The rain was lighter now, warm and misting, creating a hushed quiet in the air. He pulled the door closed behind him, then started down the stairs.

The canoe drifted near the middle of the river, the slow, wide current taking him toward the inland sea. The sun was low in the western sky to his left, but the day was still hot. Samuel held the wide-bladed oar across his knees and watched the makeshift piers slip past him on his right as he continued to drift downstream. There was a town here at the mouth of the river, but he wouldn't stop; he needed to go farther.

Would he have gone with her? He still didn't know the answer to that question, and suspected he never would, but he was content with that, and he didn't think a lot about it anymore. He didn't think much about Lear, either, and what Div-Com might have done to him. The old man was either still alive, or he wasn't. It didn't concern Samuel anymore.

The canoe bobbed in the water as the river met the gentle swells of the inland sea. Directly ahead of him, as far as he could see, was a vast expanse of water, tiny wavelets flashing golden orange and red reflections of the sun into his eyes. Another world, another life, it seemed, was out there for him. There were, he understood, small towns and villages scattered all along the shores of the sea. One of them would be the right place for him, the right place to stop.

As he drifted past the spit of land that marked the boundary of river and sea, he saw a few boats out in the water, others pulled up on the beach, and people on shore, some apparently watching him. He dug his oar into the water and headed east, away from the setting sun.

Telescope, Saxophone, and the Pilot's Death

THESE THINGS HAPPENED TO ME IN 2138. FIVE YEARS and several previous attempts to write about them have gone by, but it is only recently that I've more fully understood what they really meant to me, to my life, to my art.

I still live in the same apartment I lived in then. It's on the top floor, the fifth, of a brick and wood building. There are two large rooms, and a kitchen with a stained porcelain sink, cracked counter tile, and cold water from both taps. The recycler no longer works. Hot water does run in the bathroom, which has toilet, sink, and a small wall shower. I keep a garden on the balcony facing away from the launch fields, over the street. Rent is low because the port facilities—launch pads, repair sheds, maintenance hangars, warehousing units, gantries, terminal arms, subterranean rail systems—begin a block away; the noise level is extremely high, the air quality low. Still, the garden thrives.

The spaceport is the main reason I live here. Day and night a constant ring and clatter, small explosions and high whines, pounding and grating of metal against metal, all fill the air, periodically overwhelmed by a series of sirens followed by the massive rumbling and roar of a rocket launch that shakes the walls of this building, and vibrates the air for several minutes. I cannot sleep without the noise.

I am an artist, a craftsman, a hack, or a fraud, depending on who you listen to. I produce welded sculptures from pieces of debris I collect on the grounds of the port, often from inside the hangars or sheds. Though they vary in size, shape, function, and condition, all are pieces either from space vehicles—the freight or troop ships, the streamlined passenger liners, the smaller, more numerous shuttles—or from the machines that service and maintain them.

At night, on the roof of this building, directly above my apartment, I weld the pieces of debris together in the light of the moon, in the glow from the spaceport, and I construct my sculptures, large and small, creating abstract representations of humanity's accelerating expansion throughout the galaxy.

For relaxation, I play the saxophone.

Before I met her, I had made very few sculptures. I had started dozens, but was unable to finish most of them. And I had not completed a new sculpture in almost a year.

I earned my living at the spaceport, changing jobs once or twice a year when I grew bored. I was proficient at almost everything, and the Port Authority accommodated me, shifting me from position to position, retraining me at each new job; when emergencies arose, and they regularly did, the Port Authority knew it could call on me to fill in with whatever needed to be done.

It was during an emergency that I met her. One of the two loaders for a troop ship had broken down less than three hours before launch; the soldiers were already webbed into their compartments, but crates of weaponry, uniforms, and shock equipment still waited in the loading caverns, and the one working loader would not be able to get it all aboard in time. With the threat of a Port Authority launch cancellation for the delay, the troop ship's sponsoring corporation sent a call out through the entire port for temp-jobbers to help with manual loading. Extravagant wages for two and a half hours' work were offered, and by the time I reached the loading caverns, nearly forty people had assembled, and supervisors were already forming teams for each quadrant station.

I was assigned to a five-unit team, and our supervisor led us quickly through the maze of corridors to our station. One of the other jobbers in the team was a woman in the dark blue uniform of a starship crew. As we hurried along the dimly lit tunnels, I saw the glint of the Pilot insignia on her shoulder.

For the next two and a half hours we were all too busy to think about anything but our supervisor's rapidly shouted commands. Muscles strained, machinery groaned, sweat poured freely, lungs ached and burned in the particled heat, obscenities punctuated the supervisor's instructions.

An hour into the work, the ignition sequence began, urging the others on; but in me it evoked a fleeting paralysis, a surge of adrenaline, and a block of tension in my chest—I wanted to be on that ship. Any ship.

We completed our station's loading and sealed the holds seven minutes before ignition, then ran through the passageways, our supervisor securing portals behind us as we went. Back in the central cavern, a few other teams had already arrived. I stood by the pilot, and exchanged a few words with her as we waited.

At scheduled ignition, the controller locked on a firing hold, and we waited for the last two teams; overhead the ten-minute launch-delay timer began to count off. A minute later one of the teams came in, and quiet descended on the cavern. The timer flashed green liquid light at us.

Smiles and shouts broke out as the final team stumbled in, one man limping badly, and the last portal was secured with three and a half minutes remaining. The controller unlocked the firing hold, and the ship's engines roared to life.

I have three telescopes mounted on the roof of this building. One is used to observe the orbital stations and habitats, one to track shuttles and the moon. The third I use exclusively to watch launches from the port. This third telescope is fitted with mountings for a variety of cameras; with them, I take pictures of the troop, passenger, or freight rockets that will be converted to starships in orbit above me. I capture on film those ships destined to go where I never will.

We were to be paid immediately after the emergency loading, and in currency rather than credit, so we rode underground trams to the corporation cashier (I don't remember now which corporation's troop ship we had loaded). I sat next to the pilot, and we introduced ourselves. I knew that most of the jobbers would stick together, celebrating success in the terminal bar, with the first two rounds paid for by the corporation. I asked the pilot if she would join us, though I knew protocol forbade it.

She declined, then told me this was her first time grounding in this port, and asked if I knew a good place to eat, and a clean place to sleep. I named a nearby restaurant, asked if I could join her at dinner, and was surprised when she said yes. We collected our pay, and left the terminal.

Her name was Taylor Valarento. She stood an inch taller than I at six-foot-one, was trim and muscular, strong and agile, with the arc-light reflexes needed by a pilot. Her age was thirty-nine standard years.

Gray had begun to appear in her black hair, which was thick, not quite straight, and fell just below her shoulders. Her nose had apparently been broken several times, so there was a slight kink to it. And her eyes, which were deep, dark brown, and flecked with stars of gold, were lined and bruised, and at times seemed to be gazing into some other world.

I led the way circuitously among the maintenance hangars and repair sheds nearest the launch sites. The sun had set, and red, green, and amber lights outlined gantries and buildings that jutted into the purpling sky. I spotted a small, twisted bit of metal under the lip of a shed wall, knelt, and picked it up. I felt certain it was from a rocket, though it was unrecognizable.

"What is it?" Taylor asked.

"A stellar talisman." I slipped it into the insulated pocket of my coveralls.

"Really." She smiled, shaking her head.

I shrugged, and we walked out of the port.

Talismans.

Perhaps I should have given it to Taylor that night. If anyone needed a magical charm, she did.

At dinner, she told me she had been permanently grounded. Which meant she would never pilot a starship again. Which meant her occupation, her life, had finally caught up with her, as it did with all pilots. Which meant she was dying.

Although I did not know the name of the disease, I knew

what was killing her. Like all pilots, after ten to fifteen years of guiding starships through the holes and tunnels of the universe, of interfacing her own neural network with that of a starship, she had begun to suffer from an irreversible, degenerative disease of the central nervous system. I don't understand the specifics of the condition; progressive destruction of the myelin sheathing is a major part of it, but there is much more.

What I did understand, though, was that she would slowly die from it. I also knew she would spend days, or weeks, completely incapacitated, a disconnected mind without control of a withering body, incapable of the simplest voluntary actions.

I was afraid she would want to spend that time, the last days of her life, with me.

But she fascinated me. I had always wanted, desperately, to travel to the stars. Taylor had not only been capable of traveling between worlds, she had guided the massive starships on their time- and space-distorting voyages. While I could barely tolerate the short trip to one of the orbital stations.

I had made the trip just once, years before, the entire journey spent in a state of irrational, uncontrollable panic that left me drained and almost nonfunctional. The trip back was possible only with heavy sedation, and I was unable to work for several days afterwards.

Still, I wanted to go to the stars, and did not give up trying. I went through the tests after that trip, though I knew what the results would show. My classification—NIIT. Neurologically Incapable of Interstellar Travel. It became official—I would never go.

Throughout the rest of the meal I watched her closely, searching for some sign of the disease—a tic in her face, a tremor in her fingers, anything. But I saw nothing I could be sure of.

I'm certain she knew I was watching her; she had to expect it after telling me. Still, she did not seem disturbed by it, almost as if she wanted me to watch, either to prove the diagnosis wrong . . . or to confirm it.

After dinner I took her to a small hotel, just a few blocks from the apartment, that I knew was at least clean and secure, if not luxurious. I gave her my address and com number, told her to call if she needed anything.

"I'll be here in this city until I die," she said. "I won't travel in space again. I refuse. Not that it matters. Soon they won't allow me aboard a ship anyway, even as a passenger." She laughed, nodded to me. "I'm sure we will see much of each other. Probably more than either of us really wants."

After a long silence, I said good-night, and returned to my apartment.

The piece of metal I had picked up in the port was still in my pocket. It was small and damaged. Talisman. I took it up to the roof, tossed it into one of the crates half filled with other debris.

I sat on the roof a long time in the darkness, watching the lights of the port. It seemed strange to me then that she was dying because she was capable of doing what I had wished all my life for, knowing it was impossible.

A few days after we'd first met, I stopped by her hotel to take her to an exhibition being held in the basement gallery that carried two or three of my sculptures. I had sold only one sculpture at the time, but Renaut, the gallery owner, liked what few pieces I had done, and made room for them. Taylor was ready when I arrived, but we never made it to the gallery.

On our way down the stairs from her floor, Taylor lost control of her legs. They buckled under her, she collapsed, one hand gripped the railing, and I managed to grab her with both hands before she pitched down the steps. I helped her back up the stairs, then to her room and into a chair.

After a while, feeling returned to her legs, she regained control of them, but she did not want to leave the room. She promised we would see the exhibition another day.

"I won't be able to stay here much longer," she said. She stared at her hands as though she expected them to begin shaking. "I can't expect the hotel staff to take care of me, and there are going to be times when I will need . . ." She hesitated a long time, still staring at her hands. ". . . to be taken care of."

"Where will you go?" I asked.

She looked up from her hands.

"Where will I go?" she repeated.

She stayed in the hotel another week, then I set up a sleeping mat in the front room of the apartment among the bookshelves, and she moved in.

I taught her to play the saxophone. What was usually most difficult—learning the lip pressures, lung and throat movements, the breathing methods to produce a clear sound—came easily to her. From the start she had a natural feel for the instrument, for the pained and mournful sounds she could bring out of it. She spent hours every day, when she was capable of it, practicing, both while I worked and when I was at home. Before long, she played far better than I did. When I play the saxophone now, it is partially her voice that emerges.

Often I would return to the apartment after a work shift, and Taylor would be seated on the mat with her back against the wall, reading in the light from a lamp on one of the bookcases. Usually there were several books beside her, sometimes as many as ten or twelve, open or marked with strips of paper.

"I've never read so much," she explained. "Occasionally, during slack times, I would take in books through the ship information banks, but it's not the same. I don't know why I need to read so much now." She shrugged, and smiled. "Perhaps I am preparing myself for the final voyage." Then she laughed and shook her head.

One day, however, when I returned, Taylor was curled against the wall, crying. Thirty or forty books were scattered about the room, some with torn pages, others bent from striking walls or furniture.

She looked up, grabbed the nearest book, and weakly threw it at me. It fell short, just past the foot of the mat.

"I can't read anymore," she said. She breathed in heavily, stared at me. "I can't read a damn thing."

We both ignored the attacks in the early stages, when they were brief and relatively mild. But as the disease progressed, as the attacks became more frequent, the tremors in her limbs more pronounced, the duration of the episodes longer, the disease became impossible to ignore.

Physicians had prescribed various medications that were supposed to help control the symptoms, but the drugs seemed to have little, if any, effect. Taylor often went for days without taking any of the medication, and with no noticeable change in the symptoms.

She apparently knew in detail what she could expect—the full range of possible symptoms, how long they might last—but she never told me any of it. I was unable to force myself to do any research on my own, and I felt as if I was walking through the darkened network of passageways in the caverns below the spaceport, unaware of how many corridors existed, where they were, or what they contained. Mood swings, tremors, temporary paralysis, and a dozen other symptoms both mild and severe, occurred apparently at random, and I became obsessed with trying to predict which symptom would next manifest itself. I was almost never correct.

The first time she became completely incapacitated, lying helpless on the mat and unable to move, though her limbs shook constantly with the tremors, I sat at the foot of the mat and watched her. I moved two lamps so their light fully illuminated her face and body.

Though she was awake, she was unaware of my presence until more than an hour passed and her gaze accidentally fell directly upon me. She became agitated, and her mouth opened and closed, a fish out of water, choked sounds emerging. The sounds became more intelligible as she continued, and I leaned forward, listening. Eventually I was able to understand her.

"What . . . are you doing? Waiting for me to . . . die?" She closed her eyes, exhausted from the effort.

"No," I told her. "I'm trying to understand what you're going through. I'm trying to imagine what it feels like."

A stuttered groan welled up from her, and she managed to roll her head from side to side. Again she struggled to get out a few words.

"Impossible . . . bastard. Go away, please, just leave me. . . ."

I remained in the chair, watching.

"Do you have any regrets?" I asked her once.

"Of course I have regrets. I'm still young, and I don't want to die. But questions like that don't really apply, or shouldn't. Neither the questions nor the answers can change anything. I became a pilot, freely and willingly, and I am dying because of it. That's all there is."

"Sometimes I return to the stars," she said after a long episode of several days during which she'd had no control of her body. I'd fed her, cleaned her, watched over her. "Call them visions, dreams, hallucinations, it doesn't matter. I feel I am jacked into a starship once again, my senses changed, transformed in a way

. . . I don't know, I can't . . . it's indescribable." She laughed and shook her head, and drank from the water glass in her hand.

"It's not always like that, is it? You don't always feel as if you've returned to the stars."

"No. If I did, it would be all right."

"What do you feel then?" I asked her. "When you're lying on the mat, paralyzed? When your mind is here, when you're aware of your body, but without any control?"

Her face twisted, in pain or anger, and she threw the glass at me. I ducked, but it struck the side of my head, cracking before it hit the floor and shattered. I put my hand to my forehead, felt blood.

"Why do you ask me that, you bastard? Why not let it be? It's agony. Not just physical pain, it's helpless frustration and burning and . . ." She clenched her fists, unable to go on, and pounded at her thighs. "No, it's nothing, nothing at all, no pain, just a dream, a dream . . . nothing. . . ."

She sat without moving, looking at me, but her gaze seemed unfocused, or focused on something far in the distance, though the wall was only a few feet behind me. "I feel nothing," she said, and I could see that, at least at that moment, it was true.

Often at night she would go up to the roof and spend hours with the telescopes, watching not the orbital stations, nor the moon, nor the shuttles, not even the huge rockets launching from the port, but instead gazing into the vast open night skies, and the thousands of visible stars above.

For several days she became blind in her left eye. Her vision in the eye blurred, then darkened, and finally disappeared altogether within three or four hours. It did not greatly disturb her, and she waited, with some anticipation, for the vision in her right eye to fade as well. It did not, however, and when the vision in her left eye returned, Taylor seemed disappointed, as though she had looked forward to spending the remaining weeks of her life completely blind.

"There are no friendships among pilots," she told me. "We are all too jealous of what we have, unsure if what we experience is the same for other pilots, and envious of the possibility that what other pilots experience is somehow superior. We are, all of us, insecure. It is absurd. We should find fellowship, and comfort, in the fact that we all die the same slow, horrible deaths.''

During the last few weeks, our relationship, which until then had not been at all sexual, became intensely so. I had not expected the change, but I was not surprised by it.

Taylor took advantage of her lucid, controlled periods to initiate sessions of desperate, intense lovemaking, often marked by self-inflicted pain—an attempt, she told me, to confirm her continued existence. Sometimes she bit her lip, hard enough to draw blood which, when mixed with her tears, was salty to the taste. At other times she dug her nails into her own skin until she tore the flesh and shuddered with the pain.

I was not happy with the change. I was afraid of our growing intimacy, afraid that it would make her death that much harder for me to face, the grief that much more intense.

But she was dying, and I could not deny her.

When she lay helpless on the mat, awake and unable to move, sometimes shaking with mild or severe tremors, I sat beside her and played the saxophone. The music calmed her, seemed to ease the tremors, and on occasion brought on a peaceful sleep. As she slept, I would play on, watching her, wondering what images filled her dreams.

One night, while Taylor still had enough control to play, we went up onto the roof. The moon was not up, and the only illumination came from the dim glow of streetlamps below us and from the multicolored, blinking lights of the spaceport. Stars flickered softly above us. Taylor sat on the edge of the roof with the saxophone between her legs, her feet dangling over the street.

"Build something," she said to me. "A sculpture." She waved at my tools, the crates of metal.

"I can't," I said. "I told you, I can't seem to do it anymore. I can't finish anything."

She looked at me, then up at the night sky, and shook her head. "You want to go to the stars."

"I can't do that either," I reminded her.

She turned back to me. "Then bring the damn stars to *you.*" She paused. "I'll help." She brought the saxophone close to her mouth. "Create," she said. "Create a sculpture with twisted metal, and I will create a sculpture with twisted sound."

So I tried. I sifted through the crates of metal debris, picking out one or two pieces from each crate, collecting them all by the welder along with several sections of scrap metal sheeting.

Sirens cut the air, and Taylor matched each blast with a painful cry from the saxophone. She stopped playing when the sirens quit and the rumbling began. We could just see the ship in the distance, barely visible pillars of smoke rising from underground vents.

"Create," Taylor said again.

But I waited until the air began to shake and roar, and the ship rose slowly, slowly from its pad. I fitted the mask to my head, dropped the faceplate, and flipped on the welder. As the blue-white flame sprang to life, Taylor turned away and began to play.

For four and a half hours we worked on the roof, creating, and Taylor did indeed twist sound with the saxophone, as if it was being torn from her. I wondered where she found the strength and control to play for so long. Inside herself, of course; but also, I felt, from the stars.

As for me, I had never worked so intensely before. I listened to Taylor, to the music that came from her, listened to the roar of rocket launches, looked at the stars and the moon and watched the flaming tails of spaceships rising into the night. I took all that into me, and poured it all back out into the metal and the blue-white flame of the welder.

When we finished, I had produced a massive jungle of twisting metal vines and trees, unlike anything I had made before. Taylor came over, titled it for me.

"Heart of a Pilot," she said.

It was the first of the "Pilot Series" sculptures. I'd begun to work again.

Sometimes, usually at night, I climb onto the roof and bring my saxophone. I sit amidst the twisted and broken metal rejects from rockets and shuttles and starships and complex machinery, amidst the welding equipment and the telescopes, and I wait for the launch of a ship. When the sirens first cut through the air, I begin to play, a solo accompaniment to the sirens, and then to the roar of ignition and the ship's driving thrust into space.

*   *   *

"I will be completely helpless before long," Taylor said. We were at the port, on the outskirts of the launch fields. Dusk and colored lights lit the air. We were collecting debris for my sculptures. "I must not reach that point. My life has to end first." She stooped, picked up a tiny piece of metal, held it out. "Another talisman," she said, smiling briefly. Her fingers trembled, as they always did now. "I'll need your help."

I had expected it. I had planned to help her with whatever she needed. But I had not imagined the manner in which she wished to die.

Sirens warned of an impending launch and we stood at the edge of the open fields, watched smoke roll up from the underground vents around the distant ship. The rolling explosion began, intensified, then the ship rose, and flame appeared at its tail, hot and bright in the growing darkness.

"There." She pointed at the rocket. "I want to die in those flames. I want to be cremated by a ship headed for the stars."

I turned to her, and started to smile until I saw the intensity of her expression, the glowing reflections in her eyes, and realized she was serious. I turned back to the ship and watched it rise into the night.

I stand on the roof just after midnight, between launches, when the port and the streets below are relatively quiet. I close my eyes. I relegate all sound to the background, white noise that gradually fades into nonexistence. Then I hold my arms out to the side, spread my feet slightly so no part of my body has contact with another. I stand motionless, without breathing, and I try to imagine what it must be like to lose all the normal senses, to become disembodied, and to soar blindly, yet unerringly, through the night between the stars.

Soon it was time for another journey through the caverns below the spaceport.

For nearly two days Taylor controlled the symptoms by sheer force of will. She spoke without difficulty, the tremors were so mild I hardly noticed them, and she moved easily with me along the dim corridors. I accessed portals as we went, side-circuiting the monitor signals, leaving no trace of our passage. Taylor's face had a flush of life I had not seen in days, and for a moment I wondered at the possibility of remission; but I knew it was a false hope, and I rejected it.

We emerged into the dark chamber directly below the rocket. Looking up, we could see the massive thrusters above us, already leaking tendrils of smoke. The silence of the corridors was replaced by a heavy hiss and a steady ticking surrounded by a low hum. The chamber was warm, the air stifling. I checked my watch. Little time remained.

"How are you doing?" I asked.

She smiled, held out her hand. It was nearly still. I held out my own, and it shook worse than hers did. We both laughed quietly for a moment.

"Don't. . . . It will be instantaneous," she said. "I'll feel no pain."

I nodded. We embraced, both our bodies trembling slightly.

"You should have brought the saxophone," she said. Still smiling.

She moved out to the middle of the chamber, knelt on the metal floor, then turned to me.

"You'd better go. There's not much time." An intense spasm shuddered through her, then passed. She lay on her back, gazing up at the thrusters. Smoke drifted about her. She smiled.

I stepped to her, dropped to my knees and kissed her lightly on the forehead. "Good-bye," I said.

"Good-bye." She took my hand, squeezed, then released it. Her gaze returned to the ship above her.

I left the chamber and hurried through the passageways, securing portals behind me as I went. We had cut the time short to prevent discovery, and the sirens began while I still moved along the corridors.

When I knew I was safe, I secured one last portal, then stopped and pressed against the passage wall. As the roar began, I felt the vibration of the walls pass through my body. The sound increased, a roaring in my ears, and with a terrible ache in my chest I shook with the walls around me as the ship blasted away from the chamber and into the sky above.

Over the next three years, I produced the "Pilot Series" sculptures, one after another. *Pilot Dancing. Pilot in Camouflage. The Pilot's Interstellar Dream.* I produced twenty or twenty-five in all, all leading toward one final piece, which took me months to create. Then, freed, I moved on to other subjects.

The final sculpture in the series is in two parts. From one half of the base rise two tall, spindly projections of welded metal debris, one with a tilted crossbar, the other with a bulbous cone at its foot. On the other half of the base rests a flat and shiny, fused pool of metal.

I titled the sculpture *Telescope, Saxophone, and the Pilot's Death*.

It is not for sale.

Cities in Dust

ATURDAY NIGHT, MARTIN STOOD OUTSIDE THE NIGHT-
club, knowing it would be half empty. His legs felt weak,
and he couldn't believe he was going through this again.
He hesitated at the entrance, his stomach queasy, and
almost walked away. But a dry, cold ache in his chest urged him
forward, and he entered.

A funk band played halfheartedly on stage, backlit by rows
of stationary yellow lights so their faces were partially shadowed. Only two couples were out on the floor, a large gap
between them as they moved in and out of the shadows cast
by the band. The air smelled of stale smoke and alcohol. Martin
breathed in deeply, exhaled, then stepped up to the control
gate.

"Certificate and ten bucks," the woman in the booth said.

Martin nodded. He withdrew his Health Certificate, slid it
under glass. Gloved hands slapped it and spread it flat. The
woman studied the picture, stared at Martin, looked back at the
picture. She ran the certificate through two scanners, and green
lights flashed on both.

"Your arm," she said.

Martin rolled up his left sleeve, held up his arm. When she

saw it was unmarked, she slid the Health Certificate back under the glass. Gloved hands took his ten dollars, released the gate, and Martin pushed through into the main part of the club.

He sat at an empty table flanked by other empty tables. A waitress came by, looked at him, but didn't say a word. Mouth dry, Martin ordered a double Scotch, and as she left he closed his eyes.

Why didn't he just leave, go home, forget about it? Nothing would ever come of this, nothing *could*. But he couldn't leave, he couldn't just give up. Martin felt sick; he leaned forward and rested his head in his sweating hands.

The music stopped. The band announced a fifteen-minute break and the lights came up slightly. For the first time, Martin looked around the club. Half the tables were empty, only a few of the others had couples.

Martin finished his drink, waved at the waitress. One more drink and he should just go home. She came by with another drink for him, shook her head when he tried to pay. "The woman paid," she said. Tipped her head toward the far corner, a table in shadow. Candlelight illuminated the face and hands of a dark-haired woman; below the table, her legs were partly hidden by shadow. "She asks you to join her," the waitress said. Her voice was flat and dry, and she walked away without another word.

Join her? His breath caught for a moment, and he wanted to look away. But wasn't this why he was here? Oh, Christ.

More than two years since he had made love to a woman. Made love? No. No love, no caring. It had been fast, blinding and driving sex, over almost before it had begun. He had no memory of her name, nor what she looked like, but he remembered her smells—sweat, and smoke, and musk. He remembered muted shades of color—dark brown nipples, pale rose of lips and nails, light brown hair between her legs. And he would not forget the months of panic afterward—listening to his heart, his lungs; watching his skin; waiting for infection; waiting for disease. Waiting for death. And for two years he had wanted, *needed*, to repeat that brief and desperate act.

Join her?

Legs weak, Martin rose, breathed in deeply, and started for the woman's table.

*   *   *

"I used to be a teacher," she said. "But with schools closing down . . ." She shrugged. Martin watched her, breathing slowly, silently, trying to keep his heartbeat under control as it tried to accelerate, pound away at his ribs. He watched her breasts rise and fall with her own breathing, rippling the patterned shadows of her blouse. He could see her heartbeat pulse up along her neck. The woman was young, around thirty, and he did not know her name; she did not know his. "I'm still looking for work," she said.

"What did you teach?"

She hesitated, gave a wan smile. "Junior-high science. What about you? Job?"

"I'm an accountant. Freelance. I do almost all the work at home, no office to go to. It's . . . convenient."

She nodded, drank from her vodka gimlet, her bare arm and hand moving smoothly to her mouth. On stage, the band was tuning up for the next set. There was silence between them for a while, and Martin could not think of anything to say to her. What had happened to him?

"When the band starts playing again," he said, "would you like to dance?"

"No," she answered. "I'd rather we just left now." She looked at him, and he thought he saw her lips tremble. "We are leaving, aren't we?"

Once more his breath caught, and he wanted to get up and walk away, go home alone once again. Instead, Martin nodded. "We can go to my place," he said. "I don't live that. . . ."

"No." She shook her head firmly. "I don't want to know where you live. I don't want you to know where *I* live. We can go to a hotel."

"But—"

"A nice hotel. A clean hotel." She paused. "Certified. A safe hotel."

Safe. Martin nodded, finished off his drink. Together they stood, left the table, and, not touching, walked out of the club.

They drove in separate cars. Martin followed her pale yellow compact through the streets, the sidewalks nearly deserted. With windows rolled up tight, he felt enclosed by a shell of quiet air, stale and dry.

He could easily turn off at the next street, he thought, let her go on without him, drive back home and never see her again. But Martin stayed close behind her.

At a stoplight, he pulled up beside a bus. Though on one of the main thoroughfares, the bus was nearly empty, people sitting apart from one another. A woman at the window held a thick scarf over her mouth and nose.

The light turned green, and the bus pulled away spewing a cloud of smoke so black it was visible even against the night. Martin remained motionless, watching the smoke dissipate. Only after someone in the car behind him honked a horn did he realize the woman had already driven off. He started forward, panicking slightly when he did not immediately see her car. But within half a block he spotted the yellow car, accelerated to catch it. Relief and renewed fear swept through him, and he followed her into the night.

The hotel was near the top of a small hill, and even at ground level there was a view of part of the bay. Martin could see the slowly flashing lights marking Alcatraz, and the bobbing light of a vessel approaching the island. Supply boat, maybe.

He met the woman in front of the hotel, and they entered the lobby without a word. The air inside was hushed, nearly silent but for hints of paper rustling.

At the registration desk, the woman asked for a room for the night.

"With a view of the bridge?" asked the clerk.

The woman hesitated, glanced at Martin, and he said, "Yes."

The clerk nodded, glanced at his terminal, made a few keystrokes. He reached for a pair of keys—Martin noticed he was not wearing gloves—and set them on the lower ledge in front of him. Looked up at them, smiling. "Certificates, please."

Martin took out his Health Certificate, set it on the counter; the woman placed hers next to his. The clerk waited for a few moments, long enough for Martin to look at the woman's certificate (certain she was looking at his) and note the date. Only two weeks old, more recent than his. Still.

The clerk took the certificates, inspected them, ran them through the scanners. The woman slid a credit card across the counter, shook her head when Martin removed one from his wallet.

"Arms please."

The woman held out her bare arm, and Martin once again rolled up his sleeve. The clerk nodded, returned their certificates, then began processing the woman's credit card and registration.

As the clerk worked, Martin watched the woman, saw something in her he had not really seen before—a glow of life in her skin, her face. Suddenly she seemed very beautiful to him, and he wanted her, needed her, needed to be close to her so terribly that his entire chest seemed to collapse in on itself, taking his breath away.

With the paperwork complete, the clerk handed them each a room key. "We hope you have a pleasant stay," he said.

The room had a view of the Golden Gate Bridge. Martin stood at the window, looking out on the illuminated towers, the looping strings of light spanning the water.

The room was immaculate: walls a bright, clean white; fabrics in light, pale blues; everything freshly made and pressed. A bed, a padded armchair, a table and two chairs—all the furniture clean and polished. Martin smelled traces of disinfectant in the air. He cracked open the window, let in a slight, damp breeze.

While the woman showered, Martin listened to the water spraying against tile, to the shifting patterns of sound as she moved. He could hardly believe he was here, that it had come this far.

Martin turned from the window, walked over to the bed. He turned on the clock radio on the nightstand. There was no sound except a steady hiss. He ran through all the frequencies, and a couple of stations faded in and out, but he still got little more than static. He switched it off, and opened the nightstand drawer. Inside were a bible, a packet of condoms, a notepad and pen. Who would he write to? He took out the condoms, set them on the stand, quietly closed the drawer.

The water stopped. Martin stood motionless, listening to the sounds coming through the door and walls—water dripping; glass door sliding with a gentle rumble; tiny, nearly inaudible sounds he could not identify.

A few minutes later the door opened and she stepped out, a large white bath towel wrapped around her from just above her breasts to mid-thigh. She held a smaller towel in one hand, and over her other arm were her neatly folded clothes.

"You can go ahead," she said.

Martin nodded. They had hardly said a word to each other since entering the room. He entered the bathroom, undressed. He turned on the shower, stepped inside after adjusting the temperature. Two sets of everything—two bars of soap, two tiny bottles of shampoo, two white washcloths. The woman had placed hers on one tray. Martin picked up the unused soap from the other, carefully unwrapped it, set the paper on the tray. The water was hot, almost stinging on his skin; he breathed in the steam rising about him, slowly, deeply, trying to relax. Then he wet the soap, rotating it in his hands, and began to scrub.

When Martin came out of the bathroom, towel around his waist, he noticed the light in the room had been dimmed. Only the two bedside lamps were on, glowing orange through their shades.

The woman had pulled back the sheets and blankets, now lay on the bed, naked, waiting for him. He looked at her breasts, watched them rise and fall with her breath, and for a moment his own breath hesitated, became shaky. His gaze moved to her belly, and the light wisps of fine hair around her navel. Then he looked down at the dark, curly hair between her legs, which he expected to glisten with moisture, either from her shower, or from anticipation. But there was no sign of moisture at all, and the hair looked stiff and dry.

Finally he looked up at her face. Her lips were parted slightly, not smiling. Her nostrils moved in and out as she breathed. Her eyes, almost as dark as her hair, were large, open and gazing intently at him, and he wanted to tell her that he, too, was scared.

But he said nothing. Aroused, the sense of desperation and need returning, Martin dropped the towel to the floor, slowly approached the bed. The air was warm, and he saw she had closed the window. He sat on the edge of the bed, looking at the woman, who turned onto her side, facing him. Mouth closed now.

He lay on the bed, parallel to the woman, facing her. They were only inches apart. They lay without moving for several minutes, watching each other. He ached with need, the ache spread all through his body now, clutching at his breath.

Finally he reached out, touched her lightly on the shoulder. Goose bumps rose across her skin in silent waves, trembling. Her mouth opened again, wider, and her eyes started to close, lids and lashes quivering. An audible sigh escaped from her.

He ran his hand down her arm, watched her own hand open, reach out to brush against his belly. A shiver ran through him at her touch, and he moved closer to her, their bodies still not quite touching. He continued to run his fingers across her skin, down her side, over her hip, then back up along the inside of her thigh.

But when his fingers touched the tangle of hair between her legs, he abruptly pulled them back, an involuntary reaction. He hesitated a few moments, breathing rapidly, afraid he had broken the mood, then moved his hand back to her shoulder and moved his face toward her breasts.

Martin kissed her dark nipple, barely touching it with his lips. He kissed the skin around it, lightly in a circle, then felt her breath against his neck, her fingers lightly moving across his back, her hair sliding along his shoulder. He began trembling again, kissed the nipple, now hard and erect, once more, then raised his head to face her.

Then their arms were around each other, pulling and holding tightly, both bodies trembling. He kissed her ear, her neck, her hair; she kissed his cheek, his throat, his chin. Their mouths came closer together, quickly at first, then slowly, but closer . . . closer . . .

They stopped moving, lips not quite touching. Her eyes were open, staring into his. A terrible pain rolled through his belly, and a violent shudder tore through him, shaking limbs and head and heart, and he just could not bring his lips to meet hers. She, too, was shaking, and her lips closed tightly, and with a stifled cry she pulled back and pushed him away.

He rolled away from her, slid off the edge of the bed; he managed to get to his feet, stood swaying beside it. He looked at her; one of her hands clawed at the sheet, the other moved back and forth, reaching toward him, pulling back, reaching, pulling back. . . . He staggered, bumped against the armchair, dropped into it. He was still looking at her, unable to turn away, and her gaze was still on him. Then he took hold of his erection, and she plunged her fingers down between her legs and into the tangle of hair.

Watching each other, mouths open, they worked at themselves, hands and fingers moving in desperation, bodies shaking, breaths coming shorter and shorter. Then a sharp pain arced up his neck, to the base of his skull, muscles cramping, and he tipped his head back, no longer seeing her. And as he climaxed, eyes clamping shut, there was no pleasure, no joy, nothing except pain, and a dry, stinging and empty release.

He stood by the window, looking out at the bridge, the strings of light obscured by the incoming fog. The lights on Alcatraz spun slowly on his right, flickering at him.

The woman showered again, giving him the chance to leave. She hadn't said anything, but he knew she expected him to be gone when she came out. Still, he didn't move from the window, didn't even turn to look at the door. He had no energy, no will to do anything at all.

Leave. Stay. What difference did it make? If he were still here when she came out, it wouldn't change anything. If he were gone, it wouldn't change anything. Leave. Stay. It didn't matter. Nothing mattered anymore. Nothing.

Martin stood at the window and listened to the shifting sounds of water coming from another world.

Liz and Diego

L IZ WALKED MILES EVERY DAY—AMONG THE DENSE TREES of the nearby jungle, along the river, through the hot mazes of streets and buildings that made up the town. Her short, thick hair was almost completely gray, and though she would be sixty-six next month, Liz was in good shape despite the heart attack three years before and the smoking she could not quit. She walked in the mornings and early evenings when the air was cooler, hoping someday she would find a place or a state of mind that would allow her to be happy again. Until then, the walking kept her alive, and kept her sane.

Liz sat at a sidewalk café table, tall plants threatening to engulf her from behind and above, and slowly smoked a cigarette. It was late afternoon, and the breeze drifting among the tables was warm and humid.

She finished her coffee, signaled the waiter for a refill. She wore lightweight, tan cotton pants, a bone-colored shirt, and dusty brown walking shoes. It had been years since she'd worn a dress, and what she wore (among other things) made her stand out in this town; here, all the women wore skirts or dresses. Liz knew what the people thought of her, but it didn't matter.

A young girl in a ragged brown dress came running down the street, headed for the café. Barefoot, she dodged through the pedestrians and the few cars driving slowly along the dusty road, then made her way through the sidewalk tables to Liz's side. The girl stopped, staring at Liz.

"*El Diego necesita verla a usted,*" the girl said, trying not to laugh. Diego needs to see you.

Liz nodded, sighed heavily. "*Pues, sí.*"

The girl ran off without looking back. Liz put out her cigarette, set money on the table. She sat for a minute without moving, gazing across the street without really seeing anything. Then she stood, put on her straw hat, and started walking down the street toward the river.

Just outside of town, Liz left the road, started down a wide path through the trees. The heat increased, closed in on her, but the warm, damp air felt clean in her lungs. Samuelson, her doctor, wanted her to move somewhere else, where the air was dry. Back to the States, he'd suggested, where it would be easier for him to see her. Some godawful place like Arizona. But then, he also wanted her to quit smoking. Liz stayed here instead, willing to take her chances with the smoking and the damp heat.

Liz came out of the trees at the edge of the river, into cooler, fresher air that caught her breath for a moment. She stood on a large rock jutting out over the river and breathed deeply. The water flowed past beneath her, tumbling over moss-covered stones, pouring through deep trenches. Then she stepped back and down onto rough gravel, and started upstream toward Diego's place.

Liz had been living here nearly three years now, and in that time, she knew, most of the people in the town had seen the scars across her wrist, but no one had ever asked her about them. Except Diego. The first time they'd met he had looked at her wrist, then up at her face, and said, "Why the *hell* did a woman like you try to kill herself?" That was before the old Italian went blind. Now, sometimes, when they were alone together, he would take her hand in his and lightly brush his fingers along the scars, shaking his head and sighing.

When she came around the final bend, bringing Diego's hut into view, she saw smoke rising from the metal stove chimney. Mata must be in, cleaning and cooking for him. The hut looked ramshackle, built of stone, wood, sections of sheet metal and aluminum siding, blocks of concrete and brick. But it was much more solid than it appeared, Liz knew, and would probably outlast half the buildings in town.

She called out as she approached the open doorway, and stepped inside expecting to see Mata at the stove. But Diego was alone, sitting on a tree stump in front of the big old stove, a piece of wood in his hand. The stove door was open, and he gazed into the flames with his sightless eyes.

"Hello, Liz," he said.

"You're going to burn this whole place down someday you keep building fires when you're alone."

The old Italian shrugged, said nothing. Liz sat in one of the metal and plastic folding chairs several feet from the stove, away from the heat of the fire. There was several days' growth of black and gray stubble on Diego's face, and she knew he had been out in the jungle on one of his "treasure hunts," as he called them. She lit a cigarette, handed it to Diego, then lit another for herself.

"You wanted to see me," Liz said.

Diego turned toward her, widened his white-fogged eyes. "Never again, Liz." Then he nodded, grinned. "I've found more stuff that goes with the helmet."

"You sure?"

Diego nodded. "I'm sure. Couldn't really tell what it all was, couldn't bring much of it back. So I need you to go back out there with me, see exactly what it all is."

"How *far* out there?" She had been on a couple of his expeditions when they didn't get back until after dark, and she knew he often went a lot farther.

"We can go part way by boat, up the river. A day on the water, another day on foot, I don't know how long we'll need to stay there. . . ."

"Diego, you're out of your mind. You expect me to spend several days out in the jungle? I'm an old woman, remember?"

"Yeah, and I'm an old man. Christ, you're in better shape than I am."

It was true. Still, spending hours walking was not the same as trekking through the jungle, and at night she always had her room to return to, running water and electricity, a comfortable bed.

"Wait a minute," Diego said. "I'll show you what I *did* bring back." He jammed the stick of wood into the stove, got up and walked into the back room. When he returned a few minutes later, he was wearing the shiny black helmet, and carrying a dark meshed bundle over his arm.

It was the helmet that had blinded him, but it was also the helmet that now allowed him to somehow sense his surroundings, to "see." With the helmet on, he could go out into the jungle on his own and make his way without running into objects or even getting lost, though it gave him intense headaches when he wore it for long periods. It was a strange sight, one she had seen several times—Diego in his hiking boots and ragged khaki clothes, wearing the shiny black helmet, picking his way among the trees. Even the visor was black and shiny; Liz could never see through it to Diego's face, and she doubted if anyone, at least anyone human, could have seen *out* through it.

Diego unfolded the mesh bundle, which was in the general shape of a sleeveless vest with a stiff, banded collar at the neck, then put his arms through the side gaps. "Watch this," he said. He pressed the front opening closed, and the vest was far too large for him. But then he snapped the banded collar shut, and suddenly the vest began to contract. Silently, without bunching, the vest compressed and tightened to mold itself to Diego's body, shoulders, and neck.

That was basically what the helmet had done when he had first put it over his head, Diego had told her weeks before— interior padding had expanded to mold itself to his head so the helmet, at first too large, became a perfect fit. But then, unable to see through the darkened visor, Diego had touched the largest of several silver depressions on the side of the helmet; an explosion of sorts had gone off inside it, and inside his head. When he had removed the helmet, he was blind.

"The vest definitely goes with the helmet," Diego said. "Like this, sealing at the neck." He brought the helmet and vest collars together, they clicked shut, and suddenly part of Diego was gone.

The helmet and vest, and the parts of Diego's body they enclosed, disappeared entirely, his arms apparently dangling in mid-air.

"Diego!" Liz called.

"What?" His voice came from where his head had been, from where, presumably, his head still was, though she could no longer see it.

Then Liz realized what it was—instant camouflage, the helmet and vest high-tech chameleons, so good they were able to create the perspective of the surroundings into which they blended. The wall behind Diego had been replicated across the surface of the vest and helmet, and only when she stared closely at it could she see the blurring at the edges, the slight inconsistencies. She stepped forward, reached out and touched his chest.

"It's awfully good," she said.

"What, for Christ's sake?"

"You've disappeared."

"*What?*"

Liz explained to him what she was seeing, and what she wasn't seeing.

"So that's what it is," Diego said. "There's something like a hum when I connect the two. I don't exactly hear it, I just feel it, real soft in my chest and head. I couldn't figure out what it was."

"It's pretty incredible."

"Well?" Diego asked.

Liz stared at the arms hanging in space, at the legs and waist standing without trunk or head. It seemed to her then that this might be what she had been looking for—it brought out a sense of excitement and energy. She nodded. Then, remembering he could not see her (but wondering if he could sense her nodding), she said, "Yes, Diego, I'll go with you."

They started upriver at dawn the next day in a narrow boat that rode high on the water and was powered by a quiet prop motor. A light, warm mist rose from the water, drifted across it, and broke apart as the boat pushed through. Diego, wearing the helmet, handled the motor and guided them upstream without any direction from Liz. She wondered what it was he "saw" with the helmet, wondered how he could pilot the boat, blind, better than she could have with full sight. He skirted rocks with ease, negotiated twisting channels, and avoided branches and other debris floating down the river, often making adjustments long before Liz saw that they needed to do so.

On the banks and half hidden by dense foliage, or underwater and obscured by the silt and flow of the river, were the remnants of all the years of armed conflict—the stripped, empty husk of a crushed helicopter; enormous rusting wheels; rotting wood and melted plastic; chunks of jagged metal no longer recognizable. Though there had been no fighting in the area in more than two years, the periodic, almost regular battles and skirmishes over the last several decades had littered the jungle with the detritus of war. Diego made his living from it as a scavenger.

The day grew hot, and Liz sat in the bow with eyes half closed, her face protected from direct sunlight by her straw hat. The damp heat and the quiet shushing of the water and the purr of the motor all suffused her with a peaceful, relaxing lethargy, and she wished she could do this, or something like it, for the rest of her life.

Shortly after mid-day, they stopped at a deserted, cratered village of rotting huts. While Diego built a fire to cook their lunch and make coffee—removing the helmet to ease the head-aches—Liz wandered through the village. She made her way among blackened craters, partially burned rubble, huts now beyond repair. The air was still and quiet; even the buzz of insects and the cries of birds and animals were muted, barely audible. She half expected to stumble across a burned or decayed corpse. The village made her think of Zeke.

Back at the fire, Diego gave her a plate of fried polenta and a cup of coffee, and she sat on a rock beside him.

"Remember Vietnam?" she asked.

Diego grunted. "Couldn't hardly forget."

"Some people have." She paused. "Were you there?"

"Yeah."

She waited for him to say more, but when he didn't she said, "So was my brother, Zeke."

"Did he come back?"

She nodded. "Yes. But he came back with most of his left foot blown off. And he came back a junkie. Three years later he got shot in the head trying to break into the apartment of some drug dealer. In sunny Oakland, California."

Diego breathed deeply. "Sorry to hear it."

Liz nodded again, this time to herself. "When it happened, my husband said Zeke got just what he deserved. We'd been married about a year, and I should have known then to leave the son of a bitch. Would have saved myself a lot of grief." Liz sighed, then shrugged. "But I didn't."

"And here you are," Diego said.

She smiled. "Yeah, and here I am."

*   *   *

Night fell quickly over the river, but Diego said it didn't matter, he could see just fine. The stars came out, glittering brightly, and before long the moon, waxing and over half full, began to rise above the treetops. The river, mostly dark, became irregularly patterned with shifting silver reflections.

Diego put the boat in at a short, narrow strip of beach, and they pulled it up out of the water. Together they set up the tent, then Diego, his head in a lot of pain now, removed the helmet. He lay inside the tent while Liz started a fire and put on a pot of stew. As the stew cooked, she smoked a cigarette and sat back against a tree, relaxed and content, listening to the night sounds of the jungle around her.

When the stew was just about done, Diego emerged from the tent and staggered toward the fire. Liz guided him onto a seat of stones, then gave him a full plate of stew. Diego ate quickly, stuffing chunks of meat and vegetables into his mouth as fast as he could swallow.

"Damn thing doesn't just give me headaches, makes me hungry as all hell," he said between platefuls.

"How are you feeling now?" Liz asked.

"Better. Pain's almost gone. By morning . . ." He shrugged, resumed eating.

Diego drank two cups of wine while they ate, and several more afterwards. He'd brought several bottles, which surprised Liz, since she hadn't known him to drink much. When the fire was out and they went into the tent and crawled into their sleeping bags, she could smell the wine in the closed-in air. She wondered if he would snore.

"You ever think about going to bed with me?" Diego asked.

Liz wanted to laugh, but she didn't, afraid Diego would misunderstand. "No," she eventually said.

Diego grunted, then said, "I think about it." He paused. "Are you what some of the people in town think you are?"

"What's that?" she asked, knowing.

"Dyke."

This time she did laugh, quietly. "No. I just lost interest a few years ago."

"It was that husband of yours, wasn't it? The one you should have left."

"Partially."

"He still alive?"

"Yes." She stared up at the tent ceiling, wishing Diego would fall asleep or pass out.

"What did he do?" Diego asked.

Liz hesitated. She knew Diego would misunderstand, would imagine something simplistic—that Frederick had beaten her, or raped her, something like that. Of course it wasn't that simple, but she didn't have the desire or the energy to try to explain, at least not tonight. So she said, "Good night, Diego," and then nothing more.

The old Italian was silent for a minute, then he grunted again, and she heard him turn over, face away from her. She closed her eyes and tried to sleep.

The next day they traveled on foot. By noon, despite a slow pace, Liz was tired, but Diego had been right—she was in better shape than he was. She could hear his labored breathing emerge in hisses from the helmet, and he needed to rest frequently, which was fine by her.

They stopped briefly to eat some wild fruit, then resumed hiking. The trek through the jungle, though tiring, brought Liz a sense of peace and contentment. She felt she had at last crossed the barrier from her old world, her past, and had crossed into a new and different world, an unknown but freer future.

Sometime in the late afternoon it rained, drenching them for half an hour, then ceasing abruptly. The clouds vanished, and the sun blazed down on the jungle, bringing up a steamy heat from the dense vegetation. A shifting cloud of brightly colored butterflies swept over them in a nearly silent flutter of hundreds of wings. Birds and animals cried out and screeched on all sides.

Then, before long, the sun was nearly gone, so low it was no longer even indirectly visible in the leaves high above them, and darkness began to fall.

"Not far now," Diego said. He sounded exhausted, and in great pain. Liz wanted to help him, somehow, but knew she couldn't.

They climbed over a low stand of large, lichen-covered stones, and came out on the edge of a bowl-shaped clearing carpeted by low ferns and thick mosses and patches of crumbled, blackened stone. On the far side of the clearing, Liz could make out the remains of a fire pit. Several feet away from it, at the border between the clearing and the dense jungle, barely visible in the growing darkness, was a large, round disk on a low mound of earth.

"You see it?" Diego asked.

Liz nodded, then said, "Yes, something. It's getting dark."

Diego led the way across the clearing, directly to the thick metal disk, which was about three feet in diameter. He pulled it back, which revealed an opening into darkness. The metal around the rim of the opening was torn and jagged, as if something had blown its way out. Inside was complete darkness, but Liz had the impression the opening led into a metal structure buried in the earth.

"What is it?" Liz asked.

"I don't know," Diego said. "Spaceship?"

"The helmet, the vest, you don't suppose we have technology like that, do you?"

"This damn helmet wasn't made for human beings, that's all I know." With that, Diego pulled the helmet off his head and sank to his hands and knees. "Explore tomorrow," he said. "Daylight. I can't do a damn thing right now." He dropped the helmet and held his head in his hands, pressing palms into temples. Liz replaced the disk over the opening, then helped Diego to his feet.

This time Liz put up the tent alone, helped Diego into it, poured some wine for him. Now she understood why he had brought so many bottles along. She hadn't realized how debilitating the headaches could be.

While Diego rested, Liz finished making camp. She strung a large, slanting tarp over the fire pit, built a fire, then put another stew on to cook. While the stew simmered, she collected firewood, and stones and wood and branches to construct two makeshift seats in front of the fire. Following Diego's directions and using one of the flashlights, she found a small stream just a few yards from the camp, and refilled all their canteens and water bottles.

When she returned from the last trip to the stream, Diego was up, sitting in front of the fire, gazing into it. Liz wondered what it was he could see or sense in the flames with those sightless eyes. Maybe the warmth eased his pain.

They ate in silence, the smoke from the fire rising and slipping upward along the slanting tarp, escaping at the higher end while water dripped slowly but steadily from the lower. When the food was gone, Diego brought out the red wine, and Liz joined him. She added wood to the fire, and they sat watching it, smoking cigarettes and drinking wine.

"Why did you try to kill yourself?" Diego asked.

Liz didn't respond at first. The question didn't surprise her —she'd been expecting it since they'd started out the day before —but she still hadn't decided how she would answer. Ever since that first time he'd asked, almost three years before, she'd known the day would come when she would tell him the story. She supposed that this was it.

Of course there was no way to really tell the story as it had all happened, the way things had affected her, and what she had thought, especially since she still didn't understand it completely herself. All she could do was give him the outlines, and hope it would be enough for him to understand.

"One day," she started. And then she stopped, almost began to laugh.

"This a funny story?" Diego asked.

Liz shook her head. "No. I don't know why I want to laugh, but I do. Maybe because it's all so absurd." She put out her cigarette, lit a fresh one, then resumed.

"One day I came into the house, and found my husband in bed with another woman. Only the other woman was my daughter."

She paused, and Diego said, "Your daughter?"

"My daughter. Not a typical incest situation, though, since she was in her thirties, married, had two daughters of her own, and was very willing." She paused again, her gaze on the fire, though unfocused. "And it was not a new thing. Apparently it had been going on for years, since before she was married, though they both said never while she was living at home. Not that it matters." She shook her head to herself. "All those years, my husband, my daughter. I felt like a fool, a blind fool, that I hadn't been able to see it in all that time, all those years it had been going on. I couldn't believe I hadn't known, that I hadn't a clue." She dragged on the cigarette, held the smoke a long time before releasing it. "And then it got stranger, or at least I thought so. They told me they had no intention of stopping, they were going to keep on sleeping together, and if I didn't like it, well, it was too damn bad." She shook her head again. "I tried to get them into counseling, all of us together, or the two of them, or individually, at least that, but there was no way they'd agree to it. Finally, they told me to piss off, and so the only one who tried getting any counseling was me."

There was a long pause, then Diego said, "So you tried suicide."

Liz shook her head. "No. I had a heart attack. Wasn't that bad, I suppose, didn't really come close to killing me. I spent three days in the hospital. Three days of lying there, alone, thinking. Three days, and they let me out. *Then* I tried. As soon as I got home, I went into the kitchen and slashed my wrist. Frederick found me, got the paramedics out in time, and I was back in the hospital."

Liz tossed the cigarette butt into the fire, and sipped at her wine. She started to get another cigarette, then changed her mind.

"First few days, I was kind of numb. Stunned, I guess, that I was still alive, not too sure how I felt about that. Eventually, though, I was glad I hadn't been successful. But I knew I had to get out. Out of my life, out of that world, since it seemed to me I certainly didn't belong. I couldn't see how it worked any- more. I had lost touch somehow. So I came here."

She turned and looked at Diego, who was directly facing her, eyes locked on hers as if he could see her.

"And are you happy here?" he asked.

She thought about it a minute, then said, "I'm not *un*happy."

Diego nodded, turned back to the fire, and didn't say an- other word.

In the gray, early morning light, Liz and Diego stood before the opening. The helmet lay at Diego's feet; the headaches had not completely faded, and he wasn't going to use it unless abso- lutely necessary.

Liz knelt at the edge of the opening and peered inside. She could see a little now, mostly shadows and indistinct reflections from dark metal.

"I really don't know what the hell it's like inside," Diego said. "I went in wearing the helmet, but I might as well have been blind, the damn thing didn't seem to work right in there."

"What do you mean?"

"It's hard to explain, the way I 'see' with the helmet. I sense what's all around me, somehow, by getting . . . Christ, I don't know, lines or something, some kind of input that *means* something to me, enough so that somehow I can interpret and understand what's around me, creating pictures in my head. But when I went inside, all that input, it didn't stop, but it became gibberish, it didn't mean a thing. Well, it wasn't *all* gibberish. I could sense spaces when I was in a corridor or a room—the general outlines—so that I could move through them. But as for what's actually inside? The vest was, I found that by feel and just took it. And there's another helmet somewhere, but other than that . . ." He shrugged. "That's why I needed you."

"How nice to feel wanted," Liz said, smiling. "I assume, then, that I'm going in there by myself."

Diego shifted his feet, shrugged again. "Yeah, I figured. I'm useless in there."

Liz nodded. "All right."

Just inside the opening was a short, narrow ridged shaft angling down at about forty-five degrees and leading to a room or chamber of some sort. With two large flashlights strapped to her hips, Liz went through feet first, careful to avoid the sharp metal at the edges of the opening. She worked her way along the shaft, then lowered herself to the floor of the chamber.

Liz felt slightly disoriented and unbalanced for a moment; the darkness was nearly total, and the chamber floor was tilted slightly. She unstrapped one of the flashlights, and turned it on, directing it at the wall in front of her.

The wall was almost featureless, a smooth, dark gray metal broken regularly by thin, uniform vertical fissures. She played the beam across the entire wall, but there was nothing else. The adjacent wall was much the same, though about a foot or two above her head were highly reflective horizontal strips of some material that didn't quite look like metal. The next wall was like the first, and the fourth wall was divided by a wide passage leading farther into the structure. Liz started through it.

She came into a larger room, the floor littered with loose, mostly unrecognizable objects: clumps of fabric dotted with metal lozenges, long hollow tubes, half a dozen clear globes, and one opaque globe with interior clouds that seemed to swirl as the flashlight beam moved across it. A single helmet like Diego's rested at her feet. Bolted into one wall was what looked like a thickly padded lounge chair, and above it were more reflective strips like those in the first room.

Liz moved carefully through the room to the passage at the far end, through it, and into a third room smaller even than the first. One wall was covered with depressions and sockets and hundreds of tiny, needle-like projections. The other walls were blank.

She went through one more passage, then entered a cylindrical room with open panels revealing storage lockers filled with more hollow tubes and clear globes. One locker held more helmets and vests like Diego's, and several sets of what she decided must be the other attachments that completed full suits of some kind. This was what Diego really wanted. She tried to remove them, but most were attached to the interior walls, and she couldn't free them. A few, however, weren't completely secured, and eventually she managed to work loose another vest, two larger pieces, and four smaller. She set them together on the floor, then went on.

Liz didn't get far. Beyond the cylindrical room was an L-shaped passage that ended abruptly at a ridged wall. She tried pressing on the ridges, then against the walls on both sides, but nothing she did created any kind of opening.

She returned to the cylindrical room, picked up the larger new suit sections, and carried them through the rooms and passages to the foot of the shaft leading back out into the jungle. She thought of calling to Diego, who wasn't visible through the shaft opening, but decided to bring the rest of the suit sections first.

It took her two more trips, one for the four smaller suit sections and one for the helmet and vest. There was still no sign of Diego, so she called out his name. A few moments later his face appeared in the opening.

"You all right?" he asked.

"I'm fine. I've got some things you might want to look at. If you reach in, I think I can push them up far enough."

Diego knelt in front of the opening, then reached into the shaft. Liz picked up the helmet, pushed it up through the shaft until she felt Diego take hold of it.

"Another goddamn helmet," he said. "What do I want this for?"

"There's more," Liz said.

One by one she handed him the rest of the suit sections, then crawled up the shaft, through the opening, and back into fresh air and sunlight. The brightness of the morning light hurt her eyes, and she realized she was tired. She sat on a soft patch of moss beside the pile of objects she had retrieved.

"More that goes with the helmet?" Diego asked. He was holding one of the larger suit sections, running his fingers over it. It was made of the same dark mesh material as the vest, and looked like it connected to the bottom of the vest, but there were no divisions.

"I think so," Liz said. She handed two of the smaller sections to Diego. "These two seem to be arm sections." She smelled wine on his breath; he had been drinking while she had been inside the buried structure.

Diego remained kneeling for a minute amidst the suit pieces, running his hands over them. "What the hell?" Diego said, turning his blind eyes to her. "You get enough to put together a suit for yourself, too?"

Liz shrugged. "I just wanted to make sure we had enough."

Diego mumbled something, then put on the original vest. He closed it up, snapped the collar shut, and it compressed, molding itself to his body. When it stopped, he worked his right arm into one of the limb sections, attached it to the side of the vest. The attachment, like the vest, began to constrict. First, the end formed around Diego's hand and fingers, like a skin-tight glove, then compressed around his arm while forming a web-like flap from his elbow to his waist. Then he worked his left arm into another limb section, and the process repeated. Diego waved the web flaps under his arms.

"Like a damn flying lizard," he said. "I told you this stuff wasn't made for people." He picked up the large final section, which was shaped more like a sack than anything else. "Might as well go all the way," he said. "You going to help?"

Liz stood and went to his side, supported Diego as he climbed into the mesh sack, worked the rim up around his waist, then attached it to the bottom of the vest. Once again the material contracted, formed tightly over his boots and legs, dividing roughly into two appendages. But when it was done, another web-like flap of material stretched between his legs from crotch to knees, loose enough so he could move freely.

Diego stepped back, held out his arms. "How do I look?"

"Ready for space, I guess."

"Except for the helmet," Diego said, frowning. "Where is it? Mine, not the one you brought up."

Liz picked up Diego's helmet, handed it to him. "You going to put it on?"

"I said 'all the way,' didn't I?" Diego sighed, and put the helmet over his head. He brought the helmet and vest collars together and clicked them shut . . . and disappeared.

The effect was stunning even though Liz had expected it.

Even looking closely at him, sensitive to inconsistencies, odd visual tics in the air before her, she had trouble believing he was still there.

"Diego?"

"Yeah, here." His voice was more muffled than usual, like a hollow whisper. "Can you see me?"

"No."

Diego didn't say anything for a long time. Then, catching vague glitters of reflection out of the corner of her eye, she realized he was moving. She tried to follow the movement, which was silent and quick, but after a minute she no longer had any idea where he was, even knowing what to look for that might give him away.

"Diego?"

No answer. She turned in a slow circle, searching for him. "Diego?"

An invisible hand gripped her shoulder and she jumped back, heart pounding.

"Jesus Christ, Diego, you want to give me another heart attack?" She stepped back a few paces from where she thought he must be.

"Sorry, Liz," came the hollow whisper from in front of her. "I was just testing things out."

Liz closed her eyes for a moment, breathed slowly and deeply. She needed a cigarette. When she opened her eyes, she could not see Diego, of course, and she wondered if he had moved again.

"Diego?"

"I'm still here," he answered. "I'm going to try pushing some of these other slots on the helmet," he said. "See if anything happens now I have a whole suit."

"Diego, don't. Look what happened last time."

Diego snorted. "Think anything worse could happen?"

He didn't say anything more, and Liz stood looking toward where his voice had come from, wishing she could see what he was doing. But she could neither see nor hear anything from him.

While she waited, wondering what, if anything, she should do, the heat from the sun seemed to intensify, and the animal sounds from the jungle around her—whirring and clicking of insects, screeching of birds, snuffling of ground creatures— began to pulse, growing louder, then fading, then louder, then fading again. Sweat trickled down her sides, her face.

A bright flash of light, then a muffled explosion of sound and a blast of cold struck her, knocking her backward and off her feet. Liz hit the earth, breath knocked out of her. Then there was silence. Even the jungle had gone quiet, and she lay without moving, trying to regain her breath. For several moments she could not breathe, but then something released in her chest and air rushed into her lungs, and she began breathing again in huge gulps.

Liz sat up, saw steam rising from the ground a few feet in front of her, the mosses and ferns crushed and covered with a white, crystalline film that looked like frost.

"Diego?"

No answer.

"Diego?"

Still no answer.

On hands and knees, still breathing hard, Liz crept forward until she was at the edge of the steaming, white-frosted patch of earth. She reached out, touched one of the crushed ferns.

Cold. The coating *was* frost, now rapidly melting and evaporating in the heat of the jungle. What the hell had happened?

Liz sat back on her haunches and called out one final time, as loud as she could manage. "DIEGO!"

Nothing. The air was nearly silent, but as she sat there waiting, hoping to see or hear *something* of the old Italian, the jungle sounds gradually returned—tentative and quiet at first, then growing louder and louder until it seemed to her that thousands of creatures surrounded her, and were closing in.

Diego was gone. Dead or alive, he was somewhere else. Liz slowly rose to her feet, and the jungle sounds seemed to subside, return to normal. But there were other sounds now—her heartbeat pulsing in her throat and pumping through her skull, a slight rushing in her ears.

Liz walked over to the extra suit pieces she had retrieved from the buried structure, looked down at them. She should go back, she told herself. Leave everything here, cover the opening and camouflage it, then return to the town. Return to the States, as Samuelson wanted.

But she knew she was not going back—not to the States, not even to the town. She picked up the vest, put it on, closed up the front, and pressed the stiff, banded collar shut. The vest began to contract, molded itself to her, and the pressure, tight but not constricting, reassured her. She felt strengthened, somehow.

She stood nearly motionless and studied the clearing around her. With luck, this would be the last time she would see this world. Or at least the last time she would see it this way. She wondered where Diego had gone, and whether or not he was alive, but she knew she would never have the answers. Unless she followed him. Dead, maybe; but maybe not. There was hope, a possibility. A new world, a new place, a new life. One way or another, she had been ready to leave this world for a long time, and this was her chance for something better.

Liz put on the limb sections one at a time, attaching them to the vest. As they molded to her, she felt as if she was becoming encased in flexible armor, providing her protection and strength. Then she climbed into the lower section, secured it to the vest, and waited for it to contract, forming into legs and boots. She took a few steps, but the web-like flap did not interfere with her movements.

She was ready. Liz picked up the helmet and pulled it down over her head, adjusted it. The interior padding began to swell, encasing her, and for a moment she panicked as the padding closed over her nose and mouth; but within moments air passages had formed, and she could breathe again. She worked the vest and helmet collars together, then sealed them. A faint hum vibrated through her, barely perceptible.

As far as Liz knew, she was now invisible to the world around her. She could not see anything through the blackened visor. She wondered what it was going to be like, to sense the world as Diego had. And wondered what kind of world awaited her.

Liz breathed deeply, felt for the depressions on the side of the helmet, chose one at random, and pressed.

No Place Anymore

SIMEON STAGGERED THROUGH THE FOG, A MIST IN halos around the streetlamps. His feet hurt. He wore shoes, but his socks were missing, left behind somewhere; he couldn't remember.

He stopped beneath a streetlamp, looked up at the halo around the pulsing amber globe. He put a hand up in front of his eyes, fragmenting the light between fingers. The air was cold; his breath was cold. He walked on, leaving the halo behind.

Simeon's ears ached with the cold. That's why he was in this strange sector, searching for a hat. That last place he had gone to, maybe he had forgotten his socks there. Where was it? A hostel near the port, he thought. He remembered loud roars, and heavy vibrations in the walls. They were people he didn't know—a woman, a man, and two cats. That was what he remembered most, the two cats. It was still amazing to him that cats had made it off the world alive, enough of them to start up again. Well, maybe not so amazing, even people had managed it.

He rubbed his ears. They were so sensitive to the cold, especially when there was a wind, that sometimes the pain would shoot through his whole head. And even here inside the dome there was wind, though nothing like it had once been. . . .

So Simeon had gone to them, the woman and man and their two cats. He had asked for a hat, and they had told him he was too old. Too old for what? A hat? It was, he knew, because he was a Revenant; they must have sensed it. They would have nothing to do with him. They rushed him out and now he was on the street again.

The street was quiet, few lights in windows, fewer people about. The dome above was invisible, hidden by the fog. A door nearby opened. Two men emerged in a cloud of smoke, one smiling, the other expressionless. The first stumbled, was caught by his companion before he fell, smile becoming a strained grunt. They looked up at Simeon, stared, then staggered away, muttering at him.

Simeon looked up at the numbers above the open door. Was this the place? He didn't understand; nothing looked right. Still, someone had sent him into this sector to find a hat—first to the woman and man with the cats, then to this address. With nowhere else to go, he stepped through the door, into dim light and heavy smoke, and closed the door behind him.

A woman in green approached. She tried to sell cigarettes to him, tried to sell him poppers or veinmelters; finally, she tried to sell herself. Her teeth were white, like porcelain, which no longer existed.

Behind her, tables lit by dim orange candles surrounded a circular stage. The stage hovered above the floor, and a number of figures moved about on it, illuminated by blue footlights. Some were men, some women, some apparently both; most were fully dressed, but a few wore only shirts or trousers. It was unclear to Simeon what they were doing, if there was any purpose at all to their movements.

The woman in green touched his arm, tried once again to sell something to him. He asked about a hat, but received no response. He walked past her, toward the stage, and she followed.

Simeon sat at an empty table, facing the stage. The woman stood next to him, weaving from side to side until he ordered something to drink—Scotch. She laughed, shaking her head, then abruptly went quiet, staring at him. He tried vodka, and she slowly nodded, turned, and left.

He loosened his coat, looked down at the table. The wood was darkly grained, thick and rough in texture. Real wood! It must be worth a fortune. Or now worth nothing at all, forgotten like everything else. He sighed. The candle, though, was artificial. Melt one of us down, he thought, make a real one.

Vague noises drifted from the stage, varying in pitch and volume, an indistinct mixture of vocal sounds and the scrape and hiss of shoes, bare feet, hands. Simeon took off his own shoes to rest his feet; without socks, the skin was beginning to blister. He stretched out legs and feet, wiggled his toes with relief.

On stage, the people continued their movements and noises. Their intention, their purpose if any, was still unclear to him, though some movements involved a continual, apparently random exchange of clothing. But there were so many other actions, gestures, flailing and waving of limbs, that he could make no sense of them.

The number of performers grew, their movements becoming increasingly frantic, violent, confusing. A woman from the next table leaned over and spoke, her gaze still directed at the stage.

"When I first arrived," she said, "there was only one performer on the stage. A woman. She stood motionless, in silence, her eyes closed. This continued for what seemed an unbearably long time. Then a man stepped onto the stage, and everything started from that. I think it's called 'Heat Death of the Earth'."

Simeon shivered, pain knotting in his chest; he wished she had not told him the title. "How long have you been here?" he managed to ask.

"I don't know. Years, perhaps." She laughed, turning toward him, baring sharp white teeth that were certainly not real. Then she froze. The woman stared at him, eyes widening, clamped her mouth shut and turned away, sliding her chair around to the other side of the table. She began to whisper to her companions.

Simeon had no intention of being trapped here for years. He stood, began walking toward the front door. The woman in green approached, holding a tall glass; she looked at him and shrugged; she drank the vodka herself and walked away. Simeon pushed through the door and back out onto the street.

Outside, the fog was clearing, but the cold remained. His feet, especially, were cold. He looked down, unbelieving, at his bare feet. He had forgotten to put on his shoes; they were still inside, under the table. Simeon looked at the door, considered briefly going back in, but then thought of the woman in green, the blue lights and smoke, all the people on stage, and the woman who had been there for years. He walked on instead, barefoot.

The fog was nearly gone, but the air was still dark; darker, actually. He looked up. Night outside the dome, as always. He glimpsed a star through the thinning fog, then another, and wondered if they were real or projections. Not that it mattered, unless one of them was . . . Earth. But that was impossible, wasn't it? He didn't know anymore.

The walkway was rough and sharp on his feet. Ahead, there were no window lights, no flashing signs, no people strolling along the walk. The streetlamps formed two converging lines of hazed light. Overhead, dark clouds replaced the fog.

Simeon arrived at an intersection. There were no vehicles in sight. He started across the street, and it began to rain.

But the droplets were small, light, almost warm, and he stopped, raised his face to the sky that was not a sky, and let the water drizzle over his skin, tiny rivulets running into his ears, down his neck. He remembered standing in a field, with grass, real *grass* under his feet, rain clouds hiding the sun and the blue skies that now no longer appeared even as projections in the dome. . . .

Suddenly the rain became a downpour. The water flooded Simeon's face and he began choking. He put his head down and hurried forward, his feet splashing in growing puddles.

Simeon ran along the sidewalk, searching for shelter. Doors were closed everywhere, nothing was open, not a shop, not a drinking place or café, nothing. Everything was dark.

Finally, he spotted an alcove, a dry spot across the street. He stepped off the curb and started across. A horn blared, there was a slush and skidding sound, approaching lights. Simeon closed his eyes and broke into a run, rushing blindly until he stumbled against the opposite curb, twisting his ankle. Nothing had hit him. Opening his eyes, he limped into the dry alcove.

He leaned against a metal grate covering a cracked plate glass window, his breath harsh and fast. Dim light from a nearby streetlamp entered the alcove, but no rain.

A stifled sneeze sounded at his feet, followed by a shaky whimper. Simeon looked down, and saw he was not alone. A dog huddled in the corner of the alcove, shivering, its thick fur wet and tangled. One eye looked up at him, the other hidden by drooping gray curls.

He had not seen a dog in years. They were even more rare than cats. Dogs didn't breed well, though Simeon couldn't remember why—the wrong gravity, perhaps; the wrong light; the wrong *feel*. He understood that.

Part of a black collar and a metal tag were visible. He squatted beside the dog, reached cautiously toward the neck. The dog sneezed twice, but did not snap at him. He turned the metal tag, read the etched letters in the dim light. ''Phoebe's Dog,'' it said. No address, no number, no other words or symbols. Who was Phoebe? Should he know her? The name was vaguely familiar, but then all names were that way to him now—those of people he had known for years, those of strangers, those of the long dead.

Phoebe's Dog. Was it possible he was *on* Phoebe? He didn't remember shipping out this far, ever; he certainly didn't remember Saturn's rings. And would they want a Revenant out here? Hardly. No one wanted *anything* of Earth out here. But he had to admit he didn't know which moon this was, or which city. He had not known, or cared, for a long time.

The dog continued to shiver, violently at times. Simeon watched for a minute, and when it didn't stop he took off his coat and wrapped the dog carefully within it until only mouth, nose, and uncovered eye could be seen. A cold tongue licked his wrist.

He stood with his weight on one leg to ease the pain in his ankle, and wrapped his arms around each other. Simeon waited for the rain to stop, or let up, but he wasn't sure why. He didn't know what he was going to do now. He had no place to go; no one to see; nowhere else to look.

At his feet, the dog had stopped shivering. Simeon knelt to pet it once again, but the dog growled, low and deep within its throat. Apparently it was quite content now, warm and dry, wrapped inside his coat.

He pulled his hand back and stood. There was nothing to keep him here any longer. He walked out into the rain, colder now, wetter. His ankle still hurt, on and off, on and off.

Two blocks up the street was a marker for the glider busses. Simeon looked down the street, saw nothing coming, and stood beside the metal pole to wait.

A glider bus approached, slowed, and Simeon started forward, stepped to the edge of the curb. Then the bus accelerated and sped past, horn blaring. Simeon waved and called after it, but the bus continued on, the lighted windows rapidly shrinking, dimming.

Waiting, again. He had always waited, it seemed, and he had become used to it. Many of the things he had waited for had never happened, and most of the people had never arrived. But some did, and those few were always enough. They had to be.

Another bus appeared. Simeon stepped out into the street and put up his arm. The bus came smoothly to a stop, the door directly in front of him, and he smiled. The doors shook open, and Simeon stepped into the bus and out of the rain.

The warmth inside stunned him; a wave of dizziness curled and rushed over him. He headed back toward a seat when the driver called sharply out to him, snapped something about money. The fare, of course. Simeon had forgotten. He walked back, searching pockets for coins.

The driver was impatient; he wouldn't start from the curb until Simeon had paid. The passengers were impatient as well, he could sense it; he could hear them mutter, could nearly smell their irritation. Finally, though, he discovered a few coins, just barely enough, dropped them into the fare slot. The driver asked him about his shoes. What could he tell him? "I've lost them," Simeon said. The driver stared, didn't respond.

Walking toward the back, the bus jerking away from the curb, Simeon lost his balance. He reached out and grabbed for support; his fingers latched onto the shoulder of a woman. The woman roared at him, swung her fist upwards and hit him solidly on his right ear. She yelled obscenities at him, all referring to various sexual perversities. Then she told him to go to Earth.

Simeon wondered if she knew what pain she caused him with those words. He pushed away from her, staggered all the way to the rear of the bus, away from the other passengers, and dropped onto a seat warmed by the heat of the motors.

Go to Earth.

Simeon remained in the back of the bus, where the heat was greatest, hoping his clothes would dry. The seats were poorly maintained. Many had sheared bolts and threatened to collapse, and most had large words and phrases scrawled over them in thick, black ink. Of the writings, the majority were simple, absurd expressions of love. A few were racial slurs. The rest were indecipherable—a literary gold mine. Some things never changed, even over several decades and millions of kilometers of dead space. Simeon gave up reading and leaned his head back, closing his eyes.

Simeon rode through the night and the rain. He watched the street through the windows. There were more lights now, bright signs, open shops, people inside and people out on the walks. He thought that here he might be able to find what he was looking for, a hat for his ears; but he had no energy to even rise from his seat. The heat was too great, a drain on his strength. He could do nothing but sit and watch.

The rain lessened. Soon, he decided, it would cease altogether. Something else to look forward to. But the lights were becoming rarer again. People, too. Now, passengers left the bus, but none boarded. Before long, Simeon was once more alone.

The bus drove on. All lights were gone. Even the streetlamps had disappeared, no light anywhere. They had to be nearing the end of the city.

The bus slowed, coasted quietly for a minute or two, then stopped. The motors were shut off, bringing silence. The driver turned to look at Simeon.

"End of the line," he said.

Simeon didn't move, and the driver repeated the words. But all was darkness here, black without light or color. Simeon told the driver he wanted to ride back with him into the lights, but the driver shook his head. Not without the full fare again, he said.

Simeon went through all his pockets, knowing he had no more money. He held out empty hands, and the driver told him to go. Sighing heavily, Simeon stood and left through the back door. Outside it was still wet; no escape from that, it seemed. Not rain, exactly—there were no clouds here, the dome too low and close—but water dripped from the dome itself in heavy, irregular streams. Simeon stood under dripping water and watched the bus, listened to the motors start again, gazed after it as it pulled away.

Where to go? All directions seemed the same. He looked up, but there was nothing to see, just the black, not even a star.

His feet hurt worse than ever. Sharp stones cut into them with the wet and the cold. There wasn't even a walkway out here. And his ears, of course, were aching again.

He started forward, blind though his eyes were open. After several steps, he bumped against an invisible wall. The dome.

Simeon ran his hands over the rough interior surface, felt cracks and pitted areas. He could not see through it. There was only black; no stars visible, no dimly lit terrain of some barren, frozen chunk of orbiting rock (Phoebe, perhaps?); nothing.

The dome here was shielded, he thought. Or was it possible that there was absolutely nothing at all on the other side? The thought of a complete void so near him, a region of nonexistence, was somehow comforting. There was no way through, however. The dome was cracked, deteriorating like everything else, but for Simeon it was solid and impenetrable. He turned away.

His vision had adjusted somewhat to the dark, and he could now see outlines of objects; it was not quite as barren here as he had thought. He saw a scootcycle, several trash cans lined up together, then two slipsters—crushed hulks. Nearby were dark buildings, low and squat. Abandoned shops, perhaps, or warehouses.

Simeon turned and began walking, not into the city, but not away from it either. Perhaps he was following the perimeter of the dome. That, too, was a comforting thought. It struck him that it might be possible to endlessly circle the interior of the dome, the outer edges of the city, around and around. . . .

His feet touched smooth rockmelt—a walkway. He kept on, and streets appeared, all dark. He continued to walk from one block to another; he was cold and wet, exhausted. What would he do when he could not go on anymore? Force himself to keep on, he supposed. Keep on.

Then, a light.

Simeon stopped, turned. Yes, there it was, down along the street, several blocks from the dome, a small and orange light. He picked up his pace and started toward it. The streams of falling water did not seem to matter so much anymore, and even the cold did not seem so bad. And yet, he knew he should not hope for much.

He could tell, from the buildings and windows and the signs, that this wasn't a residential zone. All around him were small businesses, all of them closed now. Only in the distance, several blocks beyond the light, were there more lights, signs of life.

He slowed, nearing the light. Something odd occurred with his breathing—like jumping into icy water, his breath left him for a few moments. He reached the light, stopped in front of a glass door.

It was a café, small, only a few tables inside. In the window hung a sign stating that the café was open twenty-four hours—an homage to ancient time structures, to a world and time now gone. It would be warm inside, he thought, warmer certainly than out here. And dry. He smelled coffee, hot pastries. Simeon couldn't believe the coffee was real, but the smell! He pushed open the door and stepped through, then closed the door softly behind him.

There was no one inside but a young woman behind the counter. She stepped out, smiling, and walked toward him. She told him to sit anywhere, and waited as Simeon chose a small table next to the window.

"Coffee?" she asked, still smiling.

Strangest of all, to Simeon, was her smile, which looked natural, as though she was truly pleased that he had come into the café. Perhaps she didn't realize what he was.

Simeon nodded, then remembered he had no money. No, he told her, slowly explaining that he had no money for coffee, for anything, that he had forgotten. He should not have come in.

"Don't sigh so heavily," she said. "It sounds so . . . sad."

But Simeon had been so looking forward to the hot coffee, real or not. He didn't tell her that, however, he just started to get up. The woman shook her head, told him to stay seated and that she would bring him coffee. He told her again that he had no money. But she insisted, said he could have the coffee anyway, that she could see he needed it.

The woman walked back behind the counter, and Simeon felt a release of tension, felt his body relax into the metalform chair. Coffee. Real or not, he would accept it. Her kindness was what mattered, not the coffee. He didn't understand it, though; she didn't know him at all. They had never met before, and look at him, his appearance.

She came to the table with the coffee and a small plate with a hot pastry. She set both in front of him. "I thought you might be hungry," she said. "This is all we have right now. I can fix you something else if you like."

Simeon shook his head, sipped at the coffee. It was hot and strong, not real, but the flavor was so close. Close enough. He tried to thank her, he wanted to ask her why she was doing this, but he couldn't get the words out.

She looked down. "I didn't notice at first," she said. "You have no shoes, no socks. It must be cold."

Simeon agreed with her. "No coat or hat either," he said.
"Did you have them once?" she asked.

Just the coat, he told her, along with the shoes and the socks.
He explained that he had been searching for a hat to keep his
ears warm. Somehow he kept on talking, with hardly a pause;
he told her all he had been through this night, all for a hat, any
kind of hat, just something for his ears. He told her that he had
been searching for a long time, for nights on end, and that all
he had accomplished was to become even colder.

The woman sat at the table and listened intently. Why did
she listen to him, Simeon wondered? Why did she sit with him,
give him coffee and food when he had no money? Why did she
care?

When his cup was empty, she poured fresh coffee, then
poured a cup for herself. They drank together. Simeon talked,
and she asked questions. She asked him who Phoebe was, but
he didn't know, so he couldn't tell her. Maybe they *weren't* on
Phoebe after all.

And then . . . and then Simeon almost started to talk about
the life he had before, a life from so many years ago, on a world.
. . . But he stopped, catching himself.

"You're very old," the woman said.

Simeon nodded. What was there to say? Did she. . . ?

"You're from Earth, aren't you?" she asked. "You're a . . ."
She didn't finish.

"A Revenant," he said.

"I've never known someone who was . . ."

"Earth was my home. I want to go back."

Her expression saddened. "It's not there anymore," she
said, surely knowing he knew that more deeply than almost
anyone. "I mean, it's there, but you can't . . . no one can. . . ."

"I know," Simeon told her. "I'm sorry, I shouldn't have
come in here, I shouldn't have said anything."

She told him to wait, and went through a doorway into a
back room. When she returned, she held a brown bag in her
hands. After sitting down, she said, "I can't help you with the
shoes and socks, or the coat, but here's something. I'm not sure
where it came from."

Carefully, she unfolded and opened the bag, slowly withdrew a black knit cap. "Here, try it on." She held it out, and
Simeon gently took it from her hands.

He put it on over his head, pulled the sides down so they

covered his ears completely. A perfect fit! His ears were snug and warm, and he could hardly believe it after all this time. He thanked the young woman, over and over; he felt tears rising in his eyes, but he forced them back. He could not cry in front of her. Simeon put his hands up and adjusted the hat, unable to look into her face.

"For when you go out," she said.

He breathed deeply. Go out. He nodded once, then looked up. "I have no place to go," he told her. Silence. Why did he say that, why did he tell her? She didn't want to know, it was too much to put on her. Silence. She watched him, intent.

Then, with a gentle shrug, she poured him another cup of coffee. "I don't know. You can't stay here permanently," she said. Then she smiled. "But you can always come back here and sit and talk to me."

Somehow, that was enough. More than enough. Simeon turned away, and this time could not hold back; a few slow tears slipped down his face. He wiped them away, touched the hat again, warm on his head, his ears. He turned back to her, and she was still smiling.

"Talk to me," she said.

Simeon picked up his coffee, drank some, and then began to tell her of a life under open skies with a sun that actually warmed the air and brought life to a green and blue world.

Prayers of a Rain God

JANET WATCHED HIM TREMBLE IN THE MOONLIGHT
slanting through the window. Garrett was dreaming again,
the same "vision" that now repeated itself three or four
times a week. She could tell from his constricted face, the
sweat on his neck, and the abrupt, irregular gasps, as if he were
short of breath. . . .

They pray to him for rain.

Disembodied, he hovers above them, above the vast expanse
of barren rock and sand, dirt mounds, a dying forest in the
distance. The sun is fierce, leeching all moisture from the air. A
few thin plants still grow, spindly and brittle. A dry riverbed
weaves through rock and sand, then flows into what was once
an enormous lake. Several tiny pools of water remain scattered
about the riverbed and the lake, and the abandoned hulls of
several small sailing vessels lie on the sloping beach.

Here, at the mouth of the dry river, they have gathered, fifty
or sixty in number, and they pray to him.

They are not human, but clearly they are intelligent. Bipedal,
lightly furred in varying shades of rust, orange, tan—one, the
tallest, is dark black—they stand at the edge of the barren lake
and raise their faces to him.

Their eyes are small, recessed, their noses long, stiff and narrow. If there are ears, they are hidden among the tufts of fine fur covering their heads. Their narrow mouths open and close as they speak to him. Some raise their long, gangly arms to the sun and sky, fingers outstretched. In their gestures, and in their faces, he recognizes their supplication to him, their god.

They are dying, his people. They whisper and sing at the river mouth, praying to him for rain, and for life.

Garrett woke in a panic, his throat dry and constricted. He gasped for breath in the darkness, reached out frantically and tossed the sheet and blanket from him. Janet gripped his hand, held it to her breast.

"Garrett," she whispered. "It's okay, I'm here." Her voice soothed, eased away the fear.

He turned, and in the light of the moon could see her face, the smooth skin, her large eyes gazing at him. She released his hand, wiped at the sweat on his forehead. "Water?" she said.

Garrett nodded. He swung his legs over the side of the bed and sat up. A slight tremor went through his hand, then faded. He filled the tumbler with water from the glass pitcher he'd begun to keep on the nightstand. Moonlight reflected through the clear water, and Garrett quickly drained the glass. He refilled it, drank down the chilled water, and replaced the glass on the nightstand. He was still thirsty, but felt bloated and queasy.

Garrett looked out through the lace curtains at the nearly full moon. He could not shake the feelings of dread and responsibility. And guilt.

"The dream?" Janet asked.

"No dream," he answered. The exchange was becoming a tense ritual. Janet persisted in calling them dreams, and he refused to give them that name. Garrett pulled open the window and let in the cold night air; he still felt the heat of the parched world drawing moisture from him.

Maybe it was time to go back into space. Just a short trip, back to the moon, or even a shuttle up to one of the stations. Something to give him some perspective. He shook his head. Perspective on what? People, intelligent beings, were dying on some other world, and a trip to the moon wasn't going to help them. Nothing would. Except rain.

*   *   *

It was early evening, but Garrett was already in bed. Janet sat in the kitchen, drinking tea. She considered fixing a drink, a Jack Daniels on the rocks, but she really didn't want one. She turned on the small table radio, tuned in to a classical station. Something she didn't recognize, as usual, was playing. The quiet music was just loud enough so she would not hear Garrett snore, or toss in the bed.

Janet wondered if he would have the dream again, his vision. She didn't know what to think about it anymore. His dreams had driven them apart from each other, though they both fought to remain close. She felt she was fighting a losing battle.

There had always been a distant quality to Garrett, even before they were married. Janet had often felt his mind was only partially attuned to the world around him, that part of his thoughts were somewhere else—in another room, another city, on some other world. It seemed quite appropriate that he had chosen the space program for a career, that he had striven to become an astronaut. And she had not been surprised at his success.

So Garrett had begun to go into space, making several trips a year to the two stations and the moon, training hard and long as plans were made to venture to Mars and beyond. Janet had little trouble adjusting to his long absences; they seemed a natural part of Garrett's makeup. And she was busy herself, teaching German at State. There was no real distance between them, and his trips into space had put up no new barriers.

Then came the second Mars Mission, which had gone smoothly, a huge success. Garrett was a part of it, had been gone nearly two years, and came back home to her relatively unchanged—until the dreams began. Now she felt him drifting completely away from her, despite their efforts. He had become obsessed with his visions.

Janet looked at the wall clock. It was nearly eleven. She turned off the radio, put her mug in the sink, and went into the bedroom.

Garrett was sleeping peacefully on his side, one arm on top of the blankets, his head between the two pillows. If he was dreaming, it was a normal dream.

She undressed, put on her knee-length nightshirt, and crawled into bed next to him. She turned onto her side, her back to him, and eased against his body. In his sleep he moved closer so their bodies fit snugly together, put one arm over her which she held to her breast, both hands clasped around his fingers. As she drifted into sleep, she let the silent tears drip freely onto the pillow.

The drought continues. The sun and the heat remain. The people below him, these intelligent, furred beings, move slowly about their village near the dry riverbed. He can now distinguish males from females, though the differences were not immediately obvious.

Their dwellings are made of wood and stone, small rectangular structures built against rock mounds or small hillocks. Several large cooking pits are spaced regularly among the buildings. Most of the cooking pits seem to be abandoned.

The distant forest is now a skeletal maze of thin dried trunks and branches without leaves. Occasionally a small, light-skinned animal scurries over the ground, hurrying from shelter to shelter. Scattered about in all directions are the skeletons of larger animals, the bones clean and bleached; no carcasses remain, no shred of meat or skin on any of them.

A few of his people wander in the riverbed, searching for food or small pools of water. One male, the single black-furred being, searches farther upstream, and periodically pokes a long digit into the dry bed, feeling for moisture.

Toward noon most activity ceases. All members of the village gather lethargically at the riverbed then amble slowly toward the lake. As they walk, many of them ruffle the fur around their necks and under their arms, an apparent attempt to keep cool.

At the lake's edge, they form patterns, all facing the dry lake bed. The younger ones form a double row in front, each an arm's length from those on either side. The adults then form two half circles behind them, the black-furred one in the center of the back row.

A chant begins from the children and is taken up by the adults. The dark one reaches up to the sky, reaches up to his god and howls, his voice cracked and anguished. Several others raise their arms, and the prayer increases in intensity.

I want to bring you rain, Garrett thinks. *I am trying.*

But he knows they do not hear his thoughts, and he feels helpless. What good is a god who can do nothing for his people? Of what use is a god who lets his people die?

He and Janet walked through the eastern end of Golden Gate

Park on a Monday afternoon. Overhead, dark clouds rolled past, threatening rain. Garrett and Janet were dressed warmly, in coats, scarves, and boots. In the nearly deserted Children's Playground they sat on a bench facing the main play area. Two boys, about seven or eight years old and bundled up in parkas and mittens, moved unsteadily across a bridge of chains and tires while a woman stood nearby, watching and smoking a cigarette.

"You need to do something," Janet said. "It's getting worse, not better. You don't sleep enough at night anymore, you're always tired. All right, for now it's okay, but when your leave is over, and you have to go back . . ." She stopped, shrugged. "It's not doing a hell of a lot for our relationship, either."

Garrett closed his eyes, leaned his head back. He tried to will the clouds overhead to open, release a downpour, or at least a drizzle. No water fell.

"I know they seem like dreams to you," he said. He felt for her, put his hand on her knee. "I'd probably think that's all they were, except . . ." He opened his eyes, sat up and looked at her. "There's too damn much logic to them. And a regular pattern. If they were simply repetitive, but they aren't. The drought goes on, everything is drying out, getting worse. Each 'dream' is a slight progression from the previous, and they never go back. I can't believe dreams could do this over such a long period of time."

Janet pushed both hands into her coat pockets. "What else could they be? Visions? A door into another reality? Telepathic contact with another world? Jesus, Garrett, we've been through all this before, and none of it makes any sense. Every idea sounds absurd."

He stood and began to pace back and forth in front of the bench. Several times he started to speak, but couldn't. Finally he breathed in deeply and stopped pacing.

"Look, something I haven't told you. The first time it happened, the first time I had this . . . 'vision,' whatever you want to call it, I was not asleep. I was awake, and I wasn't dreaming." He paused, but she remained silent, waiting. "I was not even here on Earth." He started to pace again.

"It was just after we'd burned out of orbit from Mars. I was awake, we were all awake. Suddenly I was . . . there. On this strange world, *above* the world, looking down on drying streams that had obviously once been rivers, on a pond that had once been a large lake, on a dying forest. Looking down on a dying race of intelligent beings. It went on a long time—hours it seemed, as I watched these alien creatures moving through their world, trying to survive. And when it ended, and I was 'back' in the ship, no one had noticed a thing. Practically no time had passed. I hadn't gone into any kind of trance, and I sure hadn't been asleep to dream.''

He stood watching the two boys, who had stopped playing on the bridge and were wrestling in the sand. It began to rain lightly, and the woman called to the boys. They ran over to her and the three of them hurried away.

"You didn't tell anyone, did you?"

Garrett shook his head. He found it difficult to turn around and look directly at her, but he managed it. A few strands of hair were wet and pressed against her face. Her face was so clean and smooth, and her eyes were so large and open. Water dripped from her hair.

"The craziest thing," he began, "the hardest thing, the most absurd part of all this is that they were praying. They were praying to me, their god." He looked down at his open hands, then back at her. "I am their god."

Garrett stood in the rain watching Janet, waiting for her to respond. After several minutes she stood, put her arm through his, pressed tightly.

"Let's go home," she said.

They had not spoken for hours. After coming in from the rain, and showering separately, Janet had fixed up a fire while Garrett worked on dinner. She sat in front of the fire with a Heinrich Böll novel and sipped at a Jack Daniels. The flames drew her gaze, and she spent more time staring at them than reading.

She didn't know what to think about Garrett. He was not an irrational man. He was not given to mysticism, or astrology, or beliefs in paranormal powers, dreams that foretold the future, nothing like that. If anything, he was a skeptic, in the true sense of the word. He questioned everything, always with an open mind but needing to be logically convinced. Garrett just did not take anything on faith.

And yet, it was clear he believed what he had said. Believed it deeply, so that it caused him pain.

Garrett came into the front room and sat in the chair closest to Janet. She put the book aside, looked at him.

"I made a casserole," he said. "Should be ready in about an hour." He breathed deeply once. "Janet, do you think . . . we've never discussed one explanation. We've discreetly avoided it," he said, smiling. "But do you think I've lost touch with reality? That I've lost my sanity?"

"Do you believe that?"

"No." His answer was firm and sure.

"I don't think so either," Janet said. "But it *is* a possibility, and has to be considered."

He nodded, and they were silent for a long time. Janet sipped at her drink, finished it while Garrett stared into the dying fire. He got up from the chair, added a log.

"A god?" she said.

Garrett shrugged. "I know how it sounds. But I am a . . . presence above them, and they are praying to me." He stood, turned to her. "I *know* it, Janet, deep in my gut. There is no doubt in me. I may not be helping them, but they are praying to me, and I am their god."

Janet slowly shook her head. "You're a human being, Garrett, you don't have any special powers. Isn't it more likely that you have made some kind of contact, and are just observing this world?"

He looked away and into the fire. "You think I want to be a god? You think I have a choice?"

The silence returned. Janet shook her head slowly, watching him. "You are not a god," she said.

For the first time, it is night.

He can barely distinguish the outlines of the village dwellings below. In the dim moonlight it appears that most of the villagers are asleep.

A huge fire burns in the riverbed. Tending the fire is the tall, black-furred being. He is placing the ends of long pieces of wood into the fire, forming a circle of the pieces around the edge. The ends seem to be coated with something flammable, for as each one is placed into the fire, a small burst of flame and sparks erupts from it. Fifty or sixty of these lengths of wood ring the fire.

The dark one picks up one of the lengths, a torch now with one end burning brightly, and walks along the riverbed, downstream twenty paces. He plants the torch in the dry earth. The torch burns steadily, flames tossing slightly in a breeze. He returns to the fire, picks up another piece and carries it farther downstream, where he plants it as far from the first as the first is from the fire. The next time, he picks up two torches and plants them still farther downstream, one at a time, equally spaced.

The lone figure continues the procedure, carrying two torches at a time, hiking farther downstream with each trip to plant them. From above, it seems the course of the river is being slowly charted by fire, a long, curving string of equidistant torches marking the way.

Eventually the course of the riverbed is traced by fire all the way to the dry lake. Once the concluding torch is planted, the black-furred being returns to the fire, picks up as many of the torches as he can safely carry, then bears them to the edge of the lake. He plants them carefully in a small circle at the end of the line of torches.

All the torches continue to burn without signs of fading. The lone, dark figure paces about the circle of fire at the lake's edge, weaving from side to side. After a time, he steps inside the circle, raises arms and face to the sky, and howls. When there is no answer, he hangs his head, then suddenly drops to a kneeling position above a dark patch of earth within the flames, and sticks a finger, then his entire hand, into the ground. Wearily, he shakes his head from side to side, then plunges his face and mouth to the ground. He buries his face deeper, deeper, then abruptly pulls free and stares up at the night sky. His mouth, nose, and tiny eyes are covered with dry, dry sand.

The dark one rises slowly to his feet, holds out two open palms, then violently spits into the sand at his feet.

Garrett woke coughing, unable to breathe. He pushed himself up into a sitting position, his mouth and throat dry and gritty. He gasped for air, and felt Janet reach for him as he continued to cough. After a minute or two, the coughing subsided, and he breathed easier. Garrett wiped his mouth, felt sand on his fingers.

He looked down at his hand, then felt the inside of his mouth with his tongue. More sand. He turned and saw flecks of sand on his pillow, the sheet. He held out his hand to Janet, thrusting it at her.

"Sand! Tell me this isn't real! I've got sand in my mouth,

down my throat, and where the hell did it all come from? From a godforsaken world, that's where!" He pounded his hand on the pillow and turned from her to pick up the water pitcher. He started to fill his glass, then stopped and stared at the pitcher, at the clear, bright water. Rage and frustration swelled inside him, pressuring for release, and for the first time in his life he was afraid he would take it out on Janet. He swung the pitcher back, then heaved it violently against the far wall. The glass shattered, and water sprayed over the wall and floor. Garrett buried his head in his hands and sat on the edge of the bed for a long time, pressing his palms as hard as possible against his skull.

Garrett had almost completely stopped talking to her. She had tried to offer another explanation for the sand—that they were near the park and sandy ground—but he would not listen. He spent most of the days out walking, though Janet did not know where he went. He napped in the afternoons, went to bed quite early, slept late. He stopped fixing meals, so Janet took over the cooking, though neither of them ate much any longer. Garrett had the dreams every time he slept now, and she felt he was trying to remain permanently asleep, in a constant state of dreaming.

She nearly moved out twice, certain she could not take it any longer, but had been unable to leave him alone. Now she simply waited for it to stop, or for Garrett to deteriorate to a point where he would need to be committed somewhere for care.

When, one day, he did talk to her at length, she was taken by surprise.

Garrett had built up a fire himself, then asked her to come into the front room so he could talk to her. His tone and manner seemed rational, as if nothing odd was happening to him.

"First," he began, "I want to apologize. I can imagine what you've been through, and you don't deserve it. But I can't do anything about it. I'm not going to try to convince you that anything's going to change. Nothing will. If anything, this is all going to get worse."

"Do you know of something that's going to happen?"

Garrett shook his head. "No. You probably won't understand, but I wouldn't end this now even if I could. Not in the way you're thinking. I . . . I feel responsible. Responsible for lives. They are dying because of me."

Janet closed her eyes and shook her head. She did not want to go into that anymore.

"All right," Garrett said. "I'll let that part of it be. But there is one thing I need to say. Something I need you to promise me."

Janet opened her eyes and looked at him. "Go ahead."

"If anything happens to me, and I end up in a hospital on life-support machines, or something like that, well, I know we've talked about this before, and we both felt we wouldn't want to be kept alive by machines, not in the long run. That if one of us was in that position, we would want the other to have the doctors disconnect the life-support systems."

"What's going to happen, Garrett?"

"I don't know, I told you. But if something does, I want you to promise me you *won't* have them disconnect the life-support. I want to be kept alive. I *have* to be kept alive."

"Garrett, tell me what's going to happen."

"Promise me, Janet."

"Garrett . . ."

"Janet."

They lapsed into silence. After a long time, Janet nodded to him. *Yes*, she said silently. *I promise.*

The promise received, Garrett stood and went into the bedroom. Janet sat watching the fire, drained and empty, certain now that she had finally lost him.

He has done it.

Almost.

High, white clouds move serenely across the sky, and the furred beings stagger out from their dwellings to stare up at the clouds. In shock, in awe, they lope down to the riverbed, stand in the middle, and face upstream as if expecting water to appear.

The black-furred one remains aloof, staring up at the sky. There is no rain, no hint of moisture; Garrett has not managed that yet, and the solitary figure below him seems to recognize that.

Soon, Garrett thinks. *I promise.*

It is almost as if the dark one hears him, and does not believe, for once again he turns his head to the side and fiercely spits precious water to the ground before turning away from the sky and clouds to return to the village.

*   *   *

The contacts ceased.

Garrett went into a low-key, barely contained panic. He had been gaining control over his sleep, more each day so he was able to move at will in and out of the dream state that brought him to his world. He was even gaining control of the world itself, enough to create clouds, and before long he would bring rain, he was certain of it. But now. . . .

He had planned to will himself into a permanent, coma-like state, so he'd remain in constant contact with his world. Then he could fully become their god, and save them. But if he could not get back, he could not bring them rain. They would die. He had to do something, and it had to be soon.

But what had happened? What was wrong?

There were no answers.

Once again, Janet nearly moved out.

Garrett's dreams had stopped, and for a few days she had hoped everything would return to normal, but instead the situation worsened. Now Garrett had trouble getting to sleep for even an hour at a time. He started drinking more heavily, and while the drinking often put him to sleep, the sleep did not bring the dreams he wanted. The Seconals prescribed for him were no better. So he spent most of the days half drunk, trying to sleep, occasionally jogging or running to tire himself out. Nothing worked.

But Janet stayed. She stayed, and she kept the house together, cooked and made sure he ate, and held him when he burst into tears of frustration, mumbling about the deaths he was causing. Janet became convinced Garrett *had* finally lost touch with reality, but still she could not bring herself to have him carted away like some helpless animal.

Then one day he stopped drinking and stopped taking the sleeping pills. He still spoke only infrequently to her, but he started eating more regularly, began to exercise, and stopped trying to sleep all day. Both physically and mentally, Garrett seemed to be pulling himself together, and when he had his first full night's undisturbed sleep in weeks, Janet began to think their ordeal was over.

Then the dream returned.

They are dying.

One of the young ones is discovered dead beside a pile of

rock, and the villagers gather around her. There is a hesitancy before acting, as if they are giving the young female a moment of mourning. The black-furred one whispers a few words, makes several motions in the air with his hands, then takes a knife and proceeds to cut into the dead youth. Two others hold bowls as the blood is drained, the precious liquid saved. When all the blood has been drained, the dark one begins to skin and carve the flesh.

Garrett wants to stop looking, to turn away so he does not have to watch. But he cannot, because he is their god, and a god sees all.

A fire has been built in the nearest cooking pit, and a large grill has been set up over it. The villagers crowd around the fire. Smoke rises from the grill as the meat is placed upon it.

Not once have any of his people looked up to him in either prayer or anger; it is as if he no longer exists. There are no clouds in the sky, no traces of moisture in the air. Garrett feels worthless again, an abandoned, impotent god.

There was only one chance to save his people.

Garrett had no time to regain control over his sleep and dream states. It would take weeks, and they would all be dead by then.

He fingered one of the Seconal capsules spread out on the nightstand. He put it in his mouth, drank some water, and swallowed the capsule. Garrett swallowed another, then sat without moving for several minutes.

He had worked it out as closely as had been possible. The amount of Seconal he would take should put him deeply into a coma, but as long as Janet acted quickly, it shouldn't kill him. Once in a coma, Garrett felt certain that, at a subconscious level, he would be able to maintain the state. As long as he was hooked up to a life-support system, he would be fine.

Garrett swallowed three more of the Seconals. He waited again, looking out the window at the dim light of the hidden, quarter moon.

Janet. That was what hurt most, what he had done to her, and what she still had to go through. In the last few weeks he had thought too little of her, had taken her for granted in many ways. If it could have been different . . . but he knew he did not have a choice. She was strong, and she would survive. But this was the only chance his *people* had to survive.

Garrett took the remaining Seconals and finished off the water. He set the alarm clock and put the letter securely atop it. The letter was for Janet. It told her what he had done, what she had to do, and reminded her of her promise.

He was beginning to feel drowsy, but that might be just his state of mind rather than the Seconal. Garrett lay back on the bed and stared up at the ceiling. The room was cold and he wrapped himself in an Afghan.

Eventually his entire body began to feel heavy, as though he was sinking into the bed. He did not fight it, did not try to move, or stay awake. It would be soon.

He would bring rain to his people. Garrett felt quite certain of that now, and he welcomed the heavy drifting into sleep. He would bring rain, and he would save their lives.

It was nearly dawn. Janet sat in the chair at the foot of the hospital bed, very much awake though she had not slept all night. The lights on the wall monitors moved silently in regular patterns—blue, green, white. There were no red warning lights, no sounds indicating danger.

Garrett's face looked relaxed, though occasionally it twisted as if he were in anguish. She could not tell if he was dreaming.

She still did not believe he had been in contact with another world, but she hoped that, at least in his own mind, he had succeeded in getting there. And she would keep her promise to him, would never let them disconnect the life-support systems as long as she had a choice.

She had adjusted to the distant quality about him when they had first met; later she had adjusted to his long absences during his space missions and training sessions; and now she would adjust to this as well, no matter how long it went on.

When the sun made its first appearance in the window, Janet rose from the chair and left to return home to sleep.

They are praying to him again.

They are praying for the rain to stop.

It has rained for twenty-three days now, never letting up day or night. The river is swollen, flooding periodically, and the lake is already above its full level and still rising. The village has been washed away, and many of the villagers with it. Those who survive have moved away from the river and into the dead forest.

But the forest, too, is flooding, and there is no solid earth on which to settle or build. The black-furred being is leading them all on a long trek toward higher land, but the nearest mountains are weeks away. It seems extremely unlikely that, unless the rain stops, any of them will survive to reach even the foothills.

Three times each day the dark one halts the march and leads the villagers in prayer. Garrett knows their prayers are useless. He has lost all control, if he ever really had any. Janet was right. He is not a god.

He watches helplessly as his people die, as they pray in vain to him. They push on through earth that has become swamp, through newly formed lakes and rivers and uprooted trees. They are cold and unsheltered and without food. And each time they pray to him, Garrett prays as well, prays to any god who can hear him; prays he will die so that his people will live.

The rains continue to pour from the darkened sky.

More Than Night

A HEAVY, LOUD RAIN POURED FROM THE NIGHT SKY. Half a mile away, fire engulfed a building and, undaunted by the rain, sent up dense clouds of acrid smoke; damp ash drifted in the air.

Mallon ducked into a shallow alcove, the door boarded over, security-sealed. Exhausted, his clothes soaked and water dripping from his hair, he closed his eyes and pressed back against wood and brick so the rain did not touch him. He'd come a long way in a short time, most of it on foot; he hoped it was worth it.

Sleep tried to shut down his mind, his body; concentration was difficult, and he could not hang on to complete threads of thought. An explosion rocked the air, shook the building he leaned against. Mallon opened his eyes, pulling out of a doze. On the street, a grinder roared past, chewing up the surface of the road, spraying rock and dirt to both sides, its armored body almost hidden by damp flying dust; its siren wailed as it passed.

Mallon remained in the alcove a few minutes, resting. When the grinder was long gone—the only sounds now were faint shouts, distant gunfire, the rain falling on stone and water—he stepped out into the street and pushed on.

As he neared the fire, he could see it burning in a number

of buildings, perhaps an entire block engulfed in flame on the other side of Track Canal. Just before he reached the canal, Mallon turned down a street, crossed it, and stopped in front of a three-story building of charred stone and wood—the survivor of several previous fires. He approached the metal door, rapped on it. A gray panel at eye level shimmered a moment, became almost translucent, then went back to gray. The door opened and Terril, a big man dressed in glass and steel, nodded at Mallon, stepped aside to let him in. Terril closed the door, cutting off the sounds of the streets and rain, then retreated into his cubicle built into the wall.

Mallon walked slowly along the corridor, the way lit by strings of diffuse blue phosphor lights trailing from the ceiling. The building was quiet, but muted voices and other unidentifiable sounds filtered through the doors and walls on both sides. At the end of the corridor he turned to the right and started up a flight of wooden stairs.

The second floor was quieter than the first, the corridor darker, the ceiling higher. Only one door led off from the corridor, near the end. Mallon tapped lightly on the thick wood, and almost immediately the door was opened for him. He stepped inside, and the door was pushed quickly and quietly closed.

The room was large and dark, lit only by the glow of the raging fire fully visible through the immense open windows in the opposite wall. Two chuurkas, each nearly eight feet tall, stood in front of the largest windows. With their neck membranes fully spread, they "watched" the fire with the organic arrays of infrared receptors. A small, thin human squatted just behind them, a tiny black box implanted at the base of her skull (Mallon thought it was a girl, though he couldn't be certain). She adjusted the stands of burning incense at the chuurkas' sides. The incense rose, swirling, and Mallon could see the gill-like folds beneath the neck membranes flutter, guiding the incense into the narrow, slitted openings.

The man who had opened the door for him crossed the length of the room to another door in the far wall, stepped through it, and Mallon was suddenly alone in the room with the two chuurkas and their tender.

The chuurkas did not turn toward him, but Mallon knew they were aware of his presence. Their hearing was intensely acute, their sense of touch even more so; they would have picked up the vibrations of his steps as he climbed the stairs, approached the room and entered. If they turned toward him now, they *would* see him with their small, strangely lidded eyes, but mostly they would "see" him with their spread membranes, sense his body heat, the warmth of his breath.

The room was sparsely furnished—a few cushions scattered about the floor, a small table and chairs near the second door, a cot against the wall in the back corner. Mallon wanted to drop onto the cot, close his eyes, and sleep.

He stepped to one of the windows, looked out at the fire just across the canal. Directly below, the canal flowed slowly past, now empty of boats; reflections of the flames danced across the surface, obscured by the rain striking the water.

Mallon turned to look at the chuurkas, and now he could see the small, flexible air filters attached over nasal slits and mouth. Their skin was dark rust in color, leathery. Their upper limbs, long and spidery, hung limply in front of them; their lower limbs, thick and massive and covered with a mesh of dark leather stitched to something like boots, were slightly bent so that their stance appeared awkward, uncomfortable. The chuurkas stood nearly motionless, the only movement the fluttering of their gills and the slight shifting of the wide upper membranes.

The side door opened, and the man reappeared carrying a large bowl and a ceramic mug, both steaming. He set them on the table, gestured to Mallon. Mallon sat, glanced back at the chuurkas. One of them had turned a section of neck membrane toward him, and it quivered, as though drinking in the heat that rose from the bowl and mug.

The bowl was filled with thick noodles in a dark broth; in the mug was a hot drink with a sweet and spicy aroma. When Mallon started eating, the other man sat in the chair across from him.

"Sykora has been delayed," the man said, voice little more than a whisper. "It'll be at least four hours before he arrives, maybe nine or ten. You should stay here."

Mallon nodded, continued eating. The noodles were spongy, flavorless, but the broth had a sharp, meaty taste.

"You look tired," the man said. "You want, you can sleep on the cot there until Sykora comes."

Mallon nodded again. The man got up and left through the side door.

When Mallon finished eating, he got up from the table and

crossed the room, circling wide of the chuurkas. He sat on the edge of the cot, took off his boots.

In front of the windows, the chuurkas remained unmoving. Their neck membranes were so fully spread, so thin, that he could see a glow of red and orange through them; the glow delineated the patterned arrays of infrared receptors embedded within the membrane and linked in clusters to their skulls. At their feet, the young human tender, too, remained motionless, a hand on each of the incense stands. Across the canal, the fires raged.

Mallon lay back on the cot, closed his eyes, and slept.

He woke to gray light and shadows. Just a few feet away, the two chuurkas stood facing him, the small human tender squatting between them. The tender *was* a girl, dark-skinned, dark-haired, with large eyes that rarely blinked and that seemed to look right through him.

The chuurka on the left made several *chikking* sounds, like the buzzes and clicks of insects. After a moment of silence, the girl, still expressionless, translated, the module at the base of her neck blinking green light.

"Sykora will not be coming." The girl's voice was hollow, distant. "You will go with us alone. We leave tonight, after dark."

Mallon sat up, looked at the two large aliens (Aliens? On this world, he supposed he was as much an alien as they were). So Sykora wasn't coming. Did that mean the old man was dead? He knew better than to ask, and instead just nodded.

"Do I have to stay here until then?"

The chuurka made more *chikking* sounds; the girl spoke again. "No. But return by dusk, no later."

Mallon nodded again. He put on his boots as the chuurkas retreated into the shadows of the rear walls and stood, back to back, folding in their neck membranes. Outside, across the canal, the fire was out, and only smoke rose from the charred remains of the buildings. Mallon got up from the cot, went to the door, and left the room.

The streets were crowded, but quieter in the light, the noise more like a background murmur—people talking, the scuffle of shoes along the roads and walks, the creaking of pedalcarts, and the gentle hum of the occasional pulsed vehicle working its way slowly through the crowds. He'd thought it was morning, but it was early afternoon, the overcast not quite burned off by the sun; he'd slept a long time.

Mallon walked along the canal, away from the smoldering ruins of the previous night's fire. He wondered if the chuurkas had arranged it. The odor of charred wood still drifted through the air, a surprisingly clean smell.

A few small boats moved along the canal, most headed upstream. The sight of the boats disoriented him briefly, brought up fragments of emotion and incomplete images of a dream, or dreams, he'd had while sleeping on the cot. Something about being on a boat, or a canoe, that had somehow transformed itself into a motor-driven launch. And what else? A fire on both sides of the canal, chuurkas moving along the banks on wheeled carts, and a large silver fish that kept pace with the boat just below the surface of the water. There must have been more, but he couldn't remember anything else.

Ahead, the canal temporarily widened where a makeshift set of short docks had been built into the canal wall, with ladders and ramps leading up to the top of the bank. A few small boats were berthed at one dock, and, on the bank above, people milled about their tiny shacks or sat in front of cooking fires.

Mallon approached the cluster of shacks, started through them. People nodded at him in silence; Mallon nodded back. Most knew him, and probably would rather not have seen him again. Not because they didn't like him, though most of them didn't, but because they felt he brought disaster with him. He couldn't really blame them.

In front of a small shack near the edge of the canal, a thin, older woman sat before a cooking fire; dressed in dark red wraparound cloth, she poked at a large fish sizzling in a thick black pan.

"Hello, Rhea," Mallon said.

The older woman nodded without looking up, gestured at a tree stump in front of the fire. "Sit." She poked again at the fish with a wooden stick. Mallon sat, and Rhea turned toward the shack and spoke, raising her voice only slightly. "Katja. Mallon's here. An extra plate, another bottle." She picked up a bottle of rice beer, drank from it, shook it. "Two bottles," she added. Finally she looked at Mallon. "How long have you been back in the city?"

"Since last night."

"You working with chuurkas again?"

"Yes."

Rhea nodded, turned her attention back to the fish. He expected her to spit violently into the fire, an old gesture of hers when talking about the chuurkas, but this time she did nothing. *They're using you,* her silence said to him, words she'd spoken aloud several times. *They use all of us.* And she would spit—into the fire, into the canal, and once, into his face. Now, her silence said it all again.

Katja appeared in the doorway with the plates, sticks, and bottles. Gray had just begun to streak her long black hair. Mallon tried not to look at her left hand, but his gaze shifted to it anyway, to the stumps of her three severed fingers. As she approached the fire, he looked into her tensed, expressionless face; he could see the tiny, slashing white streaks in the shadows beneath her eyes, scars that had never quite cleared away. Mallon breathed deeply, trying to release a growing tightness in his chest.

Katja handed him a plate, a set of sticks, and a warm bottle of rice beer. She gave the same to Rhea, then sat with her own across the fire from Mallon, looking at him.

"It's good to see you again," she said.

Mallon nodded. "You're looking okay, Katja."

She gave a chopped laugh, shook her head. "I look like hell, but it's probably as good as I'll ever look again."

Rhea broke the fish apart in the pan, divided it into their plates. Mallon began eating with the sticks, lifting delicate chunks of the hot, white fish to his mouth, blowing on them, chewing and swallowing. The fish had practically no flavor.

No one spoke. The sun, low in the sky and slowly sinking, was distorted and colored orange by a thick haze, remnants of the overcast. Maybe he *should* take Rhea's unspoken advice, Mallon thought, forget the chuurkas, quit the current project he'd not yet quite begun. Stay here instead of going back to the room where they waited for him. Or leave the city, return to the mountains and isolation.

No, not this time. *This is it,* Sykora had told him. *They're bringing us in on the big one, the one we've been working for. Their big one, whatever the hell it is. Now we find out, I know it.* But Sykora hadn't shown at the building, and maybe he was dead. No way Mallon could back out now.

It was something he'd never been able to explain to Rhea,

something even Katja only partially understood—his obsession with the chuurkas, with trying to understand these alien beings, and his intense desire to learn what it was the chuurkas, all of them on different worlds, were after. Now, he no longer tried to explain.

The food and beer were gone; the fire smoldered, wisps of smoke drifting upwards, and the edge of the sun began to disappear behind the low buildings. Katja looked at him, said, "Are you staying here tonight?"

Mallon looked at her, didn't say anything at first. After all this time, despite everything that had happened between them, Katja would still take him to her for the night once again. Better for both of them that he couldn't stay.

He shook his head, slowly. "No. I have to leave now." He stood, set plate and sticks on the tree stump. "Thanks for the meal."

"Will you be gone long?" Rhea asked, looking not at him but into the glowing coals of the fire pit.

"Maybe," Mallon answered. "I don't know how long."

"Will you survive?" This time the old woman looked up at him, smiled crookedly. "Will you?"

Mallon smiled back, said, "Sure." But when he looked at Katja, *she* wasn't smiling, she wasn't looking at him at all.

The chuurkas were more animated when he returned to the room, their neck and head membranes fluttering; the green light on the tender's neck module blinked frantically as the two spoke to one another, but the tender remained silent, without expression.

Then the chuurkas became abruptly silent, turned to him. One began speaking again, and this time the tender, too, turned to him, and translated.

"It is time," she said. "Follow us."

The chuurkas, trailed by the tender, turned and started toward the side door, their gait, like their stance, awkward in appearance, though familiar to him now—a shift of weight to one side, that side's "knee" bent at an odd angle, then the other limb swinging out and forward, planting, ready for the process to begin again. Their gait should have been loud, noisy and clumping, but there was a deceptive grace and softness to it, and the chuurkas were actually far quieter than humans were as they moved.

Mallon followed them through the side door and into a high-ceilinged corridor lit by infrequent strips of pale red pulselights. The passage continued in a straight line for some distance, then angled to the right, ended. Another door was opened, this to a landing outside the building and a stairway leading to the roof. The chuurkas ascended the stairs, followed by their tender, and then Mallon.

On the roof, the chuurkas moved out near the center and stopped, silent. Mallon remained near the edge and looked out over the city, which was lit by fires, torches, clusters of electric colored lights, strings of massive pulsers. The noise had increased again with the darkness, and he could hear sporadic gunfire in the distance, an occasional explosion.

The city had been in a constant state of unrest for several years now, since the churrkas had arrived and settled in, appropriating whatever city resources they apparently needed for themselves. It had been expected, if not welcomed, a pattern that had been repeated in cities on half a dozen other worlds over the past few decades, ever since first contact had been made with the chuurkas. The fighting, disturbances, and occasional riots, which had become a regular part of life in the city, almost never involved the chuurkas themselves, but took place between those people who worked with, or for, the chuurkas, and those who worked against them. And after all these years, still no one knew what it was the chuurkas wanted, or what they seemed to be pursuing. Mallon hoped he would soon discover it for himself.

Someone tugged at his arm, and he turned to see the tender's wide eyes gazing up at him. He shuddered at their complete emptiness, an emptiness suggesting that no mind existed behind them any longer. The young girl gestured toward the two chuurkas, who were quietly talking to one another. They faced the east, membranes fully spread again.

Pale lights appeared in the sky, blinking green and blue, approaching. A few moments later, the sound of the driftship reached them, a fluttering pulse laced with a hollow whine. As the driftship approached, its size became clearer, growing, and Mallon backed away, closer to the roof's edge though he knew the vehicle would not land.

The driftship swerved around them and banked in toward the roof; the lights darkened a moment, then a crumping sound (implosion?) shuddered the air, caused a popping in Mallon's ears. The driftship halted, hovered motionless above the roof, lights blinking again.

Four large, basket-like bundles dropped from the ship, each connected to a lifeline. The two chuurkas and the tender each climbed into a basket, leaving one empty for Mallon. He approached the basket, stepped over the rim and settled into the flexible seat that adjusted to his body.

As the nearly solid gel-foam poured out from the basket's walls and began to encase him, Mallon fought down the panic, the fear of being unable to breathe that struck him each time he boarded a chuurka driftship. Light faded as the foam rose over his face. He closed his mouth, his eyes, and sleep (unconsciousness? induced coma? death?) overtook him, his last sensation the abrupt ascent as the basket retracted into the ship.

When he came to, the last of the gel-foam was receding, melting away from his legs and feet. The ship and baskets were gone, and Mallon was propped against a rock, slightly groggy. It was still dark, still night, but there was no way to know how long the trip had taken, nor how far they had traveled, and the chuurkas wouldn't tell him anything if he asked. They were outside the city, though, that much was clear—no buildings in sight, no lights, no sounds.

A few feet away, the two chuurkas were bent over the tender. Mallon approached, circled around them so he could see the girl. Her eyes were closed, and the two chuurkas were running their upper limbs across her body, prodding, pulling, checking the module at her neck. Mallon knelt beside the girl, put his fingers to her throat. There was still a pulse, and when he watched closely, he could see her chest rise and fall.

The churrkas stood, spoke with each other for a minute (the girl's module blinked steadily, but she didn't speak, didn't move at all), then they walked away, up a gentle slope of rock and dirt.

"What about the girl?" Mallon called, knowing the chuurkas wouldn't answer, wouldn't even turn around in response. They would leave her behind, let her die.

Mallon picked up the girl—she was small and light—draped her over his shoulder, and stood. The chuurkas were nearing the top of the rise, and Mallon started up after them, in no hurry. They needed him, they wouldn't leave him behind as they had the girl; if they got too far ahead, he would stop, and wait for them to come back to him.

The ground was uneven, rocky, but the sky was clear and there was enough light from the stars to make his way without stumbling. The girl was so light he hardly noticed her, and she didn't hinder his progress up the slope.

At the top of the rise he stopped and looked down the far slope, which led into a small valley; the descent would be steeper. Ahead and below, the chuurkas wound their way downhill through rock and squat bushes. Mallon thought he could see the outlines of a large, low, dark building at the base of the slope. No light emerged from it, no light reflected from its surfaces—it was a darker, blacker form against the lesser darkness of the valley floor. Mallon gently shifted the girl to his other shoulder, and started down.

The chuurkas waited for him at the bottom of the slope in front of the low structure. As he reached them, a wall panel slid quietly aside, and they all passed through the opening. The panel slid shut behind them, bringing darkness, as they stopped in front of another wall. After a few moments another panel slid open, letting in light, and they stepped into the building.

Inside, lit by patterned webs of glowing red overhead lights, a maze of corridors branched and curved in all directions away from them. A constant, faint hissing sound glided along the walls. Mallon, still carrying the girl, followed the two chuurkas into one of the corridors.

Though the walls were metal and smooth, the floor was of earth and rock, uneven beneath his feet. The chuurkas walked more quickly now, large limbs swinging, feet planting solidly and quietly, and Mallon had to strain to keep up. They shifted frequently from one corridor to another, and it wasn't long before Mallon felt completely lost, disoriented.

As they continued, Mallon began to realize that the building was enormous, probably built into and under the slopes of the valley. Occasionally they passed open chambers of different sizes, and inside some of them were other chuurkas, most working in near darkness. At one point, they passed a trio of chuurkas in the corridor, the three linked to one another by cables implanted in their spines.

The two chuurkas stopped in front of what appeared to be a blank wall, and one ran its long fingers across a strip of metal that changed color at the chuurka's touch—from steel-blue to deep amber. A wide door slid aside, and they passed through it into another passage, this one short, ending abruptly at the top of a stairway hewn from solid rock. Without a pause, they descended.

The steps were uneven, and their height made the descent

awkward for Mallon, especially with the girl over his shoulder. The chuurkas, though, were completely at ease, their movements smooth and graceful, almost gliding down the steps. The stairs curved gradually, then ended at a doorway that opened out into a room.

The room was enormous, a cavernous chamber filled with dark metal machinery, pulsing red light, a quiet thrum punctuated by loud clicking sounds, and clouds of swirling incense. A dozen chuurkas were in the chamber, working at the machinery, and several tenders moved among them, adjusting the incense burners, replenishing them. The ceiling, at least thirty or forty feet above, was barely visible through the clouds of incense that collected just beneath it.

One chuurka, larger and darker than the others, legs and trunk wrapped in a mesh of black leather dotted with tiny pouches, approached, trailed by a tender. The tender was a thin, full-grown woman who limped on a left leg distinctly shorter than the right. Mallon could see that her left arm, too, was shorter than the other. Even the left side of her face was somewhat deformed, the facial muscles tight and twisted, her left eye dull and clouded over.

The larger chuurka spoke, the two who had brought him here responded, and the three conversed for several minutes, producing a constant buzz of *chikking* sounds. Finally they stopped, the larger chuurka made a few more sounds, and the woman tender turned to Mallon, looked at him with her one good eye.

"Put the girl down," she said. "If she is still alive she will be recovered, cared for. You/we have other concerns now."

Mallon nodded, gently laid the girl on the ground at his feet; with the chuurkas, there was nothing more he could do. The three chuurkas and the woman tender started across the chamber, and Mallon followed.

They moved slowly through the rising, shifting columns of incense, past vibrating machinery and banks of glowing pale lights, mostly red and amber. The incense made him lightheaded, slightly nauseated, and Mallon tried to restrict his breathing to the pockets of fresh air between the burners.

In the far corner, fifteen-foot-high rock barriers, with a single opening, partitioned off a large section of the chamber. As the chuurkas and the tender passed through the opening, electricity crackled and sparked around them. Mallon hesitated, started forward, but felt only a slight tingling along his skin as he stepped through.

Inside was darker, though a pale glow from the rest of the chamber leaked over the walls. A tall, skeletal, cage-like structure of metal and cables rose from the center of the floor. Some of the cables curved down into the floor, while others snaked across the floor to a wall of more machinery. The two chuurkas who had brought him from the city approached the banks of machinery, began working at them. Panels of colored lights blinked on, monitors and displays of strange, oscillating glows came to life, a deep thrum shook the air; the cage-like structure began to vibrate, pulse with a pale glow.

The large, dark chuurka stood alone near the cage structure, turned to Mallon, spoke with the *chikking* sounds.

"Are you ready?" the woman tender translated.

"I don't know," Mallon answered, confused. "Am I?"

More sounds, then the woman spoke again. "No, of course not." She crossed to a set of plasteel cabinets, opened one and took out a shock suit; she handed it to Mallon. The chuurka resumed speaking, and the tender resumed translating.

"Put on the suit, you'll need it for protection from the fall," she said.

What fall? Mallon wanted to ask, but knew not to. The shock suit was light, the exterior lined with pockets along the trunk and all limbs; as he fit his legs and arms into it, sealed it along the seam from crotch to neck, the suit tightened, adjusted to his body. It was relatively thin as well as light, not at all bulky, but he knew it provided an astounding amount of protection. Mallon walked around the floor, getting used to the suit; he moved arms and legs, flexed elbows and knees, turned and twisted. The suit didn't impede his movement, and the snugness, the support, gave him the sensation of better body control, quicker reflexes, a bit more strength. He had worn shock suits twice before when working for the churrkas, and they always felt this way to him.

"You will wear the helmet during transport," the woman said. She held a helmet out to him, and he took it. As he listened to her speak, Mallon could almost block out the chuurka's sounds, could almost make himself believe the woman was speaking of her own volition, with words that originated in her own personal thoughts; he wondered if she had any now. "When you arrive, you will set the helmet's beacon, then hide it well. The suit is linked to it, will guide you back to your arrival/departure point.''

Mallon located the beacon switch, turned it on, then off. There was no seal on the helmet, no way to attach it to the suit, so it would be worn loose; he held the helmet at his side.

He listened carefully to the woman tender, aware that he would get information in bits and pieces, not necessarily in the most logical sequence, and knowing that they would not answer any questions.

''You will have forty-two hours after arrival before the shift-portal reappears for your return. We can maintain it only for ten to twelve minutes, and if you do not come through it, we will try once more an hour later. If you still do not come through, you will not have another chance.''

The chuurka, and the woman, paused a long time. Then the chuurka moved across the floor to the other two, spoke with them for a few minutes; the woman tender remained motionless, staring vacantly at Mallon. The chuurka returned, began a new string of *chikking* sounds, and the woman resumed speaking.

''The shiftportal will take you to a place. Where it is, on what world, we do not know. That is what we want you to learn for us. You will arrive inside a vast cavern, you will need to find a way to the outside, photograph the stars at night, do spectral analysis of the sun in the day, make other measurements as we request, bring all that information back to us. Or. Find some artifact, document, some remnant of this alien civilization that would indicate where in this galaxy this world lies.''

What alien civilization? Mallon wondered. Don't bother asking.

''The shiftportal will materialize within the cavern, but not within solid matter. We have little control over the height, so there will be a fall. Perhaps only half a meter, perhaps several. Note the height, because you will need to reach it to return. Simply pass through, you will return here.''

The more that was explained to him, the more risky and uncertain the whole thing became. Typical.

''There may be others in the cavern, also searching. You must eliminate them, they are working for rival . . .'' Here the tender stopped, her neck module apparently unable to translate —it blinked red now. The chuurka tried several new bursts of sound before the module blinked green again and the woman resumed. ''. . . rival sects. They will try to eliminate you as well. Do not hesitate.''

Others. Humans? Chuurkas? Both?

''In the shock suit, and in the backpack you will carry, will be all necessary equipment, weapons, instrumentation, food, tools. We will show you how to operate all items.''

A hollow pop sounded, followed by crisp, loud snapping sounds, interrupting chuurka and tender. A bright globe of white light appeared behind the chuurka, throwing the chuurka into silhouette, and Mallon stepped to the side to see a brilliant shimmering form pulsing within the cage. It hung in the air, undulating like a translucent, flexible mirror of light. Mallon thought he saw brief glimpses of his own reflection twisting and fading within it. The object (was it solid?) hovered a foot above the ground, twisting inside the cage; it was about five feet high, maybe three feet at its widest when, in its twisting, it momentarily flattened.

The chuurka spoke again, and the woman translated. ''This is the shiftportal,'' she said. ''It will be fully operational in an hour.''

Mallon gazed at the undulating light—it still seemed a mirror to him, or some strange and alien silver fish caught and, in slow motion, wriggling on its hook. *Simply pass through*, the chuurka/tender had said. He had no trouble believing it *could* transport him to another place, another world. Sykora was right, this was what they had been working for.

''An hour,'' the woman repeated. ''Until then, we will go over your equipment, the instruments and your weapons and supplies.''

Mallon broke his gaze from the shimmering mirror, turned to face the chuurka, and nodded.

Mallon stood before the cage, gazing at the shiftportal, the undulating and opaque reflecting mirror of white light waiting for him. Had the chuurkas built this themselves, or had they found it, an ''artifact'' of the alien civilization the chuurka had mentioned? Probably the latter, Mallon thought. The chuurkas seemed to have limited control over the mirror, and access only to the interior of the cavern. Otherwise, why not transport him directly to the world's surface?

The thrumming sound faded, became a soft, regular purr, and the shiftportal seemed to cease moving. But no, it hadn't stopped, not completely, Mallon realized. It continued to twist, but much more slowly now. As Mallon watched, he *did* see distorted reflections of himself in the mirror, incomplete and insubstantial.

The larger chuurka spoke, and the woman said, "It is operational. It is ready for you."

Mallon touched his hand to the packet of inhalers strapped to his side; he'd have to pop one as soon as he arrived, then activate another every eight hours to keep his lungs accommodated to the cavern air. He put the helmet on over his head, adjusted the fit and lowered the visor, leaving a narrow open strip for unobstructed breathing. Then he darkened the visor until he could see nothing but the pale shimmer of the mirror within the cage.

The chuurka spoke, and the tender said, "Down two more settings. The light will be blinding as you pass through."

Mallon darkened the visor again. The shiftportal was barely visible, a ghost in the night. He started toward it.

As he entered the cage, the glow brightened, and he felt the mirror pulling at him, like a vacuum. Mallon hesitated, forced himself to breathe deeply, slowly, fighting down panic. The fear gradually dissipated, leaking out of him, and he stepped forward again.

He took three more steps, the pull and brightness increasing with each. Then, as he started the next step, he was sucked off his feet, up and into an explosion of swirling white light.

A tremendous pressure enclosed his entire body, compacting him. Held him in stasis. No air in his lungs, all squeezed out. The light blazed, even through the darkened visor, and he closed his eyes, yet still saw a glow of white tinged red. His heart was crushed, strangely without pain.

Something struck him, and he felt himself popped out of the pressure and into freedom, out of light and into darkness.

Then he was falling.

Mallon was off balance, disoriented as he fell. He swung his arms out as he dropped, reaching, then a second or two later he hit the ground, feet first, then crumpling to hands and knees.

He was down. In. Somewhere.

Still disoriented, Mallon cleared his visor—the world remained black. He turned to look up, and in the darkness a few feet above him, the mirror hovered, barely moving. Remember the height, he told himself.

The mirror flickered once, twisted violently once, and disappeared. Everything was black again.

Mallon lay without moving, breathing deeply. The air was quite cold, breathable as the chuurkas had said, but something about it did feel, or smell, odd. He pulled off his helmet, snapped one of the inhalers from the packet, put his lips around the opening, and popped it, sucking in the rush of air and chemicals. When it was empty, he clipped it into a refuse pocket, and sat up.

He could see nothing. The sound of trickling water, faint and irregular, came from his left. The ground beneath him was hard and rough—dirt, gravel, stone. Mallon retrieved a small hand light from his hip pocket, switched on the narrow beam. All around him was more rock—jagged and dotted with reflecting crystals—and chunks of what looked like concrete, and formed stone, and a long strip of dulled metal. Low, thick patches of vegetation (moss? lichen?) lay across some of the larger rocks, a dark gray-green that was almost black.

Mallon stood, aimed the light farther away. The terrain, though uneven and broken by rocks and gullies, was relatively level and seemed to continue without end in all directions. No hills, no cavern walls. He turned the light up toward the cavern ceiling, but could see only empty air laced with reflecting dust; far, far above, the light beam seemed to simply disappear into the blackness.

He switched off the light, and with a sharp rock dug a hole in the dirt and gravel, up against a larger rock. He activated the silent, invisible beacon, detached it from the helmet and checked the suit's monitor, then buried the beacon, covering it with a layer of gravel and small stones. Mallon stood again, put the helmet back on, sliding up the visor, and looked around him, now without the light.

It was a strange, oppressive darkness, more than that of night because there were no stars, no clouds carrying traces of the day's light, no glow from city lights, no glow from a moon. Without boundaries—the darkness seemed to go on without end—yet closing in on him as if solid boundaries *were* there, only a few feet away, just beyond his vision. Still, something, somewhere, must have been a source of light, because the blackness was not quite complete. As his eyes adjusted, he *could* see—dark forms against dark forms—three or four feet in front of him.

But where the hell was he supposed to go?

He was reluctant to use the light, remembering what the chuurka had said about others in the cavern prepared to "eliminate" him. Mallon felt his way to the largest rock he'd seen, climbed it (it was only about six feet high); crouching atop it, he switched on the hand light again, swept it slowly in a full circle around him.

There was nothing new to be seen—uneven terrain that appeared to stretch out in all directions without end, clusters of concrete blocks, rocks and boulders of all sizes, tangled webs of twisted metal, all without apparent structure, without apparent pattern. He switched off the light, shifted from crouch to sitting position, legs dangling over the edge.

How the hell was he supposed to find a way out? And was this really a cavern? If so, it was enormous, almost beyond his comprehension. He would take the chuurkas at their word for now, but there seemed to be no ceiling above him, no cavern walls anywhere in sight; of course, there was no sky, either. How did the chuurkas know this was even a world somewhere, and not a . . . a what? Some *thing*, some *place* completely different from what anyone had ever seen before. Still, there was air, breathable air, so that was something.

Where to go. All directions seemed to be the same. He closed his eyes (why bother? he wondered), listened carefully. There were still no sounds but the distant, faint trickle of water. Water. Why not? Find it, and if it was a stream or river, follow it (up or down?), and maybe it would eventually lead to a way out.

Mallon stood again, slowly turned in a circle, listening, until he was fairly certain of which direction the trickling sounds came from. He started to climb down from the rock when a staccato burst of silent, incredibly bright flashes of light exploded far above, temporarily blinding him. He lost his balance and tumbled from the rock. As Mallon hit the ground another burst pummeled him, this time with sound and shock waves, vibrating him violently for a few brief moments.

Just as quickly, the lights and sounds were gone, leaving behind popping afterimages in his vision for a minute or two. Then the sparkling afterimages, too, gradually faded, and the darkness was once again complete.

Mallon got to his feet, looked up at the blackness above him. Nothing. Solid and empty as before. What the hell had done that?

It took several minutes more for his hearing to return to normal. Eventually he could make out the trickling water again, and, glancing occasionally at the blackness above, he started toward it.

He picked his way among large stones and shattered blocks of concrete, walking over sand at times, then gravel, and sometimes over the rock itself. Increasingly he came across twisted networks of jagged metal that had apparently once formed some kind of structures; metal beams, girders, tubes, and poles emerged from the ground or protruded from the concrete, and were cold and rough to the touch.

A new crunching sound began under his boots, and Mallon stopped, knelt, carefully picked up a handful of what felt like tiny bits of glass. He flicked on the hand light for a moment. It *was* glass, or something very much like glass, clear and broken into tiny pieces not much larger than coarse sand. The ground was carpeted with it for several feet in all directions before it gave way once more to gravel and rock. Mallon turned off the light, rose to his feet, and continued on.

He listened for the water, and hiked through the darkness, his mind filled with questions, more questions all the time. Too many, with no answers, and too few guesses. His thoughts became almost chaotic, a jumble of questions and speculations without control or order.

Why didn't the chuurkas come here themselves? Too dangerous here in the cavern? Or maybe the shiftportal itself was dangerous to them. Were they sending "expendable" humans, like sending out unmanned, automated exploratory probes to other worlds?

And what was at stake here, what were they after? Alien technology? What were rival "sects" fighting over, and why? And this alien civilization, was it extinct? Gone, to some other part of the galaxy? Or still on this world, somewhere? Still in this enormous cavern? Hidden? Dormant?

Why had the chuurkas sent him here with so little knowledge, so little instruction, so little help? And why send him into the middle of nothing, with what seemed like no chance at all to find a way out, if there *was* a way out? Maybe they didn't know that much to tell him. And maybe they had no choice over where they sent him.

Questions, and really no answers. And the biggest question of all: What *was* this place? No answer to that, either. Mallon tried to forget all the questions, all the doubts and uncertainties, and concentrate on his march through the darkness. That was all he really had now to hang onto, a search for a way out and, he hoped, return.

He had no idea how long he'd been walking when he finally found the stream. Actually, it was hardly even a stream—just a few inches wide, an inch or two deep, twisting and curving through the rocks. Still, it was something, it led somewhere, and Mallon decided to follow it, downstream.

Nothing changed much as he walked on. He saw nothing except more rock, more concrete, more metal, and large stretches of shattered glass, so much in spots that it seemed as if there had once been huge structures built all of glass which now lay in ruins all about him.

The longer Mallon hiked on, the more insane it seemed to him to continue. He was learning nothing, finding nothing, and, as far as he knew, going nowhere. Maybe he'd be better off dropping the whole thing, just lock on now and return to the beacon, then wait for the shiftportal to take him back.

But that wasn't why he was here, he didn't work with the chuurkas to take the safe way out of everything; he'd never learn what this was all about that way. What could he do, really, but go on? Mallon continued marching, following the stream, picking his way slowly through the ruins.

The stream of water swirled around a stone, poured down into a hole in the ground, and disappeared. Mallon knelt beside the opening and watched the water, his only guide, vanish. Jesus. This whole thing *was* insane.

He stood, listened to see if he could hear more water. Maybe the stream reappeared somewhere nearby, and he could pick it up again. He could hear nothing but the trickling of the water at his feet.

Mallon started away from the hole, picked his way back and forth through the rock and metal and glass; he'd make a thorough, patterned search for the reappearance of the stream. He had to find it, or he *would* be better off returning to his arrival point. Without at least the stream for guidance he would be wandering aimlessly through the dark. Or, he thought, he'd have to reverse himself, try following the water *up*stream, to its source.

Mallon stepped around a large, misshapen chunk of fused

metal, stopped. The vague form of a motionless, outstretched hand was visible just a foot or two to his left. Mallon stepped closer, and the rest of the body came into dim view: sprawled face-up across a flat rock, immobile, lips frozen in a grimace, eyes open and staring sightlessly at the blackness above. It was Sykora.

Mallon reached out, touched the old man's shoulder. He had known Sykora for years. They had worked together several times for the chuurkas, and they had become friends of a sort. Mallon wondered what had killed him.

Sykora's arm moved, the hand clamped Mallon's wrist, and Sykora pulled himself upright, grabbing at Mallon's head with his other hand, making choking sounds deep in his throat.

Mallon pulled back, twisting away and falling to the ground, but Sykora held on, landed on top of him and grabbed Mallon's hair, wedging his hand inside the helmet.

"Sykora! It's me, Mallon!"

Mallon tried to roll away, throw Sykora off balance. The old man wouldn't shake loose, kept his grip on Mallon's wrist, on Mallon's hair, tried banging Mallon's head against the ground.

"Sykora, don't you recognize me? Jesus!"

Sykora hesitated, lifted Mallon's head, then brought his own face down close and stared into Mallon's eyes.

"Mallon?"

"Yes, *Mallon* for Christ's sake."

The old man continued to stare. "Mallon?" he asked again. "Mallon?"

"Yes."

Sykora pulled his face back, released Mallon's hair and freed his hand from inside Mallon's helmet. "Mallon," he said one more time. "I know you."

"Of course you know me."

Sykora clambered off, stepped back a few feet, sat on the rock where Mallon had found him; his breath was rapid, deep, and harsh. Mallon sat up, watching the old man, prepared for another attack. Sykora's feet, Mallon now saw, were bare, and he wore only a light shirt and trousers.

"It's not so clear," Sykora said. "I need . . ." He held out his hand, made squeezing motions, ". . . inhalers," he finally said. "Air is funny here, I can't always . . . think."

Mallon touched the packet on his shock suit, counted the inhalers, made some mental calculations. He'd pop the last one two hours before he returned; if he held off a half hour on each, he could spare the last. He unclipped one of the inhalers, held it out toward the old man. "Here," he said.

Sykora stared at the inhaler a long time, then shook his head. "No, I can't. Probably too late. I know you. Mallon? Yes. Why are you here?"

"Why are *you?*"

"I'm dreaming. The chuurkas sent me . . . here? Now, dreaming. I'll wake up when the lights come on. The lights will come on in here, but it will still be night."

"What happened to your shock suit? Your boots? You did have them, didn't you?"

Sykora grinned, closed his eyes. "Sure. I got a crazy idea, took off the boots, took off the suit. I don't know where I put them. It's damn cold in here." He began to hug himself.

Mallon didn't know what to do about Sykora. Could he take the old man back through the shiftportal? Maybe, but what was he going to do with him until then? Sykora was a little out of control.

"How long have you been here?" Mallon asked.

Sykora shrugged, opened his eyes, shook his head. "Too long. The air . . ." He didn't finish.

"Sykora, is there a way out of here? Out of this cavern?"

Sykora nodded. "Through the fish-mirror. I couldn't get back to it, something happened, I got . . ." Again he couldn't finish, shrugged.

"No, is there *another* way? To the outside?"

"Maybe. I couldn't find it. Wait until the lights come on, maybe you can find it then, wake up from your dream. *My* dream."

Mallon shook his head. He looked at the inhaler still in his hand, held it out again to Sykora. Maybe it would help, bring some coherence to the old man's rambling, help him gain control. "Here," he said. "Please, Sykora, take it, I can spare it."

This time Sykora took the inhaler. He stared at it for a minute, then threw it at Mallon's head. Mallon instinctively ducked, heard the inhaler clatter on the rocks behind him. The old man sobbed once, then darted into the darkness; almost immediately, he was gone from sight.

Mallon hesitated a moment, then ran after him, guided by sound—gravel or glass crunching (cutting Sykora's bare feet?); rocks clicking; the occasional ring of metal; once, the splash of water. Mallon stumbled through the dark, unable to see any-thing, hand out to keep from crashing into something large and solid; the shock suit protected his shins and knees as he struck smaller rocks and blocks of concrete.

But the sounds grew fainter, more distant, and within a few minutes faded completely. Mallon halted, listened. He heard nothing but his own harsh breath, and the quiet trickle of water. He remained motionless, resting, and continued to listen. Noth-ing. Sykora was gone, or holed up nearby, impossible to find.

A long, low moaning sound began, apparently from far away. It slowly, steadily grew louder, rolling through the cav-ern. Like a monstrous foghorn, the sound surrounded him, swept over him. A stiff bitter wind shook his body. Then sound and wind rushed past and released him, trailing dull echoes that grew fainter, farther apart. Then silence again, except for the bubbling of water.

What was going on in this place?

Mallon remained motionless a while longer, listening again for Sykora, hoping the old man would still be nearby, or inad-vertently circling back. Nothing.

He knew he should go back, find the inhaler Sykora threw at him. He might need it later. And he needed to find the water again. Mallon homed in on the sound of the stream, turned, and started toward it.

And then, just as Sykora had said—the air remaining dark and black—lights came on, from far away, and from beneath the ground.

The cavern was still dark, but now like a sparsely populated city at night with scattered, wide beams of light rising from the ground like immobile searchlights. Mallon climbed a rock, and could now see, though dimly, quite a ways in all directions.

The lights were far apart from one another, several miles, probably, but they revealed the vastness of the cavern, or at least hinted at it. Now more than ever the cavern seemed to stretch on and on without end as far as he could see, the dark-ness broken irregularly by one beam of light after another, mile after mile. The beams of light, sometimes broken with shadow, rose at different angles toward the upper reaches, then disap-peared, swallowed by the darkness far above—there was still no ceiling to see.

There was enough light now, reflected from stone and metal

and glass, for Mallon to make his way, but it definitely *was* still night, as Sykora had said, and all around him were the dark, indistinct forms of the ruins of this place. The looming, immobile shapes and shadows were almost more disconcerting than the total darkness had been.

These *were* ruins, almost surely, but was this a world? Able to see more, now, there were other possibilities—the interior of a vast starship; a self-contained habitat orbiting a planet, a sun, or a moon; or something quite incomprehensible.

He climbed down from the rock and started back toward the stream. When he reached the hole in the ground through which the stream disappeared, he began to search for the inhaler.

After a while, using the hand light in short bursts, he thought he found the rock where Sykora had lain, and he searched the area more closely. He crawled on hands and knees over the rock and gravel and sprays of shattered glass, looked into crevices, gaps between rocks, felt along ridges of concrete and metal. There was no sign of the inhaler.

Eventually he gave up, returned to the stream. He had a decision to make again, but now there were more options: return to the beacon and wait, follow the water upstream to its source and hope to find a way out of the cavern, or head for one of the lights shining up from the ground.

An easy decision, really. Mallon turned toward the nearest of the lights, a mile or so away, and started off toward it.

It took Mallon more than an hour to reach the light, fifteen minutes just to cover the last hundred feet through a jungle of twisted metal, tangled and webbed with broken cable, coils of frayed wire, large shards of broken glass. As he worked his way closer, everything grew steadily brighter; the light rising from below reflected in all directions from the metal and glass, adding and canceling, casting distorted shadows and angled streams of light all about him. Large crystals attached to some of the metal girders reflected prismatic colors as he moved past.

Mallon climbed onto an enormous block of concrete with metal posts jutting from it, and came to the edge of a large, well-like hole in the ruins, the full blaze of light rising up through it. He kept a foot or so back, lowered the visor, darkened it several settings. Mallon inched toward the edge, and looked down.

Thirty or forty feet below him, bright even through the darkened visor, was a huge round disk of light, a gently curved partial globe embedded in a solid black substance. Sprawled across the light, covering less than half its diameter, lay the prone, motionless body of a chuurka. The light shined a bright orange through the thin, fully spread membranes, revealing the complex patterns of dark receptors.

Mallon leaned back and sat, propped against one of the metal posts; he cleared the visor, gazed up at the dark void above, which seemed to swallow all the light rising up from below him.

He felt suddenly very tired, and now didn't want to move at all anymore. What was there to do anyway? He thought about making a descent to the light and the body of the chuurka; there were enough hand and footholds so it shouldn't be too difficult.

Still sitting, he leaned forward, darkened the visor and again looked down at the light and the dead chuurka. There might be something down there, something worth finding, something about the light. Mallon stood, breathed deeply, prepared to descend.

The light went out.

All the lights in the cavern went out, and the blackness, darker than night, returned again.

Vision gone, Mallon lost his balance. He felt himself tipping forward, flung his hands out, struck one of the metal posts and grabbed it. His feet slid across the concrete, went out from under him and he collapsed, but he hung onto the post somehow. He pulled, grabbed it with his other hand, then dragged himself back from the edge.

He remained motionless, holding onto the post with both hands. When he felt secure, he let go with one hand, slid the darkened visor up, then struggled to his feet. He still didn't go anywhere, waited a few minutes for his eyes to readjust to the darkness.

New sounds drifted through the darkness—the crunch of gravel and glass; the clatter of stones; something that sounded like whispers, hushed voices. The sounds faded in and out, seemed to come from two or three directions at once, but were definitely getting closer, converging.

Mallon crouched within the jumble of metal posts, hiding in case they used a light. The sounds continued to come nearer, then several minutes later the footsteps ceased, though the hushed whispers, broken by full voices occasionally, continued. A few moments later a flickering glow appeared about a hundred and fifty, two hundred feet away, a red-orange in color from a source at ground level, hidden by rock. A fire? What would burn here? Or was it something else?

Mallon crept forward, careful with each step to remain quiet, making sure each handhold was secure, his footing solid. The closer he got to the glow, the more it looked like it did come from a fire. Then he began to smell cooking meat.

Suddenly hungry, his stomach reacted immediately with a hollow pain. He had plenty of food in the suit, but hadn't once thought of eating until now.

He continued forward. The shadowed figures of people sitting around a fire came into view. Mallon made a wide approach until he found a spot no more than thirty feet away that gave him a full view of the fire and the people around it.

There were seven figures altogether—two women (one obviously pregnant), four men, and a tall, skinny girl naked from the waist up, probably fourteen or fifteen years old; the girl had the look of a chuurka tender, though there was no chuurka in sight. One of the men wore a torn shock suit, the woman who wasn't pregnant wore the sleeveless upper half of another shock suit, and the rest were dressed in worn clothing.

Mallon could hear them talking to each other, sometimes in whispers, more often in low voices. The fire came from the smooth surface of a black metal box, but there was no wood, no apparent fuel, as if the fire burned only air. A large kettle hung from a tripod over the flames. The people passed a wide-mouth cylinder among themselves; all drank from it except the girl.

Mallon heard something behind him. He started to turn, but someone was on him before he could move, one arm around his shoulder and chest and, incredibly, a knife inside the helmet and touching his neck.

"Don't," a harsh voice whispered at him. "Don't . . . do . . . anything."

The man's hand wasn't steady, and Mallon could feel the knife blade make tiny slices in the skin just under his chin. He remained motionless and, despite the crashing of his heart against his chest, spoke to the man in a calm voice.

"You're cutting me," he said.

He felt the blade ease back a bit, but the knife remained in under the helmet collar.

"To . . . your . . . feet," the man hissed.

Mallon rose slowly, the blade nicking skin twice as the man rose with him.

"To the . . . f-f-f-fire." The man made a choking sound, then a sob, and pushed Mallon forward.

Most of those around the fire looked up as Mallon and his captor staggered into the small clearing; but the pregnant woman glanced quickly at him, then looked away, while the young girl seemed oblivious to everything around her. The man wearing the torn shock suit shook his head, set the cylinder on the ground at his feet.

"Let the man go, Tyrone."

The man's grip on Mallon tightened, and the knife sliced skin once more.

"Tyrone."

Tyrone abruptly released Mallon, jerked the knife away (making one final cut across Mallon's chin), and made another choking sound. "Stick it," he whispered. "Just . . . stick it." He turned to Mallon, glared at him, held the knife up to his face. Tyrone grabbed the knife blade with his free hand, gripped it tightly, then slowly pulled the blade out of his grip. He opened the hand, which now bled from deep cuts in the palm and fingers (there were a number of scars on the skin), wiped his hand across the side of Mallon's helmet and the shoulder of his shock suit. Then Tyrone twisted away and, with a pained sob, ran off into the darkness.

"Your name."

Mallon turned back toward those around the fire. None of them had moved. "Mallon," he said.

The man in the shock suit nodded. "Mallon. New in here, aren't you?"

It seemed such a casual question, but a tightening in his chest warned him that the answer was probably important. He tried not to hesitate too long, thoughts working.

"Not really," he said. "A few days."

The man laughed, then shook his head. "A few days," he said. "Then you've been stranded here."

Mallon breathed very deeply, nodded once. "Yes."

The man didn't say anything at first, head cocked slightly. Then, "You *are* new though. A few days." Shook his head again. "I've been here a few years."

Mallon looked more closely at the man, then at the others. Years? Was it possible?

"My name's Rugger," the man said. "That's Charl." Nodding at the balding man on his left. "Trask." A gesture at the man nearest Mallon, who had to turn to see him, and who looked at him through eyes almost completely closed. "Ashley." The woman on Rugger's right wearing the partial shock suit. "Bollondi." The man next to her. "Lisa." The pregnant woman. "And the girl. We don't know her name. She's a tender, Trask found her beside a dead chuurka about two years ago."

"You!" It was the woman, Ashley, who spoke. She smiled. "I know about you." She nodded slowly, still smiling, but didn't say anything more. Mallon was certain he didn't know her.

"Sit down," Rugger said. "Join us. Maybe you'll join us on a more permanent basis. Tough to make it in here on your own." He waved at a flat stone between Trask and Charl.

Mallon sat, questions surfacing, though none he felt comfortable asking, at least not yet.

"You found us at a good time," Rugger said. "Most of us are somewhat lucid, though that's likely to change soon. You've noticed it by now, I imagine. The air."

"Yes," Mallon said, remembering Sykora. "It comes and goes. Sometimes I don't really know what I'm doing."

Rugger nodded. "You'll get used to it after a few weeks, a few months." He picked up the cylinder, sipped at it, passed it to Charl. "If you live that long."

Charl drank from the cylinder, handed it to Mallon without a word. Mallon passed it to Trask without drinking.

"It helps," Trask said, holding it back out to Mallon. Helps what? Mallon wondered. He shook his head. Trask shrugged, drank, then got up and took it over to Lisa, who still looked away from the fire, away from Mallon, maybe away from all the others.

No one spoke for a long time. Bollondi watched the food cooking in the kettle, stirring it occasionally with a plastic stick. Mallon watched, wondering where the food had come from, wondering how the black box produced the fire. Was the black box a remnant of the alien technology, the kind of thing the chuurkas were looking for?

Next to him, Charl began to visibly tremble, then began pounding his thigh with his fist, each blow accompanied by a stifled gasp. He was staring at the girl, grinding his teeth now, lips pulled back in a grimace.

Charl stood with a hushed cry, seemed to calm down a little. He nodded once, then walked silently around the fire to the girl.

He took her hand, tried to pull her to her feet, but Lisa got up and grabbed his wrist. She jerked at it, hitting him with her other hand, slapping him across the face and arm until he finally let the girl go.

Charl stood looking at the girl and Lisa, put his hand into his trousers, working at his crotch. He whimpered once and staggered back, then he turned and lurched slowly away into the darkness.

The girl had remained motionless, without expression, and now Lisa sat back down beside her, crying for some reason. Still crying, she gently stroked the girl's hair, and murmured quietly into her ear.

"Food's ready," Bollondi said.

Ashley dragged a pack out from behind her, began removing plastic plates from it. Rugger stood, looking intently at Mallon.

"Let's go talk," Rugger said. "I'm not that hungry." He started walking away from the fire. Mallon got up and followed him.

"Hey, Mr. New Man Mallon," Ashley called after him. "Remember, I know about you."

Mallon looked back at her, but she was busy passing out the plates to the others, and he continued after Rugger.

Rugger stopped about twenty-five or thirty feet from the fire, far enough so their conversation would not be overheard, close enough to keep everyone in sight. He found a low, flat block of concrete, sat. Mallon leaned against another concrete block, but remained standing.

"We all have lucid periods," Rugger said. "Regularly. I just happen to be the lucid one now. And Ashley, though sometimes it's hard to know with her."

"What was she talking about?" Mallon asked. "That she knew about me. I don't know her at all. I'm sure I've never seen her before."

Rugger smiled. "Probably she meant she knew what *I* know about you. That you were lying. About being stranded." He leaned forward, reached toward Mallon, touched the packet of inhalers. "Only two gone, which means you've been here something under sixteen hours."

Even less, Mallon thought, but he didn't tell Rugger about the inhaler he'd lost. He wondered if he was due to pop another. He didn't want to check the time, though. Not yet. "How long have *you* been here?" he asked.

Rugger's smile faded. "Difficult to know for sure, but I think about four and half years. I was one of the first ones the chuurkas sent here. Of course I don't even know which faction sent me. There appear to be quite a few." He turned to look at the people sitting around the fire. "All of them have been in at least a year, most longer."

Four and a half years? In this place? Jesus. Mallon looked at Rugger, all the questions still rising into his thoughts, and he finally asked the one he could not ignore.

"Is there a way out of here?"

Rugger turned back to him, laughing harshly. "No." He shook his head, still smiling. "I've never seen one. No one I've ever met in all these years has ever found one, or heard of one. This place doesn't end, it just goes on and on, and there's no way out, there's only . . ." He paused, smile gone again. "There's only going *back*, through the portal. And for those of us stranded here, there's not even that."

Was that resentment in Rugger's voice? Mallon would have been surprised if it wasn't. Four and a half years.

"Do you suppose the chuurkas know that?" Mallon asked. "That there's no way out of here?"

"Probably." Rugger shrugged. "Doesn't matter much, not to them, though I'm sure they *would* like to know where in the universe this place exists. But that's not really what they're after."

"What *are* they after, then?"

Rugger gave him a half smile, said nothing for a minute or so. Then, "Maybe you'll find out before you go back. It hasn't happened in a long time, so it's overdue." He didn't say any more.

Overdue. Mallon couldn't ignore it any longer, and he checked the chronometer. It had been almost nine hours now since he'd arrived. He glanced at Rugger, shrugged to himself, then took one of the inhalers, brought it to his mouth and popped it. Rugger laughed again, quietly.

"Yeah, you keep taking those things," he said. "You get too much of this air, go a little off-line, and you might forget to ever take another, might forget about your beacon, the portal, might forget to go back. It's happened. Almost everything has happened in here." He shook his head. "This damn air, the things it does." He gestured toward the fire. "We stick together, because almost always at least one of us, and usually two or three, is lucid at any given time, manages to keep things under control. Even when we're *not* lucid, we usually know enough to recognize those who *are*, and do what they say, even if we don't understand it or want to. Like Tyrone, when I told him to let you go. He wanted to cut your throat, wanted to very badly, but he did what I asked. We all do. Survival instinct, I guess. It's what's kept us alive." He shook his head again. "Though it doesn't always work out. We were better off a while ago." He turned back to Mallon.

"We were living in a good place for a long time, close to two years, I think. It was a cave, though not a natural cave, something formed out of rock by machines. It was warm, safe and secure, close to a brook, near a steady food supply. Everything we needed." Rugger paused, sighed heavily. "One day, I guess we all went crazy together, *no* one was lucid, and we all left, started wandering around. Wandered a long time, a long ways, before one of us came around, Lisa I think, and tried to get us searching for a way back to it." Another pause. "We lost one of us, Cheyenne, don't know what happened to her. Never found her, and never found the cave. We've never been able to find our way back, but we keep searching." Rugger tried to smile, didn't quite manage it, then shrugged.

"I was wondering about the food," Mallon said. "Where do you get it? And you were near a steady supply once?"

Rugger pushed abruptly to his feet, took a step toward Mallon, face tightening. "What the hell do you think I am, a goddamn information service? Maybe if you get stranded here yourself, and we meet again, *then* maybe we'll tell you. Maybe. Until then, though, you don't really have to worry about anything like that, do you?" Rugger started pacing back and forth, growing angrier. "And since you *are* going back, I'm not about to give you even the slightest bit of information that might help the chuurkas, nothing that will help those obscene creatures who keep sending more people here, either to quickly die or spend the rest of their lives mostly crazy and wandering through this godforsaken place, struggling just to survive. No, I'll tell you *nothing!*"

He stopped, pointed back at the fire.

"You see Lisa there? She's been here almost as long as I have. Eight months along, and this is the fifth time she's been pregnant. Three early miscarriages, one other carried to full term. The baby was dead at birth, and this one will be, too. They *all* die here before birth." He paused, took several deep breaths, and appeared to calm down. "Probably better that way. Still, imagine what it does to the women." He slowly shook his head, not looking at Mallon, and sat down again.

"I wonder why they don't come here themselves," Mallon said. "The chuurkas. Why keep sending more humans if this is so important to them?"

"A few *have* come here," Rugger said. "Pilgrims."

"Pilgrims?"

Rugger nodded, but didn't explain. He shrugged. "They've always been cautious. This place, I think, is more dangerous to them than it is to us. Besides, we're expendable." He looked at Mallon, smiled. "Or haven't you figured that out yet?" He shrugged again, with what was becoming a frequent, exaggerated gesture. "Still, you're working for them yet. We all did at one time. But none of us do any longer." He turned away again and looked at the fire.

They remained there without talking for a long time. Charl reappeared, but refused to eat the food Bollondi offered to him, sat huddled against a rock a few feet back from the fire. Lisa got up, walked over and began slapping him until Ashley said something, then Lisa returned to her seat, began feeding the girl.

"You didn't bring any cigarettes, did you?" Rugger asked.

"No. I don't smoke."

"Coffee?"

"No. All I've got are the food packets, water, some juice I think. You want any of that?"

Rugger shook his head. The silence between them returned. Mallon still wanted to ask him more questions, but the tension had eased now, and he wanted to keep it that way, so he restrained himself.

Somebody near the fire shouted, and Bollondi threw the kettle across the clearing, food and liquid spraying. Trask stood and shook his fist at Bollondi, then Ashley got to her feet and stepped between them. She spoke quietly to each of them, and eventually Trask retreated, picked up the empty kettle and brought it to Bollondi. Bollondi took it, then squatted beside the fire and began cleaning it with gravel.

"You should probably go soon," Rugger said. "Before one or more of the others figure you, realize you're a way out."

"A way out?"

"Sure. Kill you, use your suit monitor to track your beacon, wait for the portal to reappear, go back in your place."

"You don't have to kill me," Mallon said. "I'll take you back to the beacon, all of you, and we can all go back through."

Rugger shook his head. "Doesn't work that way. It's been tried. The portal closes down right after the first one goes through. I've seen it tried with several people holding hands, in a chain. Portal closed down after the first, slicing off the hand of the second where it was holding the first person. She bled to death." He paused. "I've thought a lot about it, when I've been able to. I can think of only one thing that might work to take *two* people through, though I've never seen it tried. There aren't really that many opportunities." He stopped, looked at Mallon, but didn't go on.

"How?" Mallon asked.

"How what?"

"How can two people go through?"

"Oh. Sorry. I don't know for sure, remember. I've thought about it, though. Maybe if one is carrying the other, on his back or in his arms, like that. So it's a single unit going through. But even then, who knows? Who knows anything in this damn place."

"Come back with me, then," Mallon said. "We'll go through together."

Rugger shook his head. "I can't. I can't leave them. We help each other. The chuurkas have abandoned us here, but we can't do that to each other. *I* can't." He smiled. "Besides, I'd probably try to kill you on the way back to the beacon, or while we were waiting for the portal. I'm not going to stay lucid forever, remember? Hell, I'd probably kill you, then forget why, or what I was doing, and miss out on the portal anyway." He shook his head.

"Maybe Lisa," Mallon suggested. "Or one of the others?" But he knew it was a bad suggestion as soon as he made it.

"No," Rugger said. "You'd just better go. Now."

Mallon nodded, pushed away from the concrete. He was reluctant to leave, but he knew he should. "Good-bye, Rugger."

"Good-bye, Mallon." He was looking toward the fire again.

Mallon took a few steps back from Rugger, then turned and started walking away. When he heard the rushed footsteps behind him, he was ready, not at all surprised.

Mallon quickly turned and dropped to a crouch, easily

avoiding the oncoming knife in Rugger's hand; he kicked Rugger's legs out from under him, using Rugger's own momentum. Rugger fell to the ground, then Mallon was up and straddling him, pinning Rugger's arms to the gravel. Rugger released the knife, smiling.

"Good," Rugger said. "You didn't trust me, even now." He stopped smiling. "Go now, Mallon. While I'm still being generous. I'll be all right for a while longer, I think."

Mallon clipped the knife to Rugger's shock suit, got up and stood over him for a few moments. Then he nodded and backed quickly away, quiet and cautious. Listening and watching for the others as well as Rugger, he felt his way along, walking backwards, losing sight of first Rugger, then the fire, and finally, when he could no longer hear a thing, he turned and pushed off into the darkness.

It was a half hour, maybe longer, before Mallon felt relatively safe again. He had no idea where he was anymore, and he didn't really care. He stumbled along, paying little attention to his surroundings. He could be traveling in circles, for all he knew. It didn't seem to matter. If it became necessary, he reminded himself, the beacon would lead him back.

Mallon was tired, depressed. He felt sick when he thought about Rugger and his companions, sick when he tried to imagine how many others like them were stranded here in this endless night, and how many had already died. All of them with no way out.

And for what?

He still didn't know.

For hours he wandered through the dark without direction, without purpose. Once, the lights came on again for a little more than an hour, but the night did not leave, and the rising beams that cut such small sections out of the darkness, seemed weak and futile.

He came across several trickles of water, including one that actually could be called a stream—nearly two feet wide, almost a foot deep. He crouched beside the stream (all the lights were out again), switched on the hand light, and directed the beam down through the clear water. Mallon remained there a long time, staring at the water flowing through the light, searching for fish, or insects, or other tiny creatures, any signs of life at all in the water.

But there was nothing.

At seventeen hours inside the cavern, Mallon popped the next inhaler, thinking of what the air could do to him, of what it had done to others—Sykora babbling away, hardly recognizing him; Tyrone gripping the knife blade with his own hand, slicing it deep; Charl trying to take the girl, then lurching off into the darkness.

And then, for the first time since he'd been here in the dark, not quite understanding the connection, he thought of Katja, and the tiny scars below her eyes, her screams (which he had never heard, but had often imagined) as her fingers had been severed.

After all these months, he still did not know what had happened to her—neither Katja nor Rhea would say a word to him about it. It had to do with the chuurkas, he knew that for certain, but whether the chuurkas had done it to her themselves (why?), or someone else had done it as some kind of punishment, he had never known. Once Katja no longer worked for the chuurkas, she had pleaded with Mallon to quit, too. When he didn't, she still forgave him. She would have forgiven him anything. That was a gift he had never appreciated.

Mallon wasn't so sure he understood any of this anymore, and he wondered what the hell he was doing here. He sat on the ground, his back against a warped sheet of cold, damp metal, removed the helmet, and rested his head in his hands. He didn't move.

Mallon was walking again, still wandering aimlessly, when the sky opened up above him and filled with stars.

He looked up, stunned, and nearly lost his balance. The complete blackness was gone, the ceiling—if there had ever been one—was gone, all replaced by a dazzling night sky filled with brilliant stars shining down on him.

Mallon stared, and stared, turning slowly in place, gazing at the hundreds, thousands of stars above and all around him. It seemed that he was outside now, nightside on a world with the cleanest, purest atmosphere, the stars almost painfully sharp and clear against the blackest of skies.

It was beautiful, unlike any night sky he'd ever seen. Not one of the stars flickered; their light blazed steadily at him without interference, without filtering, undiminished and untouched. He smiled, wonder and contentment welling in his chest, spreading through him. *This* was something worth coming for.

Coming for. He remembered the chuurkas, and why he was here—almost as an afterthought. Hardly thinking about it, Mallon unclipped the backpack, shrugged it off, laid it on the ground and opened it. In something of a daze, he began removing equipment, emptying the pack and most of the pockets lining his shock suit.

Mallon put the equipment together as the chuurkas had shown him. A few instruments he recognized or understood—still and motion film cameras, radiometers—but most were complete mysteries, and he knew only that they were detectors of some sort. What amazed him was how small some of them were, and how large others became when constructed—fan-like arrays of thin, membranous materials; patterned networks of wire; clusters of weaving, flexible projections. Who knew what they detected or measured?

Just as surprising was how easily and quickly everything assembled. Most of the equipment, self-powered, assembled automatically, and all Mallon had to do was flip the toggles or switches that set the process in motion.

In just over fifteen minutes, he had all the equipment assembled; it took only another five to position everything as indicated on the diagram the chuurkas had included, and then he was ready. Mallon went from apparatus to apparatus, starting each one, watching tiny lights come on, listening to faint clicks and buzzes begin. From now on, everything would operate automatically, and he had nothing to do but watch.

When Mallon looked up at the sky again, the stars were moving.

The movement was slow and regular, and after a minute or so Mallon realized the stars were rotating, uniformly turning around a point almost directly overhead. It was disorienting at first, and he felt slightly dizzy, legs wobbly, but gradually he grew accustomed to the motion, and his stability returned.

Mallon stood motionless among the machines, the nearly silent instruments laid out on all sides, and gazed up at the stars slowly turning above him. There was no sound anywhere except for the quiet clicks and whirs of the instruments, which he hardly noticed anymore, but he thought he could imagine what sounds these stars *would* make as they moved gracefully across the sky—something delicate and elegant, whispers of sound, soft and peaceful. Music of the spheres. An ancient phrase he felt he was only now beginning to understand.

But then the movement of the stars gradually, yet noticeably, accelerated. As the stars began to rotate more rapidly overhead, Mallon once again had trouble maintaining his balance and orientation; he staggered, and almost fell. He gave up and sat on the ground, found a place where he could rest his back against a low, slanting rock. Half lying, half sitting, and with the cold, hard feel of stone anchoring him, Mallon continued to watch.

The stars were not really moving *that* quickly, Mallon realized, just enough now to make a complete circuit every two minutes, like a half-speed sweep of a second hand on a conventional watch or clock. The stars maintained a steady speed for several more minutes, mesmerizing him; then they began to move gradually inward with the rotation and became a slow motion vortex in the night.

The stars, spiraling slowly inward, collected at the center of the vortex, and a tiny globe of light grew, increasing in size and brightness with each star that joined it.

The globe continued to grow, adding star after star, and continued to brighten. After some time (how long?), the globe was so bright that Mallon dropped the helmet visor over his face, darkened it two settings.

The globe was now the size of a large moon in the sky, spinning slowly, he thought, matching the rotation of the thousands of stars still turning about it and spiraling inward. Every three or four minutes now Mallon darkened his visor another setting until eventually, though the globe remained bright and swelling above him, he could hardly see the stars spinning about it.

When the globe was so large that it filled half the sky, and his visor darkened to the point where he could no longer see the stars around it, the globe of light began to pulse.

Mallon could actually feel the pulsing of the globe. As the globe pulsed brighter, a wave of pressure would descend on him; then as the light dimmed, the pressure would ease.

The globe ceased growing, but continued to pulse above him. Soon, the rate of pulsation had matched that of his heartbeat, and he felt as if this globe of stars, of light itself, kept his heart going, kept him alive. Mallon remained transfixed, unable to move, and lost all sense of the passage of time. There was nothing now but the steady beat of the brightness and pressure, nothing but the massive globe of light and stars in the middle of solid darkness.

The globe exploded.

The explosion of light burst through the darkened visor, and Mallon instinctively closed his eyes, but his vision remained filled with blazing orange and yellow and red and white. Then the shock wave hit him, impossibly silent, and crushed him against the rock and gravel, squeezed the air from his lungs. And still there was no sound.

A moment later the pressure abruptly ceased, breath returned to his lungs, and Mallon, as instinctively as he had closed them, opened his eyes.

The sky was in flames.

It was still a night sky, black and completely filled with stars again, motionless once more, but it was laid over by deep red and orange flames blazing as if the fabric of the sky itself was on fire.

Then Mallon realized the sky, the stars, and flames were all pulsing, just as the globe of light had pulsed. He could feel this pulse as well, beating regularly against him, down upon his body, but it was much slower now, the heartbeat of a monstrous, hibernating leviathan.

And the heat struck.

It hit him like a great wind, an incredible heat that should have incinerated him, but somehow didn't burn at all. The heat radiated through him with an intense pain that was strangely welcome, surged through head and limbs without resistance, cleansing his body and purifying it.

Cleansing. Purifying. What was this? he asked himself. Getting mystical?

But that was how it felt, he couldn't deny it, as absurd as it seemed. More than that, he could do nothing to stop it.

Mallon still couldn't move, but now he gave up trying, content to watch and feel what was happening. The heat continued to course through him as the sky blazed through the stars. Maybe, he thought, he was in the heart of a sun.

That, too, he decided, was absurd.

It began to rain.

A torrent of water poured down upon him, laced with silver and blue flames that hissed and sputtered as they struck the ground, his suit, his visor. The rain fell not from clouds—there were none—but from the blazing flames in the sky, and Mallon began to wonder how much of this was real, and how much was . . . was *what?* Hallucination? Brought on by what, or whom?

It didn't matter. It was raining, the raindrops wrapped in flickering blue flames, rain from a star-filled night sky that burned with all-encompassing flames and an agonizing heat that did not burn. And it continued, above and all around him, and so it did not matter. It was real. Real enough.

New images rose in his vision, but without blocking or obscuring the blazing sky above him. There were layers of perception, or layers of reality, somehow all simultaneously visible to him. These new images, though, had to be coming from within *him*, not from without, for they were very much his own.

. . .Charl pulling at the girl tender, with Lisa, eight months pregnant, hitting and slapping at him, then Charl releasing the girl and lurching off into the darkness, hand at his groin. . . .

. . .Sykora grabbing the inhaler, then throwing it at Mallon, turning and running off into the darkness. . . .

. . .The chuurka sprawled across the curved disk of light at the bottom of a well in the ruins of stone and glass and steel. . . .

. . .Rhea seated before a cooking fire, poking at fish in a large pan, not looking up. . . .

. . .Katja, silent but glaring at Mallon, trickles of blood seeping from a dozen tiny slashes beneath her eyes. . . .

. . .Sykora, in the heat and light of midday, making obscene gestures at three chuurkas crouching in the shade of a lean-to he had built for them, then turning to Mallon and grinning. . . .

. . .Lisa feeding the girl tender, stroking her hair. . . .

. . .Katja again, holding up the stumps of her severed fingers, long before they had healed, cursing Mallon, cursing the chuurkas. . . .

. . .Rhea spitting into his face. . . .

. . .The twisting mirror in the cage, flashing pieces of distorted reflections back at him. . . .

. . .A mob sweeping along a street in the city during a night riot, buildings all around them in flames, arms raised and flailing, hands gripping guns and clubs and bottles. . . .

. . .Rugger gazing silently at the fire coming from a plain black metal box, looking at his companions seated around the fire, tiny reflections of flame flickering in his eyes. . . .

. . .And finally, the two chuurkas standing at the windows, incense swirling up around them, neck membranes spread and quivering and fully open to the flames of the buildings on fire across the canal. . . .

This last image brought a terrible ache to his chest, an ache of realization, of growing, though incomplete, understanding, and he wondered how many people had died in that fire—a fire the chuurkas had almost certainly set themselves just so they could watch those blazing flames. How many people had died in all the other fires the chuurkas had set over the years? How many had died because of everything the chuurkas had done in their pursuit of . . . of what? And he was helping them. Mallon wanted to cry out at them, but he still could not move except to breathe.

The last image faded, and there were no more, nothing now but the star-filled night sky, still in flames. The stars seemed to grow even brighter, the flames seemed to burn more intensely and wildly, and the heat, though it still did not burn him, became even more painful, searing through him, and it all kept on, growing, the stars and the black and the flames and the heat, on, and on, and on. . . .

When Mallon came to, the darkness had returned, and the sky was gone. He wasn't sure that he had ever quite lost consciousness, but there had been some kind of break in his awareness, a gap between the heat of the flaming starry night sky and the cold of the darkness now all around him. More than night, once again, with hardly a glimmer of light.

He sat up, then stood, stretched aching muscles. He was exhausted, hardly able to move. He checked the time, saw that he'd been in for almost thirty hours, which meant he was long overdue. He fumbled with the inhalers, pulled one free, and popped it. Maybe that was why he felt so tired, something in the air? No, that wasn't it.

Then Mallon noticed one of the chuurkas' instruments at his feet, and anger rose in him, purging his exhaustion. He kicked the apparatus, sent it clattering over the rocks, scrambled after it and kicked it again. This time when he reached it, he picked up a large rock, swung it with both hands and smashed the instrument, crumpling metal projections, breaking open the main housing, cracking the glass.

Anger still surged through him, providing renewed energy, and Mallon started in on the rest of the machinery. One by one he searched out all the instruments he'd assembled and set up, and attacked them, almost in a frenzy, inflicting as much damage on each of them as he could.

He used large stones, or heavy bars of metal, and smashed the instruments. He tore the membrane fabrics to shreds, ripped apart the networks of wire, he cracked open the housings, he bent and crushed metal projections, he shattered any glass he could find on them. He pulled or smashed or broke them into as many separate, unusable pieces as he could manage, splitting open film cartridges and other inserts or attachments he couldn't identify. And as he finished destroying each one, he took all the pieces and threw them out into the darkness, scattering them among all the other, much older ruins and debris.

When he could not find another intact instrument, Mallon stopped, stood for a long time in one place, breathing heavily. The anger, the bitterness and despair, slowly leaked out of him. He was tired, tired of everything.

Eyes barely focused, he checked the time. Ten, eleven hours until he was due to return. It didn't seem to matter much anymore, except that he knew he could not stay here; he *had* to get out.

Mallon became distantly aware of an aching hunger and thirst. Mouth dry, he managed to eat enough to stop the pain in his belly, drinking three packets of flavorless juice to wash down the food. Time to go back, he decided. There was nothing else to do here.

Mallon activated the suit monitor, and it picked up the steady signal of the beacon. Without the pack, without any of the instruments the chuurkas had sent with him, he started back, making his way slowly through the darkness.

The journey seemed endless, and Mallon soon lost all sense of time, which seemed appropriate, since he had long since lost all sense of direction. Almost mindlessly, he followed the beacon's signal, paying little attention to his surroundings.

He stumbled over stones and concrete blocks, staggered through gullies, and crawled over massive collections of metal and stone debris, rarely bothering to search for an easier way around. Only the shock suit kept him from being seriously hurt as he occasionally tripped and fell to the ground, or tumbled down short inclines. Each time he fell he got up, studied the monitor, and pushed on.

Mallon crossed several trickling streams, even a large, knee-deep pool he waded through, but no longer checked to see if anything lived in the water. At one point, his route brought him back to the stream he had first followed after he'd entered the cavern, only now he was headed upstream instead of down.

Images of stars and flaming raindrops and the black sky in flames tried to surface in his thoughts, along with all the other images that had appeared laid over the burning sky, but Mallon, not wanting to think about them now, fought them down, kept them from coming into focus.

Eventually, Mallon staggered into the tiny clearing where he had arrived a day and a half earlier. Was that all? It felt like so much longer. He dropped to his knees, dug up the beacon, and replaced it in his helmet. Time. He checked the chronometer, popped his final inhaler.

Mallon thought about standing, but decided it wasn't worth the effort. He was too damn tired. He set the chronometer to wake him an hour before the shiftportal was due, set a backup, then curled against a large rock, and slept.

He waited for the shiftportal to appear.

Mallon had awakened to the alarm, eaten again, and then, remembering the chuurka's warning, had gathered several large stones and blocks of concrete, stacked them to form a mound that would bring him to the height of the shiftportal. Now, just a few minutes before the shiftportal was to appear, he climbed the mound and stood, waiting.

A crunching sound came from nearby. Mallon dropped to a crouch and turned toward it. He could see nothing in the dark, not even the ground below him, but he heard another sound, a footstep, and then a loud whisper.

"Mallon." The voice was familiar.

"Sykora?"

"Yes, it's me."

There were more footsteps, approaching, and then Mallon could see the old man just below him, hand on the largest concrete block. Sykora stared up at him, mouth open.

"Sykora, how did you find me?"

"Waited by the water, where I ran away. Waited a long, long time, left a while, I think, then came back, waited some more, I don't know. I'm okay right now, I think, a little, but I'm still having trouble. Then you came, coming back, you weren't following the river exactly, but I heard you, and I followed, listening, followed your footsteps." He paused, reached up with one hand. "Take me back with you, Mallon. Take me out of here."

"Of course I'll take you back." Mallon reached down, took Sykora's hand, and helped the old man clamber up to the top of the mound beside him.

Sykora was shivering, and Mallon could see bloodstains— some fresh, some dry—on Sykora's clothes, bruises and cuts on his skin, a rash covering his neck and the left side of his face.

"This is a terrible place," Sykora said. "But . . ." He stared hard into Mallon's eyes, just two or three inches away. "Did you see it?"

Mallon nodded.

A shudder rolled through the old man, but he smiled, an odd, lopsided expression.

"Listen to me," Mallon said. "We're going to have to do something to get through together. You can't get two people through the shiftportal, not separately, so you're going to have to climb on my back when it comes, all right? Over my shoulder, hang on so we go through as a single unit."

Sykora nodded, cocked his head. "Sure, okay, you say so, but how do you know this?"

"Met some people who have been stranded here for years," Mallon said. He wasn't going to tell Sykora he didn't know if this would work, or what would happen if it didn't.

Sykora nodded again, and another shudder rolled through him, started a hacking, dry cough; he didn't say anything more.

They waited together in the darkness, neither speaking. Mallon checked the time. The damn thing was late. A sick feeling twisted through him at the thought of being stranded if the shiftportal never appeared.

A flicker of light materialized in the air to their right, at chest level just a foot or so out from the mound. The light grew, hovering, lengthened, flattened out and twisted, and then it was fully there, twisting and shimmering, waiting for them.

"Okay, now climb on," Mallon said, turning his back to Sykora and bending his knees.

But Sykora did not climb onto his back, and Mallon turned to see the old man staring at the shiftportal, motionless, an expression of terror on his face.

"Sykora, for Christ's sake, get on!" Mallon grabbed Sykora by the shoulders, shook him. "Don't zone out on me now, dammit, let's go!"

But Sykora just shook his head, then pushed away from him. "No," he said, still shaking his head. "No." He turned and scrambled down the rocks to the ground, slapping away Mallon's hand as he reached for him. "No!" he cried out one more time.

Mallon quickly lost sight of him, though he could hear the footsteps running away from him again, just like the first time. He called out to the old man, desperation in his voice, because this time he could not attempt to follow. "Sykora! Sykora, come back, dammit, you'll be stranded! Sykora!"

Mallon looked back at the twisting mirror. How long would it stay? Ten to twelve minutes. Not long enough. Jesus. He turned back to the direction Sykora had taken.

"Sykora! Sykora!"

There was no answer, there was no longer even the sound of his fleeing steps.

The shiftportal would come back in an hour if he didn't go through it now, that's what they had told him. He could leave, try to find Sykora, then return and go through it the next time, with or without the old man.

But Jesus, what if it *didn't* reappear? He thought of Rugger, of Lisa and Charl and Ashley and the others, *all* the others—the dozens, hundreds, thousands, perhaps, that he hadn't seen— here for years. How the hell could he take the chance?

He couldn't.

Mallon turned back to the shiftportal, stepped to the edge of the rocks, dropped the visor down over his face and darkened it. He could see nothing but a tiny sliver of twisting light.

"SYKORA!" he called, a final time.

And when there was no answer, he silently cursed the chuurkas one more time, and jumped into the portal.

There was bright light and compacting pressure again, but Mallon hardly noticed it now, and moments later the light and pressure eased, and he was falling forward inside the cage, falling to his hands and knees across a cable that snaked across the floor.

He was back.

Mallon didn't move at first, unable to see anything at all. He cleared the visor, then tore off the helmet and tossed it away from him, listening to it clatter across the stone floor. He looked back into the cage, but the twisting, translucent mirror was gone.

The room seemed brighter than when he had left. Mallon struggled to his feet, and a large chuurka, the one who had given him his instructions, quickly stepped up to him, the woman tender at its side. The chuurka, with its small, strangely lidded eyes, stared at Mallon, neck membranes fully spread and fluttering slightly. The chuurka made several *chikking* sounds.

"You have seen the Heart," the woman tender said.

It was odd, Mallon thought, how he could hear the capitalization of that word. He returned the chuurka's stare.

"What heart?" he said.

More sounds, then the tender translating. "You *have* seen it, I can sense it in you, I can see it in your eyes."

It was the first time he could remember the chuurka using the word "I" instead of "we." "What heart?" Mallon asked again.

There was a long pause, the chuurka still staring at him. Then it spoke again, followed by the woman tender.

"The Heart of the Universe."

Mallon didn't reply. Yes, it had to be something like that to them, he thought, *something* worth their worship. *Pilgrims*, Rugger had said. The final connections clicked, linked with the aching realization back in the cavern.

The chuurka reached out to him, began running spidery fingers across Mallon's shock suit, feeling the empty pockets, sweeping over his back where the pack should have been. Mallon remained motionless for a minute or two, enduring it, then knocked the chuurka's arms aside and backed away.

"Leave me alone," he said. "Don't touch me."

The chuurka made sounds, and the tender spoke.

"Where are the instruments? The detectors? You did set them, yes? When you saw the Heart? Where are they?"

"Gone," Mallon said. "Destroyed. Lost."

There was another long silence, and only now did Mallon notice the other two chuurkas, the two who had brought him here. They, too, were gazing at him, membranes spread wide. Finally the larger chuurka spoke again, making the *chikking* noises that Mallon now found increasingly annoying, and the woman translated.

"You will go back, Mallon. We will give you more instruments, new apparatus, and you will go back."

Mallon shook his head. "No."

"Yes, it will not be dangerous, you have been once, you know it, you will go back through the shiftportal with new instruments, bring back records."

Mallon shook his head once again. "This means so damn

much to you, this Heart of yours, go yourselves, and stop send-ing *us.*'' He paused, glancing at all three chuurkas, then shook his head one final time. "No, I won't go back there," he said. "I'll never work for any of you again.''

Mallon stripped off the shock suit and, heart pounding, went to the cabinet. What would they do to him? Incarcerate him? Force him back through the shiftportal? He latched the suit onto empty hooks, closed the cabinet, then turned back to the chuurkas. He breathed deeply.

"Take me back to the city," he said.

The chuurkas looked at him, but did not respond. Then the larger one turned to the other two, made a long series of the *chikking* sounds. The woman tender did not translate.

The large, dark chuurka turned away from its two compan-ions and, followed by the tender, left the room amid the crackle and sparks of electricity.

"Take me back to the city," Mallon said again.

The other two chuurkas returned to the banks of machinery and worked at them for several minutes. One monitor after another went dead, lights went out in clusters, dials stopped moving. When everything had been shut down and not a single light remained, the two chuurkas backed away from the ma-chinery, crossed the room and, not looking at Mallon, left.

Mallon was alone.

The room was dark now with all the machinery down, the shiftportal mirror gone. He stared at the opening, which led out to the main chamber. Was he trapped inside?

Mallon cautiously approached the opening, stopped. He hesitated, then started forward. As before, he felt only a mild tingling across his skin, and he stepped through without resistance, without harm.

The chamber hadn't changed. It was still filled with machin-ery and clouds of incense, red lights and groaning sounds. Chuurkas worked throughout the chamber, all of them busy with the tenders moving among them. Mallon wandered through the chamber, headed slowly toward the entrance, ex-pecting at least one of the chuurkas to stop him, to at least say something to him.

But none of the chuurkas did. Mallon walked among them, walked through the entire chamber, and they all ignored him; not a single chuurka, not a single tender paid any attention to him.

He stopped at the chamber entrance and looked back at the chuurkas and tenders moving about, working at the machinery, talking to one another. Mallon nodded slowly to himself with growing understanding as he remembered how the chuurkas had walked away from the unconscious, useless tender on the hillside.

That's what he had become to them—useless—something to be discarded, ignored. He had told them he would not go back to the cavern, that he would never work for them again, and he realized now that they didn't care. They didn't care about *him* at all.

He stood in the doorway for a long time, watching, almost unwilling to leave before at least one of them took notice of him. None of them did, and Mallon finally turned away from the chamber, stepped to the foot of the stone staircase, and began to climb.

View from Above

TOMCZAK WISHED HE WERE DRUNK. THEN MAYBE HE could stand it, this damn job.

From ten stories up, on a platform of wood and rope, supported by more rope from the roof above, Tomczak looked down at the lunch crowds walking past below him. Businessmen, businesswomen, secretaries and clerks, delivery people. Let one of them come up here and wash windows!

He thought about kicking the large pail of soapy water, tipping it onto its side, spilling gallons of water onto the people below. Oh, so sorry, an accident, my sincerest apologies. Maybe if he were drunk he'd have the balls to do it.

The platform swayed in a sudden gust of wind, and Tomczak grabbed onto the rope rail for support. Of course, if he were drunk he'd probably get sick up here and vomit, sending his breakfast spraying down ten stories, scattered by the breeze. Tomczak smiled at the image, turned back to the window.

He stared at the glass, trying to remember whether or not he'd washed it yet. It didn't look too clean, but that didn't mean much; he was never very thorough. He couldn't understand why he hadn't been fired yet, for Christ's sake. Probably because he *did* clean every damn window, he came into work on time every day, stayed late if he had to, and never called in sick, not once, even when he felt like hell. With his wife and kids at home, no way was he going to take a sick day.

Well, he decided, the window looked clean enough, whether he'd washed it or not. Screw it.

Tomczak stepped across to the rope controls, prepared to lower himself one floor, when a familiar, high-pitched voice called up from below.

"Daddy! Daddy, lookit us!"

Tomczak's head jerked, he leaned over the rope and looked down into the crowds, searching. Then he saw, on the sidewalk across the street, two waving arms flanking three very familiar faces.

No, this was just too much. Ten stories below, backs against the stone wall of another tall building, faces turned upward and looking at him, were his wife and two boys. Marta was holding their hands, and the two boys each waved at him with a free arm.

"Daddy! Daddy, we're watching you!"

No kidding. Why had that damn woman brought them here, for Christ's sake?

Tomczak noticed that other people on the sidewalks, hearing his two boys, had stopped and were looking up at him. Wonderful. It was going to be a show now, was it? Damn her. He turned away from them, focused his attention back on the ropes and pulleys, began to lower himself to the ninth floor.

"Daddy, can you see us?"

Not a chance, kid, I'm blind and deaf. Tomczak tried to ignore the two boys, tried to concentrate on the ropes, prayed to God his wife wouldn't start up, too. That's all he'd need, that grating voice yelling up at him.

He worked the platform down to the ninth floor and secured it, then turned his attention to the window in front of him. Inside, two women smiled, pointed at him, then waved. Tomczak ignored them, adjusted his buckets, checked the cloths and sponges and squeegee.

"Tomczak! Say hello to your sons at least!"

God *damn* that woman!

"Tomczak! Your sons!"

Tomczak turned abruptly, bent over the rope, shouted down at his wife.

"Shut up, dammit! Go home!" He waved frantically in the direction of their apartment. "Just take them home!"

"They want to watch you working!"

"Let them into the bedroom some night, then!" he shouted back. "Let them watch me work on you in bed!" He grinned, seeing Marta's eyes widen, visible even from so high above her; grinned watching her try to cover the boys' ears while still holding onto their hands.

"Tomczak!" she wailed. "Don't talk . . ." She couldn't finish, still struggling with the boys.

Tomczak laughed, rocking the platform. No doubt about it, he was getting a bit reckless, but he was feeling better.

"Tomczak! Tomczak, the boys! Tomczak!"

He stopped laughing, stared at her. Why did she keep on ranting? Why couldn't she keep quiet, shut that damn mouth of hers? Take the boys home?

"Tomczak, tell your sons you're glad to see them, at least! Tell them something!"

What had gotten into that woman? The boys weren't looking up at him anymore, probably embarrassed by the whole thing. But it seemed that half the people on the street *were* staring at him now, the other half staring at the hysterical madwoman still shouting his name. It *was* a show.

Tomczak turned away, tried to ignore everything and go back to work. But the two women inside the building had called over three other people, and all of them were looking and pointing at him. He flipped them off, laughed at their shocked expressions. What the hell did they expect?

"Tomczak, what's wrong? Say something to us, Tomczak, something to your family! Your family!"

That did it. Tomczak knelt on the platform, violently pulled at his bootlaces, ripped off his right boot, stood again and went to the rail. He raised the boot, took aim at his wife, and let fly.

The boot sailed down and across the street, people scattered, his wife screamed. But the boot fell short, banged against a newspaper rack a few feet in front of his wife, bounced back and into the gutter.

"TOMCZAK!" Marta wailed.

Jesus, the woman was asking for it. He pulled off his other boot and hurled it, giving it more loft.

This time, just as she screamed, she pushed away from the wall and ran, releasing the two boys. The boot struck the stone wall close to where she had been standing, and Tomczak grinned again. He had the range now.

His wife was still screaming, running back and forth along the sidewalk, shouting his name, calling after the boys. Tomczak could see his sons, both laughing, pushing through the crowds, avoiding their mother. They had the right idea, Tomczak thought.

Socks were next. Why not? He pulled them off his feet, tied them in knots around each other. He was about to take aim at Marta again when the bucket caught his eye. Inspiration! He dunked the knotted socks into the soapy water, held them under until they were soaked through. Tomczak took them out, water dripping from them, turned and threw the wet clump at his wife.

Water sprayed out from the socks as they tumbled down through the air toward his wife. She scrambled away, and the socks landed at the feet of a man in a business suit, splattering water over the sidewalk and the man's shoes. When the man looked up and started shouting at him, Tomczak gave him the finger. Then he turned and flipped off the crowd inside the building again for good measure.

One after another, Tomczak repeated the process with each piece of clothing he removed—sweatshirt, flannel shirt, T-shirt, blue jeans. He soaked each one in water, tied it into a compact mass, then stood and threw it nine stories down. He no longer aimed only at Marta, whose continual screaming was beginning to fade into the background, but instead aimed the soaking wet bundles at the largest groups of spectators in range below him. He grinned and laughed, watching the people scatter, watching the wads of clothing strike the ground and spray water in all directions.

Now, standing in his underwear, the platform swinging from side to side, Tomczak paused, watching the chaos below, listening to the sirens approaching. He smiled, feeling relaxed and free, happier than he'd been in a long time. His wife was still screaming below, he recognized her wail, but her words had become unintelligible. Above, the sun shone brightly, keeping him warm.

Tomczak turned toward the window. Quite a crowd had gathered inside, fifteen or twenty men and women staring at him, some laughing, others frowning, a few appearing quite shocked but staring at him anyway. Well, he decided, he might as well give them the final show.

Tomczak slipped off his underwear, watching with pleasure

the mixture of expressions on the faces of those on the other side of the window. He dropped the shorts into the bucket, swirled them slowly in the water for a minute. Then he took them out of the bucket, held them dripping for a moment, and threw them against the glass.

The wet shorts stuck for a few moments, started to slide down, then fell away from the glass and dropped nine stories to the sidewalk below.

A free man. That's what he felt like right now.

But the sirens were getting louder, though all the other sounds were fading. Sirens. He wasn't going to be free for long.

A gust of wind caught the platform, swung it wildly for a moment. Tomczak heard a ripping sound, and the platform jerked, knocking him to his knees as it dropped a few inches. He looked up at the support ropes, saw they were fraying, tearing loose.

Impossible! He'd checked them himself, and the stuff they were made of, no way this could be happening. But more strands tore loose, unraveling, and the platform jerked again.

Tomczak scrambled to his feet, grabbing the rope rails for support. Jesus Christ, he wanted to be free, but not *this* free.

He reached out toward the building ledge, but before he could make contact with the stone, the ropes broke completely. The platform dropped and fell away from the building, Tomczak clinging desperately to the rope rails. He cried out, knowing he was going to die.

A few seconds later the platform stopped falling, coming smoothly to a stop high over the street, still seven floors above the crowd below. Suspended above the street, Tomczak stared down at the pavement and upturned faces that should be rushing toward him. Had time stopped moving? No, he could see people scattering madly out of the way, could still hear the approaching sirens, could feel the breeze blowing across his bare skin, could see some people starting to stare and point up at him in disbelief.

The platform hovered, swaying slightly in the breeze. Tomczak rose shakily to his feet, hands still gripped tightly around the rope. This was crazy, he thought, this was impossible. He started laughing, stamping the platform with his bare feet. He *was* free!

What he'd like to do right now, he thought, was fly down on this thing, buzz his wife and scare the crap out of her. He could see Marta now, staring up at him, hands over her mouth, eyes wide.

As if on cue, the platform dipped forward, went into a smooth, gliding descent. It headed down the street, looped 180 degrees at the intersection, then swooped directly at his wife, picking up speed.

Marta screamed, started running, and Tomczak grinned. Within seconds he had reached her and, as she dropped sprawling onto her belly, the platform pulled out of the dive and climbed again.

About three stories up, Tomczak and the platform leveled out, and hovered once more.

"Daddy, Daddy! Give us a ride!"

"Daddy, take us with you!"

Tomczak looked down at his two sons, who were jumping up and down on the sidewalk, reaching up to him. He wanted to take them with him, wherever it was he was going, he really did. But he knew, he *knew* he would never be completely free if he did. All or nothing, now, is what it was.

Tomczak gazed down at his sons, and shook his head.

"Sorry, I can't!" he called down to them. "Take care of your mother! She needs it!" He could see her still belly-down on the sidewalk, face turned just enough so she could look up at him.

"Where are you going, Daddy? Are you coming back?"

"I don't know," he said, holding out his hands. "I have absolutely no idea." Which was, he realized, what really made the whole thing so wonderful. "I'll send you a postcard from the moon!"

And with that, Tomczak, naked and grinning, took hold of the ropes, leaned back, and hung on as the platform shot forward and started climbing toward the sun.

Three thousand copies of this book have been printed by the Maple-Vail Book Manufacturing Group, Binghamton, NY, for Golden Gryphon Press, Urbana, IL. The typeset is Palatino, printed on 55# Sebago. The binding cloth is Arrestox B Grade #66000. Typesetting by The Composing Room, Inc., Kimberly, WI.